THE **WHISPER**

THE WHISPER

EMMA CLAYTON

Chicken House

SCHOLASTIC INC.
NEW YORK

ISBN 978-0-545-43365-5

10 9 8 7 6 5 4 3 2 1   12 13 14 15 16

Printed in the U.S.A.   40
This edition first printing, January 2012

The text type was set in ITC Avant Garde Gothic.
Book design by Phil Falco

FOR MATTHEW, MAISIE,
OSCAR, AND EDD

War does not determine who is right –
only who is left.

BERTRAND RUSSELL

Whilst this planet has gone cycling on according to the fixed law of gravity, from so simple a beginning, endless forms most beautiful and most wonderful have been, and are being, evolved.

CHARLES DARWIN

CONTENTS

1 A Glitch

As darkness fell on the cliffs of Cape Wrath, a storm blew in from the North Sea. There had been many storms at Cape Wrath before, but this one rocked around the fortress as if a DJ were spinning dark matter. Waves boomed against the cliffs, clouds rolled like molten lead, and all those elements in between warped in the night as if part of the strange event that was occurring in the fortress.

For most of the day, the dormitories had been as quiet as tombs. Thousands of children lay in rows of metal beds, sleeping so silently in the dim light that the nurses had to lean right over them to make sure they were still breathing.

The new implants glowed like moons on their foreheads. Their sheets covered them like shrouds.

The nurses treated the wounds around the implants as if they were caring for crops or things, just stuff, not the living, breathing, feisty children who had filled the arcades with rush and noise, Pod Fighter T-shirts, and talk of the game. The implants were working. Now these children were Northern Government property: pilots and gunners, weapons of war.

But as darkness fell and the storm rolled in, the implanted army began to stir.

It breathed, faster.

Eyelids flickered, as if brains were rebooting.

It whispered and writhed, frowned and tangled in its long white gowns and sheets, until it looked like a shoal of fish trying to escape from a net.

Now, this was not supposed to happen.

These children had been told to sleep until they were needed.

There were only two nurses in each dormitory. For a while they watched the children stir, not quite sure what was happening. But as the army began to rise like mist from those long lines of beds, the nurses were gripped by dark horror, as if they were witnessing a morgue of corpses rising. Some tried to bully the children back to their beds, as if they were still just children, but most ran as if a dam had burst.

Waves boomed against the cliffs.

Wind howled.

Darkness warped.

Now it felt as if the storm was inside the fortress.

The implanted army rose, and the nurses ran, gasping with fright.

Implant engineers rushed to Mal Gorman's office. The dormitory nurses were hard on their heels, followed by any other members of staff who suspected they might get blamed for the awakening. While all this was going on, Ralph, the butler, was in the kitchen next to Mal Gorman's dressing room, preparing his master's supper.

As he walked toward the door with the tray, alarms began to wail and a herd of nurses ran past with their hair flying from their buns. He paused. It was clearly not a good time to deliver cheese on toast to the Minister for Youth Development, but since Mal Gorman had ordered it, the butler decided he'd better deliver it. He valued his head almost as much as the nurses sprinting past him valued theirs.

The office was as packed as a Tube train at rush hour. It took all of Ralph's best navigation skills to carve a path through it to the desk. Mal Gorman made a frightening spectacle. While his staff crushed in around him, he sat at his desk, illuminated by the light of its giant screen. He was a government minister from a broken world; half bone, half blinking machine.

A mass of tubes and wires connected him to a life-support system on the frame around his chair.

The eyes in his skull face were poison pale.

He was building up to one of his venomous outbursts.

The butler prepared to set down the tray on the corner of the desk.

"Not there," Gorman said.

"Where would you like it, sir?"

"Not on the desk, you fool, I won't be able to see what's happening."

Images flickered across the screen. His skeletal hands touched heads and gowns. He shuffled views like playing cards and watched his implanted army run, like a cat watches a mouse it has been torturing. It would not get far before he pounced on it again. He had taken these children to fight for the vast riches on the other side of The Wall.

There was nowhere else to put the tray. Ralph looked around, but every inch of floor had a panicking person standing upon it.

"Stop hovering," Gorman said. "Get out."

The butler left, the tray still in hand.

Gorman's eyes remained glued to the screen.

The engineers were telling him the awakening was a glitch that could be fixed via a computer. But some of the children now had blood seeping from the wounds around their implants. Running around in such a state, they were damaging Northern Government property.

"Hurry up!" he yelled. "Fix this glitch before these children make themselves even more stupid!"

It did not occur to him for a moment that there was no glitch to fix, that these children had been strong enough to defy their implants and climb out of bed. For what he had unwittingly harvested, from the arcades he had built across the North, was a spectacular upgrade of the human design: children who were smarter, stronger, and more likely to survive than any born before them. And among their repertoire of strange new talents was the ability to connect with each other. Even in their sleep.

Mal Gorman did not know this, yet he was the one who'd made it happen. An hour before, he'd reunited the twins Mika and Ellie and formed the clasp that would hold this new connection together, that would cause the start of a seismic shift in the human world order. While he was thinking about cheese on toast, twenty-seven thousand sleeping children were downloading the contents of Mika Smith's mind. That quiet, clever, black-eyed boy who'd flown over The Wall . . .

There was no glitch to fix.

These children were running because they now knew what lay on the other side.

One of the nurses was trying to talk to him, trying to tell him that the army had climbed out of bed knowing impossible things. But he didn't hear her. The nurses were annoying him; they were talking all at once, crowding around his desk, hot-faced and disarrayed.

"Get out!" he yelled. "I can't breathe with you all flapping around me! Someone fix this glitch—now!"

The implanted army had awoken knowing there were trees and animals on the other side of The Wall and that they themselves had been taken to bomb them. But it wasn't going to be easy to escape from that fortress.

The implants had been shot like bolts into their heads and were still fighting for control, demanding the children obey the Northern Government, ordering them to sleep until they were needed. The children had been strong enough to wake themselves up, but moving away from those lines of beds felt like pulling against the jaws of a mantrap. The moment they ran out of the dormitories and into the fortress passages, they felt an intense, punitive pain in their minds that made them drop the connection that had formed when Mika and Ellie touched. And this connection was important. They would need it to work out what to do. For what they'd learned from Mika while they slept made the concrete feel like quicksand beneath their feet. They ran in a wild panic with it all hot in their heads.

They were born behind The Wall. They were the firstborn children of the refugees who'd fled north from The Animal Plague. And like their parents, they'd believed that The Wall had been built to protect them. That now, after forty-three years, there was nothing but poisoned dust on the other side. But in their sleep they'd flown over The Wall and run with Mika through a *dark forest.*

They'd watched dawn light pour through trees.

They'd flown over the mansions of the rich elite who had stolen their parents' land.

And seen *real animals*! And borgs too. The giant silver eagles and wolves that guarded all this beauty and would rip their parents apart if they tried to reclaim their land.

The Animal Plague had never happened.

Their parents had been tricked into moving into a giant concrete cage.

But . . .

. . . as well as shock, this made the children feel happy.

There were trees and animals on the other side of The Wall!

They'd grown up believing such beauty was destroyed by the humans born before them.

But now they were being drawn into a smash and grab, a greed-fueled fight for territory that had been going on as long as humans could stand up and hold a weapon. The Northern Government was trying to use them to fight for that land on the other side of The Wall. But no lump of metal, no glowing moon, no knife-sharpening, flickering bone machine would make children like these bomb forests full of animals, even for their parents if their parents knew the truth. They'd grown up aching for such beauty.

They knew this as they ran. But the boy Mika, who'd shown them the forest, felt lost to them now. Their connection had dropped, and without it, they had no idea how to help themselves.

The fortress passages were cramped and cold. There were cameras everywhere. The children ran in a river of heads and white gowns with the fortress watching them. Alarms began to wail, but all the passages looked the same. There were no signs, no windows, just a recurring nightmare of dormitories and bloodstained pillows. Soon the atmosphere was hysterical and they were dragging each other along. A boy, Tom, ran with a girl called Ana, and he held her hand as if his life depended on her. She felt like all he had left; she was the only person he recognized from his arcade.

"They told us we were playing a game," Ana gasped. "I thought I was playing a game!"

"I know," Tom panted. "They lied. Forget the game, Ana. It's gone. Let's just get out of here."

They found stairs and ran up, stubbing their toes on the concrete steps. At the top they felt blasts of icy wind. The children ahead had found fire doors leading out of the fortress. They felt relieved. And then they ran into the Cape Wrath storm.

They were almost blown off their feet. They pulled up sharp, gasping with shock, as the storm lurched around them. Wind howled, waves boomed, and the ground beneath their feet was rocky and slippery with rain. They couldn't see anything but the spectral forms of other children running away. In their gowns they looked like hundreds of white smudges on the darkness.

Now they had the feeling they'd left something important behind.

What?

Shoes.

No, not shoes.

This was more important than shoes.

But what?

It was in their heads, big and blurred, but feeling so much pain from their implants, they could not figure out what.

Tom and Ana were blocking the path of those behind them. As the children pushed forward, Tom lost Ana's hand. He slipped sideways down rock, and by the time he recovered, he couldn't see her. Then he was frantic, stumbling through the crowd, shouting her name over the wind. He started to run, blind in the darkness, desperate to find her again. He ran, without realizing it, toward the edge of the cliff and a brutal, deadly fall. Then he thought he saw her. Just ahead of him. But no sooner had he seen her than her feet slipped, the back of her head smacked hard on rock, and she began to slide down the cliff. Tom sprinted to save her, but others reached her first, grabbing at her wet arms, trying to pull her back as she screamed and dangled over the sea. Hands slipped, gripped, yanked, and she scrambled frantically with her feet. By the time she was standing on firm ground, her legs were cut to shreds and she was sobbing with shock.

But it was not Ana. It was another girl, who looked like Ana. Then Tom watched her weep in the arms of a boy and realized it was only fate that made Ana a friend and this girl a stranger.

They were not strangers.

And they needed each other.

The connection would return with that thought in their minds.

They backed away from the cliff and turned to face the fortress. It loomed over them like a dark and silent lord. They began to run again, desperate to get away from it, and followed its great black wall as it curved away from the sea. Eventually, they saw the nearest town in the distance — towers, factories, and traffic trunks in a haze of yellow light. They ran on, faster, thinking of the normal adults who could help them there, until a fence loomed out of the darkness, a giant chain-link fence. It buzzed and hissed where the rain touched it.

They pulled up and turned to stop their friends from running into it.

Every few feet hung yellow signs, bearing gray skulls flanked by lightning bolts, as if Mal Gorman had used a picture of himself to warn them what would happen if they touched it. The fence enclosed the land around the fortress and ended halfway down the cliffs.

They were trapped.

The screen on Mal Gorman's desktop looked liquid. As he gazed into it, he wished he could dip his hand through the surface and scoop his children up. Squeeze them until they squeaked. Drop them into their beds. But instead he was forced to watch them pour over the rocks like spilled milk. He was quite sure they wouldn't get away, but as they massed along the line of the electric fence, he felt the first twinge of panic. He hadn't expected them to stay awake this long.

"Someone tell me what's happening," he said.

"We don't know yet, sir," an engineer replied.

"I thought you were running a diagnostic program to find the glitch in the implants."

"We did, sir. But we still don't know what's wrong."

"Then look out the window!" Gorman yelled. "All those little white dots on the rocks aren't dandruff or snowflakes or marshmallows; they're children in nightgowns with nothing on their feet! Look out the window and see what's wrong! I want this glitch found and I want it fixed! I want my children back in bed, ready to fight the war!"

The children massed along the fence, realizing they were trapped. But as they stopped running, the punitive pain of their implants subsided and they were able to think again. They thought hard. The game had taught them how to strategize for survival, and they did it now.

In this state, their new connection returned.

One by one, as their minds focused, they joined like links in a chain. Then they heard The Whisper, the quiet sound of their thoughts flowing like a river through their minds. And as they listened, they realized something important, that this new connection would hold only while they were quiet like this. While they were running around, overcome by fierce emotion, The Whisper was lost to The Roar.

The Whisper was the sound of thoughts, they realized.

The Roar was the sound of emotion.

They realized this as they gazed through the fence.

The wind whipped their gowns and they listened to each other.

We have to stay calm so we can hear this.

We have to accept what they've done to us so we can work out what to do about it.

We shouldn't have run out of the fortress like that.

Now we're trapped.

And we've left something behind.

What have we left behind?

As they focused, the answer began to take shape. It had almost reached the tip of their tongues, when a noise ripped through the sky that left claw marks in the clouds. Immediately, the children felt the blood jump in their veins.

Pod Fighters!

They looked up, all at once, as if their heads were jerked on strings. Then a single thought flashed through them all, as fast as the electricity running through the fence.

"What are they doing?" Gorman asked.

He couldn't hear the Pod Fighters through the thick glass of his window.

The engineers gathered and they watched the children gaze at the sky. The children looked like a pale ring around the fortress.

"They've seen something, sir."

"Well, yes," Gorman sneered. "But what?"

"Pod Fighters. A squadron of Pod Fighters has just returned to the fortress."

Gorman laughed.

"Brilliant!" he mocked. "So they've only just realized there are Pod Fighters in the fortress! Did they think I was going to send them to war in their parents' hover cars? They're even more stupid than I thought. . . ."

But as fast as the children had frozen, they became a fluid mass again, surging toward the fortress like a noose closing on its throat.

The green worm of Gorman's heartbeat began to bolt across a screen.

"Lock the doors," he said. "Don't let them back in. If we let them back in, they'll go for their Pod Fighters. They're going to try to get their Pod Fighters and escape."

"Yes, sir."

Gorman watched the children swarm toward the fire doors.

"How are they communicating?" he asked. "They look as if they're communicating, but they can't, spread out like that. It's not possible."

The children reached the fortress and pressed hard against it.

Now Gorman felt afraid. All at once he felt as if he were watching aliens instead of children. That he'd harvested a crop of aliens to fight his war. He'd felt this unsettling sensation in the past, in the company of the mutants like Mika and Ellie, but never with these normal children.

"I don't like it," he said. "They're being weird."

"The doors are locked, sir. They can't get back in."

"That's not the point," Gorman said. "I've had enough of this now. I want these children under control. I told them to sleep until they were needed, and they're trying to run away from me."

He continued to watch them. Suddenly he felt vicious, as if he wanted to slap them down in the hardest, cruelest way.

"Release the Creeper Nets," he said.

The engineers looked shocked.

"The Creeper Nets, sir?"

"Yes, the Creeper Nets."

"But the Creeper Nets are weapons. The children will be injured."

"Good," Gorman replied. "They need teaching a lesson. Perhaps when they've felt the stab of a Creeper Net, they'll remember who's in control. I want my army back in bed."

The children pressed against the fortress, tugging on the wet bars of the fire doors. Their connection was faltering again. They were killing it with panic.

They'd left their Pod Fighters behind!

How could they have made such a terrible mistake?

It was difficult to accept they'd done it, and they continued to tug on the doors long after they realized they were locked.

But after a few minutes, they heard the grunt and grind of heavy metal. Startled, they backed away, not sure where the noise was coming from. Then they saw holes appear in the walls of the fortress where it met the rock of Cape Wrath. For a moment they considered using these as another route back in, then they heard a metallic scuttling sound and realized there was something in them.

They pulled back slowly, still reluctant to leave, but when they saw the Creeper Nets reach the mouths of the tunnels, they turned and ran in terror.

The Creeper Nets erupted in a spindly black mass and spread up the wall of the fortress. Then they spilled over the rocks, scuttling madly on hard, spike-tipped feet. It was difficult to see them through the darkness and the rain, but they looked like something hatching. Something made of scorpions and bats and spiders with some of their legs pulled off.

Each Creeper Net had five barbed legs with a black wire net stretched between them. When they reached the children, they rose and bloomed like black flowers ready to strike. They struck hard, with one leg that arched back and came down with the speed of a paintbrush stippling canvas. The attacks were so fast and brutal, the first children fell without even seeing them—jerking like starfish, collapsing like puppets, paralyzed by venom, and cocooned by a net and barbed legs before they ever hit the wet rock.

This was child control of the severest kind.

But as Gorman watched them fall, his fear subsided. He'd caught a glimpse of something he didn't like, and he didn't want to see it again.

2 What Mutant Eyes Could See

When Mika and Ellie touched, only one adult realized something strange had happened. The man with the gun, who was guarding them. He'd thought he'd seen them *glow* when they touched. As if all the energy they'd used missing each other now fused them together into something new, something even more powerful and strange. Now he was trapped in a pod with them, flying toward London.

Something bad had happened when they touched, he was sure of it. The Northern Government knew these mutant children were different, but how different? What exactly were they? Mika was born with webbed feet. Ellie was born with webbed hands. And many other children had been born with animal mutations, but no one understood why.

Mal Gorman had taken Ellie a year and a half before the others so he could explore her mutant power. But they were still a live experiment, and the man with the gun did not want to discover the outcome of that experiment while he was alone, up in the air, with them.

Ellie moved suddenly, reaching across the seat for a bottle of water, and the man with the gun almost jumped out of his skin. But Ellie didn't even look at him. She opened the bottle quickly and passed it to her brother, with her eyes still fixed out the window. Mika was thirsty, not her. The man wondered how she knew.

"Thanks," Mika said.

The man watched them carefully. He understood why Mal Gorman found them fascinating. They were beautiful beyond their blend of Italian and Indian bloods, with their long limbs, black hair, and eyes as sullen as night flowers. Their beauty was startling and unfathomable. Looking at Mika and Ellie was like staring at a wormhole in space and trying to see what was in it. But mutant beauty was deadly beauty. These children could kill with their eyes. This seemed like a useful talent to a war-mongering corpse machine like Mal Gorman, but it frightened this man with the gun.

Please don't kill me, he thought.

Children don't glow, he told himself. Glowworms glow, the sun and moon glow, but children *do not* glow, even mutant ones.

We're just flying to London to visit their parents.

Nothing bad is going to happen.

This trip home had been arranged by Mal Gorman to make Ellie safer to work with. She'd been difficult to handle because her parents believed she was dead, so this was a calculated act of weapon management. When she returned to the fortress, Gorman hoped, she'd be as calm and obedient as her brother.

The man wiped his free hand on his trousers and tried to admire the view. The passing towns looked prettier when darkness hid the mold and the pylons.

Surely, there was nothing to worry about.

They were, after all, just children.

The Golden Turrets appeared on the distant horizon. The air roads rose like ribbons attached to the glittering domes, and Mika and Ellie felt their hearts swell with happiness. This was the journey they'd longed for since the day Ellie was taken. Their parents were about to discover she was still alive.

They watched the city, full of love. It was even more beautiful viewed through mutant eyes. Every pod that flew ahead of them on the air road toward London had a trail of light the man couldn't see. Blue light streaming from the craft, gold light streaming from the people within, fluid as water, bright as sea and sun, a startling blue, a brilliant gold, buzzing and throbbing with meaning. And the traffic moved at such speed on its gentle curve toward London that all those streams wove together into a silk of inanimate and living light that was mesmerizing.

As Mika and Ellie absorbed this beauty, with their hearts so full of happiness, it didn't feel as if anything could go wrong.

But as the pod reached the first glittering dome on the outskirts of the city, the man's com began to glow.

Immediately, Mika and Ellie turned and fixed their eyes on him.

He listened and nodded.

Red spots appeared on his cheeks.

The call was brief, but by the time it ended, the golden light emanating from his body was darkened by streaks of dread.

"What's wrong?" Ellie asked.

"Nothing," the man replied. "Look, we're nearly there."

They knew he was lying. Sometimes these adults forgot what mutant eyes could see. The emotions they tried to hide with false expressions and words pulsed through their light, clear and true. It was pointless lying to a mutant child. And the pilot had begun to fly faster, nudging through the traffic on the air road. Something was clearly wrong.

Mika and Ellie looked away, reaching. They stopped thinking about their parents and let their minds drift toward the fortress. The city and its streamers passed, forgotten.

It was their turn to connect.

They felt a tug and a split second of uneasiness as they fastened. Then, as if a pipe had burst with a million gallons of water behind it, their minds were flooded by the thoughts of twenty-seven thousand stricken children.

Blood, fear, darkness, rain. The Creeper Nets bloomed like black flowers around them. All at once they were not in the pod, they were running on black rock, dressed in thin, white gowns, with lumps of metal in their heads. And all that fear, pain, and confusion was like a sudden, deafening onslaught that they could not control. The Roar rose up without a hope of suppressing it. And what remained of the sound of fierce emotions in the old human mind became a weapon in theirs.

"MIKA!"

Mika looked up and realized that the man with the gun was shouting at him. Then he looked down again and saw that the pod seat was on fire. He'd set it on fire. It caught the sleeve of his jacket and licked up his arm. Ellie grabbed him and yanked him away, slapping it hard with her hand.

"What the frag are you doing?" the man yelled. "You just set the seat on fire!"

The pod began to fill with smoke. Ellie dragged Mika's jacket off and beat the flaming seat. The man with the gun shouted frantically at the pilot, telling him to land as quickly as possible. Then they heard a click and a shunt, and a rush of air filled the pod.

"The pilot's ejected!" the man with the gun yelled. "He's left us! We're going to crash!"

Then the pod began to fall like a stone from the sky.

It was quiet.

The man with the gun thought he was dead.

It occurred to him that it hadn't hurt. Then he began to cough violently and he felt his eyes sting. When he opened them he saw Ellie and Mika through a haze of smoke. They were standing over him. Their white armored boots and trousers were smeared with soot from the fire, and Ellie had his gun in her hand. He panicked for a second, but all she did was hold it out so he could take it back again.

"Thanks," he said.

"Mika landed the pod," Ellie told him.

"Did he?" the man replied. "Where are we?"

"In the Golden Turrets, in New Hyde Park, in front of our parents' turret."

"Oh," he said, sitting up.

He tried to gather his thoughts. Only seconds ago they'd been in free fall. Now the fire was extinguished, the pod had been landed, and Ellie and Mika were watching him steadily. As if it were an everyday occurrence to set fire to yourself, scare the pilot so much he ejected, then land a pod in exactly the right place, seconds before it crashed . . . and give him his gun back.

The children looked different. Their black eyes now shone with a mercurial gleam. He didn't like it.

"We're surrounded by soldiers," Mika said. "Why are they here?"

For a moment the man was confused. He'd forgotten the call he'd taken in the pod and the message he'd received from the fortress. Then through the window he saw black helmets and guns and remembered what was happening. For a moment he considered opening the door and running away so someone else would have to deliver Mal Gorman's message.

"Tell us," Mika urged.

They stood so still he could hear his heart beat.

"There's a problem in the fortress," he began. "It's nothing to do with me, I'm just following orders. I had no idea this would happen. . . ."

"What?" Mika asked. "Just tell us."

"Promise you won't blame me."

"OK," Mika said.

"The implanted army is awake and trying to run away. Something's wrong with the implants . . . and you know what Mal Gorman's like when things go wrong. He gets angry and he changes his mind about things. He wants his army under control . . . and that means you as well. He wants you in the fortress while the implanted children are returned to their beds. I'm sorry, Ellie, but you can't see your parents today. He's sent these soldiers to escort you. . . . Please don't blame me."

Ellie flinched and he saw a split-second spark of pain in her eyes. He waited for it to morph into anger and to feel that anger turn on him, but to his astonishment, she said, "OK."

"Wh-what?" he spluttered.

"OK," she repeated. "We'll go back."

"Really?"

"Yes," she said.

That was not what he'd expected her to say. She'd almost killed Mal Gorman the last time he tried to stop her from going home; she'd spent a year and a half crying for her parents, grieving and longing to end their suffering. But he didn't want to waste time wondering why she was so willing to return to the fortress. He just wanted to get away from her as quickly as possible.

He stood up and reached past them to open the door.

It opened to reveal a landscape of helmets, guns, and gold. New Hyde Park was in the center of London, surrounded by a ring of turrets. An army freighter hung above the glittering fountain pools, and hundreds of soldiers stood around them. The man with the gun stepped down from the pod, but the children paused as they realized something within them had changed. Everything they focused on was brighter and more meaningful. As they stepped down from the pod, they watched the soldiers react and saw patterns of emotion spread through their light. Those closest to them felt hyperalert and anxious, those farther away wished they had a better view, and those in between felt a mixture of both. And they could see the people in the turrets too, standing on their balconies and looking down. Their lights shimmered with curiosity as they watched the scene in the park.

Someone barked orders, and the children began to walk

through the soldiers toward the army freighter. Ellie didn't look back until they reached it, then she couldn't resist one glance.

There!

Behind them on a balcony, she saw a pair of lights glowing brighter than all the rest. As her face tipped up, they expanded with a sudden pulse of shock.

Mum!

Dad!

They were far above her, thirty floors above her, but she could see her mother's sari flicking in the wind. Her father's hand raised, as if to wave. They shone with a great, pure love that radiated into the park.

They've seen you, Mika thought. *At least they've seen you.*

The men moved forward, urging them toward the freighter. Ellie took one last look, her heart convulsing with longing, then she turned and followed Mika to the freighter.

Their army needed them.

3 Bloody Fingers and Black Rock

"**T**hey've got guts, I'll give them that," Mal Gorman said.

Now he watched the children through his office window with a set of digital binoculars.

He enjoyed the moment a Creeper Net stuck. There was a slick brutality to their design that made them compulsive viewing. The children were struck, paralyzed, and cocooned before they hit the ground. Then they were no longer running around damaging themselves or thinking about Pod Fighters, they were laid out on the rocks in neat little packages waiting to be collected. Gorman thought this was beautiful until he noticed more weirdness: As the Creeper Nets had emerged from the tunnels, the children had scattered as if he'd dropped a stone in a puddle, but now they were coming together again, as if the water was settling. All around the fortress, they were starting to move toward the cliffs.

Gorman watched anxiously as a boy sprinted toward the

face of black rock with two Creeper Nets on his tail. The boy was fast. He didn't look as if he was going to stop. Gorman held his breath, afraid the child would throw himself off the cliff in his panic to get away, but right on the edge, he lowered himself carefully and vanished.

"Frag!" Gorman shouted. "They're trying to escape down the cliffs!"

"They can't escape down the cliffs," an officer said. "The fence ends halfway down it, and the waves almost meet it."

"But they've been trained to do this!" Gorman yelled. "We've just spent weeks training these children how to deal with situations like this! They've been running assault courses with rucksacks full of concrete on their backs!"

He turned his hover chair and returned to his desk. He shuffled views so he could see in closer detail what was happening.

Yes, there they were. A few children had already climbed under the end of the fence and were running over the patch of dark wasteland between the fortress and the nearest town. It would take them less than ten minutes to reach it.

"Send men out to clear the streets of the town," Gorman shouted. "Make the people close their blinds so they can't see out. Then release more Creeper Nets and shoot any child that hasn't been caught before it reaches the refugee towers. Those children must not come in contact with normal people. If parents see them looking like this, it will cause another riot. And you" — he pointed at the group of engineers — "you're all sacked! Get out!"

Tom ran with a red-haired boy. A big lad, the sort he would have played Fastball with in school if they'd known each other then. They reached the cliffs with a Creeper Net at their heels. They turned to fight it off, but it struck a girl to their left, and they knew there was nothing they could do to help her. After the first attacks, they'd tried saving their friends, but the barbs on the Creeper Net legs sliced their hands like razor blades. It wasn't long before they realized there was no way of helping. But they'd learned the hard way. They had blood dripping from their fingers.

As they crouched to drop over the edge of the cliff, another Creeper Net appeared, scuttling toward them like a demented spider. In their haste, they slid down the edge too fast and, for a few awful seconds, thought they'd slip straight off it and fall into the sea. The waves crashed and boomed below them, the wet rock slipped like fish through their fingers, then their feet hit a ledge on the rock below and they were saved. They leaned against the cliff, their fingertips searching for cracks in the rock, but the red-haired boy's hands were badly cut and Tom realized he was likely to fall. Children were climbing past them, down and away. He released a hand and placed it on the boy's back, willing him to survive.

"I can't hold on," the boy said. "My fingers are too bloody."

"Wipe them on your gown," Tom replied. "I've got my hand on your back. Quickly."

The boy still found it hard. They stepped sideways along the ledge, gasping with fear and willing their hands to remember what to do. They'd climbed every day in Fit Camp, but not over jagged rocks and monstrous waves. Already their fingers were numbed by cold, and each shift of their weight felt like an imminent fall into that dark, cold mass of water below them. They moved down slowly, closer and closer to the waves. Above, they could see more children coming, cold feet searching for the ledges on the rock. But just as they reached the ball of razor wire that marked the end of the fence, a monstrous wave crashed in. Freezing, salty water ran over them, making them gasp with shock, and for a moment the cliff face looked like a black waterfall and they were almost dragged down with it. They watched the surf tug through their fingers, and by the time the wave dropped back, they were so scared, it was impossible not to succumb to panic. Their climb beneath the end of the fence was dark and dangerous, and they took risks they would remember later and wonder how they'd survived. But they were all doing it, hundreds at a time—it was the only way to escape.

They reached the other side before they heard the roar of the next big wave and scrambled up as if their feet would be bitten off by it. The wave hit like thunder. They looked down as it dropped back, and saw a Creeper Net emerge from the spray.

They slipped and scrabbled, desperate to get to the top of the cliff before it reached them. But the boy's fingers were covered in blood again. He began to fall behind and as Tom gained on the overhang, the boy was still well below it.

The Creeper Net picked its way up the rock toward him. Tom dropped back as it bloomed. He grabbed the black metal leg between the joints as it came down to strike him between the shoulder blades, and he yanked hard, trying to pull it free from the rock. The boy hauled himself up out of range and then the leg attacked Tom, stabbing at his cheek. He ducked and heard a sharp *tang* as it hit the rock behind him. He yanked again and managed to pull one leg out of a crevice, but it replaced its grip within seconds. In desperation he grabbed for the processor hub where the five legs met and smashed it against the cliff.

Nothing.

He did it again.

For a split second its legs contracted as its electronic brain faltered, and that was enough. With one frantic yank, Tom pulled it off the cliff and hurled it to the sea. He watched it fall, almost following it. Then the two boys hauled themselves over the cliff edge and began to run toward the town.

4 Monkey Maggot

Mika held Ellie's hand as the freighter rose.

In the years before she was taken, they'd had a difficult relationship. They'd fought every day about stupid little things. Living in a fold-down apartment had made their parents more careful with each other. But this was not the case with Mika and Ellie. They'd never known the life their parents lived before The Wall was built, and their latent power made them frustrated and bored. Their world felt wrong. They were animals in the wrong type of cage.

Most of the time when Mika and Ellie fought, they yelled at each other and threw stuff. But they also had another state, the one they entered when they were deeply hurt. This made them quiet. When Mika felt like this, he'd go to bed with a book or a game. He'd turn his back on Ellie and refuse to talk to her. Ellie would sit very still and blink, her breath catching in her throat. She was doing it now, as the freighter rose.

Mika gazed out the window and watched the city shrink until it looked like a hot, gold coin, but Ellie gazed at the seat in front of them.

She was ten when Mika last saw her. Now she was taller and her face had lost its baby softness. She was pretty now, in a dark sort of way, and she wore her white uniform with grace. But while Mika held her hand, he saw the old Ellie. For all their frustration and anger, they were taught to love well by their parents. And they could have seen them if they'd chosen to, despite Mal Gorman's order. They could have melted every gun in the park. They could have sent those soldiers running for their lives.

But their army needed them. Ellie blinked black lashes. Her fingers felt soft in Mika's hand.

Being born a spectacular upgrade on the human design did not make them feel like one.

Awen the dream dog leaned against their legs, squashed against the seat in front. Mika's invisible friend had watched over him in the lonely days after Ellie was taken by Mal Gorman; now he would watch over them both. He lay his head in Ellie's lap and sighed a big doggy sigh. Mika wondered then how he'd ever argued with his sensitive, loving sister.

The passenger hold was hot. Soldiers filled the seats around them. They yanked off their helmets to show red faces and sprigs of sweaty hair. Ill ease swelled through their light. They'd heard about the fire in the pod and they would not relax until these mutant children were out of their hands in Cape Wrath. It would be a difficult journey for them all.

But as London was left behind, Ellie began to recover. She rubbed her eyes and gazed out the window with a new, sharper look. She'd left her parents, but Mika was still with her and they had an important job to do. For their planet was soaked in human tears as volatile as gasoline, and if the match struck, it would burn bright, but just for a few moments, before it crumbled to dust.

Many children had been born during wars before, but never had a whole generation of twelve- and thirteen-year-olds been snatched from their homes to fight one.

But they would not fight it. They would solve the problem of The Wall a more intelligent way, a way that helped their parents understand that those forests were as much a part of them as their arms and legs.

They thought about this as they flew toward the fortress.

They were no threat to the men around them.

It was Mal Gorman who had something to worry about.

Tom ran with the red-haired boy and a few other children across the dark wasteland between the fortress and the town. They ran from black rock onto concrete and glass that cut and bruised their feet, but they were now so numbed by the cold, they didn't feel it.

They could see more children running ahead and even more behind, but they were spread out over a greater distance now. It was quieter. They could still hear the boom of waves against the cliffs, but mostly they ran to the sound of their own hard breath and the howl of wind. They were beginning to feel grateful for all that training in Fit Camp. They would never have been able to survive those cliffs or run like this before.

The nearest town, Sandwood Seven, looked achingly familiar. It was a sprawl of refugee towers, factories, and waste plants just like the towns they'd grown up in. Now their thoughts turned to home and their parents, who were slowly fading like cut flowers in this concrete cage. Tom began to wonder how his mother was coping without him. She had the lung disease people caught in The Shadows.

"I have to get home," the boy managed between breaths. "I help my gran look after my baby brother."

"What's your name?" Tom asked.

"Luc," he gasped.

"I'm Tom," Tom replied. "We'll stick together. Don't worry, we'll get home somehow."

They began to run faster. But as they reached the first buildings on the outskirts of the town, they heard the rumble of freighters and turned to see several rise from the fortress and fly slowly toward them.

Panic-stricken, they ran down a road flanked by factories and warehouses. Then they spread out and banged on doors, hoping to find people who could help them. But it was late evening. Most of these buildings were serviced by borgs in the hours between dinner and dawn. All the children saw through these windows were the blinking lights of security cameras.

The freighters had almost reached them.

They'd run out of time.

They gave up on the doors and began to look for places to hide.

Tom sprinted with Luc and a few others farther up the road, then down the side of a Tank Meat factory. They squeezed behind a line of refuse containers and stood in a foul, stinking slime. The freighters came down. They felt shadows fall on their heads. Then they crouched farther, trying to make themselves as small as possible, with the stinking slime squelching through their toes. They felt as if they'd waited an hour, when they heard a heavy clunk. A container had been dropped at the front of the Tank Meat factory. For a while it was quiet again, then they heard the familiar tap of spike-tipped feet.

Creeper Nets.

They pressed their bodies hard against the factory wall, hoping that if they stayed still, the Creeper Nets wouldn't find them. But Creeper Nets didn't hunt by sight, they tracked by scent. For a few moments the wind blew in the children's favor, rushing hard down the alley and carrying their scent away. Then it changed and came back at them, whipping through their hair and blasting around the front of the factory. The Creeper Nets reacted instantly, moving en masse toward them.

The children blundered out and ran as fast as they could toward the other end of the alley. But when they reached it, they found it blocked by the tall fence that enclosed the storage lot behind the factory.

They began to climb.

The thin links of the fence hurt their hands and feet, and the structure swayed with their weight. When they reached the top, they found it covered in rolls of razor wire. They couldn't get over it.

The Creeper Nets were scuttling down the alley, up the walls, and over the refuse containers. Tom and Luc clung to the fence, below the others. They watched a girl lunge for the guttering on the Tank Meat factory and dangle from her hands, trying to haul herself up. They watched her feet scramble against the wall. The moment she was on the roof, the rest followed quickly, almost losing their minds to panic, but by the time it was Tom and Luc's turn, three Creeper Nets were just below them. Tom lunged for the gutter and missed. He lunged again and caught it. Then Luc was beside him, climbing at the same time, up and over before Tom made it. Luc shot off, blind. Tom heard a girl scream, "Watch out!" and hauled himself up just in time to see Luc run straight onto a skylight in the factory roof.

They heard a splintering crack, the ground dissolved beneath Luc's feet, and he began to fall.

The Creeper Nets were coming. They ran toward the skylight and looked down through the broken glass. The light in the factory was soft and orange, cast from long lines of tanks. Luc had fallen into one of these and they could see him thrashing on the surface, his white gown billowing in the orange fluid. He'd fallen into a tank of growing meat. They felt lots of things then, in just a few seconds: relief that he'd survived, disgust that he'd landed in such a horrible place, then panic again. He was fifty feet below them and the Creeper Nets were coming.

A girl gasped.

They all turned and saw the flash of surprise on her face as a Creeper Net struck the side of her neck. There was nothing they could do, and more were coming. They ran, leaping over skylights toward the other side of the roof. They found a service ladder leading down into the yard at the back of the factory. But there were seven of them. They could not climb down fast enough. They looked around for weapons and found rusting scaffold poles on the wet, dirty felt. Then they stood at the top of the ladder and fought back the Creeper Nets as they came. They broke the Nets' legs, smashed their hubs, and battered them down until they lay in twitching heaps.

It made a lot of difference facing a Creeper Net with weapons in their hands.

But as Tom climbed last down the ladder, he saw a Creeper Net drop through the hole in the broken skylight. Luc had not been so lucky.

"The twins have landed, sir."

Gorman looked up, alert.

He swept away Sandwood Seven and summoned a view of the hangar in the fortress. The twins' freighter had just set down.

"They agreed to come back with no fuss?" Gorman asked.

"Yes, sir."

"Really?" Gorman said.

"Yes, they behaved perfectly, sir. We haven't heard a peep out of them all the way home."

"Excellent," Gorman said. "At least some of my children are doing what they're told. I thought Mika would be a good influence on Ellie. I'm glad I've put them together again."

During the game, he'd hunted for these mutant children and selected the six best to join Ellie. He called them his Chosen Ones, and while the implanted army slept in cold, concrete dormitories, his Chosen Ones were stored at the top of the fortress in a secure white enclosure. Mika, Audrey, Leo, Iman, Colette, and Santos. Gorman's jewels. He did not know that Mika had allowed himself to be chosen only in order to be with Ellie again. . . .

Gorman waited for the freighter door to open. The soldiers had given Mika and Ellie clean uniforms so they wouldn't have to tell Gorman about the fire and get blamed for it.

Gorman watched the twins walk through the Pod Fighters.

"Ellie does look calmer," he mused. "Even though I canceled her trip home. That's good, really good."

He watched Ellie talk to a man by the elevator.

"She's asking if she can take Mika to meet the monkey."

"Yes," Gorman replied. "Let them go. But only for an hour, and then put them in their enclosure. And send four men with them."

He watched Ellie's face light up as she was told the good news, then he swept the twins away, unaware that control of his army was about to pass into their hands.

Ellie sensed Puck waiting for her.

Because she'd been with Mika for the past few hours, the monkey had been left alone. Like them, he was stored in a maximum-security enclosure, with white floors and walls and bulletproof glass. Gorman had given the monkey to her as a pet, as one of his calculated acts of weapon management, but Puck was more than a pet: He was a Northern Government secret; he was proof that The Animal Plague never happened. Puck would never see daylight as long as Mal Gorman sat at the top of that fortress.

As the elevator began to rise, with Mika and Ellie in it, Puck stood up on the branch of his white plastic tree. Then he dropped to the floor and scampered toward the glass so he could watch the door beyond his enclosure.

He would have to wait longer than usual for her to arrive. Mika and Ellie were being escorted via a long route to avoid the dormitory levels. Implanted children were being carried to their beds, cocooned in their Creeper Nets. Mal Gorman wouldn't want his precious Chosen Ones to see this. Mika and

Ellie didn't want to see it, but they saw it anyway, in their minds and through the concrete walls.

When the guard opened that last, heavy door, they saw Puck at the glass, with his small, brown hands pressed against it.

"Hello!" Ellie cried.

She ran forward and crouched down, placing her hands on the other side, but when Mika joined her, Puck startled and scampered away.

"He's difficult with strangers," Ellie said. "He bites. But he'll be fine with you when he realizes who you are."

"He's so beautiful," Mika whispered.

The monkey watched him with hurt, suspicious eyes. Mika wanted to smile and cry. To see a live Black-capped Capuchin monkey was astonishing to a boy born behind The Wall. But to see it in a white box, feeling trapped, lonely, and confused, was heartbreaking too.

I know, Ellie thought. *We have a lot in common.*

"Stay here with him. I need to get something."

Ellie left for a moment and Mika crouched down and placed his right hand on the glass. Puck scampered farther away and sat in the corner, next to the trunk of his tree. But by the time Ellie returned, Puck was sitting on a branch close to the glass, with his eyebrows fidgeting.

"I told you," Ellie said. "He's beginning to realize who you are."

She held up a bag of letter tiles so the monkey could see it.

Puck leaped excitedly through the branches of the tree. She opened the door and they joined him in his cage.

It took a while for the monkey to calm down. After he'd

greeted Ellie, he spent a few minutes pulling Mika's hair and eyelashes and searching through his pockets for things to fiddle with. But Mika carried only one object—a holopic of mountain lions that had belonged to Ellie before she was taken. The corners were curled and the image was cracked. When Puck grew bored with it, Mika handed it to his sister. She looked at it and blinked, then put it in her pocket.

Then the game began.

At least it looked like a game.

The children sat on the floor with their legs crossed, and Ellie shook out the bag of letter tiles. Then Puck helped turn them over so they were all the right way up.

The four men with guns watched through the glass, yawned with boredom, then retreated to lean against the wall by the door.

The town Sandwood Seven was now part of a war It knew nothing about. Dozens of soldiers dropped into the streets and herded people back to their homes. The residents peeked through their blinds, trying to see what was happening, but all they saw was litter blowing down the streets, and the black slabs of freighters against the sky. They would wake up in the morning and wonder what they'd missed.

Meanwhile, thousands of children were trying to reach them. Thousands of children in dirty wet gowns, with bleeding hands and feet and implants. Some of Sandwood Seven's own children were among this ghastly flight, and their parents would never know.

The rain fell hard, pelting their skin. Tom ran with the rusting bar slipping through his hands. It was heavy and awkward, but he would not put it down. The Creeper Nets were everywhere, lurking in shadows and swarming over the buildings. Sometimes they dropped from the rooftops and almost landed on their heads. It would have been safer to run in the middle of the road, but because the freighters were above them, they were forced to cling to darkness, and wherever there was darkness, the Creeper Nets were waiting. By the time they reached the center of town, three of his friends had been caught, and the remaining three knew it was more luck than anything that had kept them running.

It was strange being in the center of a deserted town. All the shops were familiar, but there were no people, and every window was dark. There were no pods or hover cars zipping through the streets.

On the outskirts of the shopping zone, they saw a reflection move across the window of Sneaker World. They dropped back and listened as a pod whined past, and they felt a pang of hope. Perhaps there were some people here after all. When they emerged again, they ran past the shop and found themselves in the town square, facing Sandwood Seven's arcade. It was dark now, the blue fountain of light turned off and the great glass doors shut. They walked toward the arcade, drawn to the place even though it had gotten them into this mess.

A heap of litter had settled against the doors, cups from the Ra Ra Shake Bar and wrappers from Tank Meat Express. Tom crouched down to pick one up, then two things happened in quick succession: They heard the whine of another pod and they were grabbed by the arms and dragged into the alley between the arcade and a shop. They struggled, not understanding what was happening, then realized they had been dragged away by children and allowed themselves to be pushed down into the litter. They listened to the whine of the pod as it flew slowly around the square.

"They've sent out snipers," one of the children whispered. "They've started shooting at us. We think they're trying to kill us before we get too close to the towers."

They were quiet while they absorbed this news. When they were sure the snipers had left, they stood up and waded through the litter toward the back of the arcade. They now formed a group of eleven: six girls and five boys in tattered, bloody gowns that clung to their skin in the rain.

There was a small yard behind the arcade, full of air-conditioning units and refuse containers. They felt like rats skulking in the debris of their old world.

The arcade was on the top of a hill. When they looked south, they could see the refugee towers, spread out in the distance like rows of concrete crops. In these towers were normal people, like their parents; refugees of The Animal Plague. If they could reach these people, they would help them, but above the towers hung more freighters and between them was a maze of streets filled with Creeper Nets and snipers.

They had progressed to a new level of the game. One they would be lucky to survive.

They leaned against the arcade and wiped the rain from their faces.

"I was happy two weeks ago. Really happy."

"Me too."

"I loved Pod Fighter."

"It was like a wish, wasn't it? As if we'd wished for something exciting to happen to us, then the arcades appeared as if by magic."

"I loved the lights. I used to get home from school and run to the arcade to see the blue fountain."

"I liked the strawberry shakes in the Ra Ra Shake Bar."

"Yeah, they were good."

"Better than the Fit Mix."

"My parents were happy too. They said it was about time the Northern Government took an interest in us. They were hoping I'd win an apartment in the Golden Turrets."

"But we didn't, did we?"

"No."

"We won a lump of metal in our heads."

"I wonder what our parents will think when they see us like this."

"They must be really upset. We went out on Sunday and never came home."

"The government must have told them something."

"But not the truth."

"I reckon our parents know we've been taken for an army. But they haven't been told whom we're fighting. The government wants the land on the other side of The Wall, but if they intended to share it with our parents, they would have told them the truth before now. They would have had a willing army to fight this war if our parents knew the truth. They wouldn't have taken us like this."

"Our parents are too old to fight, anyway."

"I wonder if they tried to get us back."

"I bet they did."

"I hope they weren't hurt."

They tried to imagine what had happened in the hours after they were taken. They didn't know about the riot in The Shadows after Mal Gorman sent out his message, but they suspected something had happened. Their parents wouldn't have given up on them easily. This idea made them anxious.

"I don't want my parents to see me like this."

"They'll have to see us like this."

"But if we turn up at home with lumps of metal in our heads, they'll go nuts. They'll expect us to tell them everything. But if we tell our parents what's on the other side of The Wall, they'll start the war themselves."

"We can't go home if that will happen. We're trying to stop the war, not make it ten times worse."

"We could go home and tell them some things but not others."

"But then we'll be lying to them. We'll be just as bad as the government. And my mum knows when I'm lying. I wouldn't get away with it."

"No, neither would I. I can't look my father in the eye if I try to lie to him. And he knows."

"I don't want to lie to them, anyway. I'm sick of all these lies."

"Then we can't go home."

They were quiet again.

"But if we can't go home, what are we going to do?"

"Sort out this mess, then go home."

"How? Look at us! We ran away from our Pod Fighters and most of us have been caught by Creeper Nets."

"I hate this. I just want to be normal again."

"I want to go home and be normal."

"What we thought was normal was a lie. There is no

normal. The Animal Plague never happened. There are forests and rich people on the other side of The Wall. Our government's corrupt and even our teachers lied to us. This is real. Our government trying to use us to bomb forests full of animals. That if our parents find out, they'll start the war themselves. This is real."

"What are we going to do?"

All across Sandwood Seven, children gazed at the distant towers and The Whisper carried their thoughts in a stream through them all.

The darkness seemed darker. The towers looked like a threat instead of a sanctuary. They shivered in their thin white gowns, realizing they were surrounded by adults they couldn't ask for help.

Behind them, in the fortress, Mika and Ellie sat facing each other with a monkey crouched between them. He watched them intently, waiting for the game to begin. Then a letter passed from their minds to his and he set off searching for it among the tiles on the floor.

C

he found first, then . . .

O

M

E

B

A

C

K

In The Whisper, this mutant message was like a gold thread running through a silk rope. As Puck laid the letters down, black against white, its meaning was bright and strong. The children saw glimpses of the hands of the monkey, black eyes, white boots, glass, and guns.

COME BACK.
COME BACK TO THE FORTRESS AND SLEEP UNTIL YOU'RE NEEDED.
COME BACK TO YOUR POD FIGHTERS AND YOUR FRIENDS,
AND THEN WE'LL FIGHT OUR WAR – A WAR AGAINST WAR.

The children looked at each other. They would never have considered going back to the fortress, but it made total sense and their decision was made instantly. In the fortress they'd be close to their Pod Fighters and their friends. The medical staff would treat their wounds. They wouldn't be shot by snipers, or hunted by Creeper Nets, or have to face their parents' questions.

They would sleep in those dormitories again, but this time because they wanted to sleep in them, and when they awoke for the second time, they would know what to do.

Without speaking a word, they began to wade through the litter down the side of the dark arcade. When they reached the town square, they lay down on the ground a few footsteps from the great glass doors. And then they obeyed the call of their implants and fell into a deep sleep.

Their gowns soaked up the puddles. The girls' hair whipped in the wind. But for the first time since their implants were fitted, their pained expressions melted away and they looked as if they were sleeping in their own warm beds. Like on a Friday night with no school in the morning. As if when they woke up, they'd be doing something they wanted to do, rather than something they'd been told to do.

In the moment before Tom closed his eyes, he remembered Luc and wondered what had happened to him. Now he hoped he'd been caught by the Creeper Net and taken back to the fortress.

"The implants have started working again."

The engineers gathered around Gorman's desk while he shuffled views of Sandwood Seven. For almost an hour, he'd been staring at a deserted town with Creeper Nets crawling all over it. Now there were gowned bodies lying in the streets, where they could be seen easily from the air.

"Excellent," Gorman said. "Get the freighters down quickly and collect them before they get too cold. Are they all asleep? Are the children in the fortress sleeping too?"

"Yes, sir. They all dropped within seconds of each other."

"Good. Very good. Well done."

The engineers left the office, knowing this turn of events had nothing to do with them. But they weren't going to tell Mal Gorman that.

Awen lay at Mika's side, snoozing on his paws. Puck sat on Mika's shoulder, poking an inquisitive finger in his ear. Mika hunched; it felt horrible, but this new monkey friendship was important to him, so he tolerated it.

"Just tell him," Ellie said, grinning. *Or think it.*

If he can read my thoughts, he would have stopped by now. I feel like I've got a maggot in my ear.

He's taking advantage of you because you're trying to please him. He's smart. Tell him again. Be firm with him. He knows who you are now, so don't worry about upsetting him.

OK.

"That's enough now," Mika said. "Get your finger out of my ear."

Puck dropped into Mika's lap and opened the pocket where he had kept the holopic.

"You've already found it," Mika said. "There's nothing in there now."

"He's an optimist." Ellie grinned.

He needs to be, Mika thought.

Then Puck dropped from Mika's lap, scattering the letter tiles. The words COME and BACK hurtled like asteroids across the shiny floor.

"Help me put them away," Ellie said, holding up the bag. Then the monkey scampered back and forth, picking up the letter tiles and placing them in her hand. When they were all tidied up, she pulled the drawstring tight. The game was over.

The men stood by the glass, waiting.

"This is the difficult bit," Ellie said. "I hate leaving him."

As they walked through the door and closed it, Puck retreated to the white plastic tree and watched them with sad eyes.

We'll be back soon, Ellie thought. *And in a few days' time, if we get this right, you'll never see a plastic tree again.*

5 Return to The Shadows

Kobi Nenko and his father waded quietly through the dark water in old Soho. This was river water, cold, filthy, restless water, that had burst from the banks of the Thames and drowned the old heart of the city. It reached their knees and tugged at their legs; a mess of litter rolled through it, and their feet were grabbed with each sodden step by inches of slime. All they could hear as they waded was lapping. All they could see was broken buildings, covered in mold. This was The Shadows. The dark city that used to be known as London. Old Soho had been its creative soul, the home of artists, actors, thinkers, dreamers. But there was no evidence of their buzz now; it had been carried away by the water long ago.

Kobi Nenko had been born in The Shadows and he looked part of it. Under his long, ragged black coat and his long, ragged black hair, he was pale, gaunt, tall, and thin, like a plant that had sprouted from a seed in darkness and grown reaching for light. But there was no light to reach in The Shadows, for the Golden Turrets had been built on top of it. As Kobi followed his father through old Soho Square, they waded around one of the giant black pillars that held up the enormous platform on which the new city was built. When they looked up, they did not see the sky, they saw a solid sheet of black metal where it used to be. The Shadows was a dying place for the poor who couldn't afford to move. Kobi's mother had died there. It was the last place on Earth Kobi and his father wanted to be. But they had no choice. Kobi had stayed away from the arcades on the day Mal Gorman took his friends. Now he was running from the Northern Government, and The Shadows was the best place to hide.

But as they waded into Greek Street, Kobi did not feel lucky that he had gotten away, he felt despondent. He'd been one of Mika's best friends in Barford North, and like him, he'd sensed there was something wrong with the game. But while Mika had allowed himself to be drawn further into it, Kobi had stopped playing and avoided it. Now he was wondering if this was a good idea. He'd sensed the change as Mika and Ellie touched. He'd seen a ripple in the water . . . felt the first stir of shifting matter. Now he wondered if he was avoiding something important. He felt as if he was in the wrong place. As he waded after his father down Greek Street, he worried about this behind his hair.

His father paused and waited for him to catch up. "Are you OK?" he asked.

"Yes," Kobi replied. He didn't want to explain how he felt to his father. Abe was taking a huge risk to help him hide, and he was proud of his son for realizing there was something wrong with the game. Abe hated the Northern Government. He blamed it for his wife's death. Government ministers lived in the Golden Turrets that had stolen the sky above them, and the moment Kobi told him why he wanted to run, Abe had given up everything. His job, his hard-earned home in Barford North, everything. He'd already lost his wife; there was no way he'd let his son be taken by the Northern Government.

"All we have to do is find John," Abe said. "As soon as we find John, we'll have a place to stay. Then if the Northern Government searches for you here, you'll have The Shadows on your side. John knows everyone. There's no safer place in The Shadows than with Soho John."

They were heading toward a pub at the end of Greek Street. It was a pub where the people of Soho had sat and talked and drank beer for several hundred years. John was Abe's best friend in The Shadows and had lived in the pub since he was born. He was one of the few people who'd not come to London as a refugee.

But as they waded down Greek Street, they noticed how much worse it looked. The last time they were there, some of the buildings were still occupied. Lights shone in windows, and people waded past them in the street. Now the old shops and restaurants looked empty and the water around them was deserted.

"John will still be here," Abe said. "Soho John would never leave."

But when they reached the pub, they looked through the window and saw water lapping against a dark bar. All the brightly colored bottles, glinting glasses, and chatting people were gone. They stepped back and looked up, hoping to see a light in the first-floor window and saw that the roof had fallen in.

"Oh no," Abe said. "I can't believe it. John's gone."

"I bet he didn't leave until the roof fell in," Kobi said.

"I bet he didn't," Abe replied bitterly. "He would have stuck it out 'til the end. I hope he wasn't upstairs when it happened. I don't know what to do now."

Abe pulled his companion from his pocket and searched through his address book. His hands were so cold, he almost dropped it in the water. "I don't know where else he could be," he said. "He's always been here."

"Try calling him," Kobi suggested. "His number will be the same."

"Oh yes, of course. I'm so cold, I'm stupid. We have to get out of this water."

Kobi sat on the slimy windowsill while his father called John. It was very cold. He shrank down in his coat, buried his hands in his pockets, and awoke the borg kittens that were sleeping there. This made him think of Audrey. He'd been building these kittens for her before he left Barford North. As they squirmed against his fingers, he felt a pang of loss.

Why? he wondered.

He'd always been a loner. When he moved to Barford North, it was weeks before he spoke to Mika. He'd been a brilliant pilot in the game, Tom's game partner, but it hadn't hurt him to stay away from the arcade after he realized something was wrong. Because he was one of those rare, lucky people who discover at an early age what they're good at. He was a talented industrial robotic engineer, like his father.

Kobi could transform scraps of metal into beautiful animals. But now his friends seemed more important.

He watched his father wade back and forth across the street, talking to his friend John, and felt cast out and alone.

Abe ended his call looking relieved and happy.

"John's moved to an old office block along the river," he said. "He's going to come and meet us. He said to wait for him here. He'll be about an hour."

"OK," Kobi replied.

This was good news. Now they had somewhere to stay, but an hour was a long time to stand knee-deep in freezing water.

His father sat next to him and hugged his coat.

Nevermore *craarked*.

The borg raven was in Kobi's rucksack, squashed between his back and the pub window.

Kobi took off his rucksack. The bird was sticking its head out of it. A beady silver eye met his. He pushed the raven down and refastened the zip. He'd built this creature with his own hands and he didn't want to lose it to the water.

While father and son waited for John, they shared a box of cold noodles. But when the noodles were gone, the cold began to get to them. Kobi tried to doze to make the time pass faster, but every time he closed his eyes and drifted, he began to feel bad and he didn't know why. At that moment, the implanted army was trying to escape from the fortress, and he was feeling it faintly, but he was not connected.

"Are you sure you're OK?" his father asked.

"Yeah," Kobi said. "What time is it?"

"Just gone eight. We've still got fifteen minutes. Let's move around a bit. I can't feel my legs."

They waded down Little Compton Street, trying to stay in view of the pub, but as they passed a dark building, Kobi noticed a camera attached to the wall, following them down the street.

"Dad," he said. "That camera's watching us."

His father glanced up. The camera was pointed right at them, and the rest of the street was deserted.

"OK," Abe whispered. "Let's walk back to Greek Street. I don't think we should worry too much, but let's go where we can't be seen by it."

They began to wade. This time they heard the mechanism of the camera move.

"It's following us," Kobi whispered. "Is it a police camera? Do you think they can see how old I am?"

"Maybe," his father said. "It's difficult to see much of you with all that hair over your face, but you're tall. Don't panic. John will be here soon. Just walk slowly."

It wasn't hard to walk slowly through the heavy water. But now, instead of feeling numb with cold, Kobi was hot beneath his coat, his back prickling where he felt the camera's eye on him.

When they reached the end of Greek Street, they saw two people wading toward them from the direction of Soho Square. When they quickened their pace, it was clear one was John.

"Good," his father said. "They're here. We can get out of here now."

They began to wade up the street, planning to meet them halfway, but when they were still fifty feet apart, a police pod flew around the pillar in Soho Square, heading directly toward them. Its engine whined. Its lights reflected off the slimy buildings and the dark water below.

Then a mechanized voice filled the street: "Halt, civilians, put your hands in the air. Halt, civilians, put your hands in the air."

"Frag!" Kobi cursed. "They have come for me! What should we do?"

"Just stick your hands in the air," his father said quickly. "And do what they say. They've got guns, Kobi. I'd rather you were taken by the government than shot."

"I fragging wouldn't," Kobi said.

"Just do it, Kobi! Please! For me! Put your hands up!"

Kobi put his hands up and watched the police pod hover over John and his companion.

A door opened in the side and one of the policemen leaned out to talk to John. Kobi watched John explain something and point toward the pub. After a brief exchange, the policeman nodded and the pod began to fly toward Kobi and his father. Then they felt like rabbits looking down the barrel of a gun.

Suddenly, they heard a loud *BANG*.

They were so startled they just stood and watched as the police pod veered and crashed through a cake shop window.

Then John and his companion rushed toward them through the water. Kobi saw a gun in John's hand and began to realize what had happened. John had shot the police pod; he'd made it crash. Now it was wedged in the shop with its siren wailing and smoke pouring from its engine. They could see the policemen struggling to get out, with their own, bigger guns.

"Quick!" John shouted at them. "Go to that black door! Move!"

The door was between the cake shop and a restaurant. They pushed through it, with John and his companion hard behind them. When they were all through, it was slammed shut and locked. Then they found themselves in a deeper darkness, still in water and wading again, down a narrow alley with strangers all around them.

They were pulled into a building with rooms sloshing with water. Then out the back and into a watery yard. Then through a gate and along another alley, through another gate and into a building, up rotting stairs, and through a hole in a wall. Then down more stairs, and out again into deeper water, far from the smoke, siren, and guns.

Now they were moving toward the river. The water was getting deeper. The people who surrounded them had faces covered with scarves. The buildings looked darker and more desperate, and soon they were wading through the old financial heart of the city toward one of many office blocks that hadn't been used since the Golden Turrets were built. At the top was the company name:

FUTURE COMMUNICATION

The foyer of the building was flooded. A flight of moldy stairs rose out of the water. They began to climb.

For ten flights, Kobi saw nothing but empty doorways leading into deserted offices. But when they reached the eleventh floor, the steps and walls looked almost dry and they found themselves facing a metal door and a security camera. The top twenty floors of this building had become home to several hundred people.

Kobi felt people watching them through the camera, then the metal door clicked and opened. John waved them in with a kind smile and Kobi felt grateful. But it was a wary gratitude. There was an intensity to the strangers around him that made him feel uneasy. Only a few days before, The Shadows' people had rioted because their children were taken. But they would not get their children back, or the sky or clean air or any of the things they wanted. They had plenty of reasons to be angry, and this did not make for a relaxing, homey environment. As John followed them through the door with the gun, Kobi wished he'd put it away.

On the other side of the door was a large room: a buffer zone between the water outside and the homes within. It contained hundreds of damp boots and coats.

A group of people had gathered to welcome them. His father was helped with his coat, but it was Kobi they were most interested in. Kobi was the only child born in The Shadows to avoid capture. He symbolized rebellion against a corrupt government. But Kobi was trying to get away from trouble, not closer to it, and he found the sudden attention difficult. Between the adults' legs were scores of curious young children, who watched him with owl eyes.

They took his coat, his long, black coat. He asked to keep it on, but they insisted he take it off because it was wet and would make him cold, so he handed it over and stood before them in a ragged white T-shirt and a black sweater with a big hole in the front. He felt practically naked without his coat, and was glad his face was covered by so much hair. But they were being kind to him, so he tried to be gracious about it.

Next he and Abe were shown their new home.

The eleventh floor, beyond the buffer zone, was fitted with communal living areas, meeting rooms, and kitchens. The other nineteen habitable floors of the office building had been divided into family sleeping units. Their walls were thinner than those of a fold-down apartment and they were only just big enough for beds and storage. But Kobi and his father were pleased when they were given a room with a desk between two beds. Abe dropped his bag onto it. They both had more tools than clothes with them.

Then the people departed, closing the door quietly, leaving father and son alone.

6 A Swarm of Shiny Flies

The next morning in Cape Wrath was gray and still. Waves lapped against the cliffs, and the blanket of cloud threatened only drizzle.

Mal Gorman had had a late night, but he was at his desk at dawn, flicking through the fortress cameras. The implanted army was still sleeping peacefully, and the nurses were treating its wounds. Some of the children had hypothermia and had been taken to the hospital unit, but most would be fighting fit again in a few days. It was mostly surface damage, cuts, bruises, and Creeper Net wounds, nothing worth worrying about.

Seven children had fallen from the cliffs and been lost to the sea, but Gorman wasn't worried about those, either. He decided their deaths were a weeding-out process. If those children weren't able to survive the cliffs like the others, it was likely they'd make similar mistakes in war.

Most of the bodies had been found. Gorman would tell the parents later. Like Ellie and Mika's parents, they would never know what had really happened to their children.

When Gorman bored of looking at the curved backs of nurses, he ordered breakfast. Ralph appeared with a heavy tray.

"Where would you like it, sir?" the butler asked.

"In front of me," Gorman said. "Where do you think?"

"Very good, sir," Ralph replied. He placed the tray in the middle of the screen, over the faces of the sleeping children, and left again.

Then Gorman ate heartily.

Mika awoke to find Awen's nose an inch from his own. The dream dog had been watching him like a sentinel since he'd fallen asleep. Mika fiddled with his ears. They were soft and warm and smelled like butter cookies dipped in tea.

"Funny dog," he whispered.

He got up and sat on the edge of the bed. The dog made room for his legs, then yawned and settled himself on his feet, looking up as Mika rubbed the sleep from his face. There had been a time when Awen only visited in his dreams. Then he began to appear during the day, whenever Mika was in danger.

In the coming days, the dog would watch his every move.

Mika's room in the Chosen Ones' enclosure was small and white, with not much more than a bed to fill it. Audrey joined him while he was still sitting in darkness.

Audrey looked cute in her regulation white army pajamas. They were a bit too big for her. Her short red hair had been punked by her pillow, and her alien, fairy face was still sleepy.

But her green borg eyes were wide awake and glowed with unnatural, nuclear light: partly because it was dark in the room, partly because she was so happy to see Mika.

"I woke up at four," she told him.

"You should have gone back to sleep," he said.

"I tried," she replied. "I couldn't."

She sat next to him, and her legs jiggled against the base of the bed. Mika grinned. He knew she'd been sitting next door, waiting for him to wake up.

"Sit still," he said.

"I can't," she replied. "I missed you yesterday, and after the army woke up, they made us stay in the enclosure watching TV."

She glanced at the camera over the door.

We could feel them connecting and disconnecting, she thought, *and it was really difficult being stuck in here, knowing what was happening outside. We wanted to do something.*

You will do something, Mika thought in response. *Next time the army wakes up, it will fly out of here, and we'll be with it.*

Her eyes became earnest. *We're actually going to do it, aren't we? Like we talked about in the forest. We're going to stop the war.*

Mika met her questioning gaze. *We're going to try. But it won't be easy. Don't get excited yet. It's going to be difficult and dangerous.*

I know. She nodded. *But I can't wait to get out of here. I hate this enclosure. I can hardly breathe. Leo was pacing around last night. The TV was driving us nuts. We're ready now.*

But everything has to be done the right way, Mika reminded her. *We can't rush it. Our main objective is to make adults listen to us, on both sides of The Wall, and consider negotiating for freedom instead of fighting for it.* He scratched Awen behind the ears. *But before the adults will listen to us, we have to make them respect us. We have to prove to them that we're not just children and that we know what we're talking about. So we'll take control of the North—this fortress and all its weapons. Then we'll take control of The Wall. Then, when we've proved how powerful we are, we'll talk to the South on behalf of our people and tell them what we've done. Ask them for freedom without a war and explain to them why it makes sense.*

Now it was Mika who looked briefly at the camera before continuing. *But the first thing we have to do is get rid of Mal Gorman. He's our main problem at the moment. We won't be able to take control of this fortress while he's sitting at the top of it.*

Audrey's eyes brightened mischievously. *And how are we going to do that?*

That's what we need to figure out, Mika thought. *Today. It's not going to be easy to move him while he's attached to that life-support system. But we've got a meeting with him after breakfast. We can get a good look at him then. He's going to get the shock of his life.*

Good, Audrey thought. *He deserves a shock. While we were stuck there staring at the stupid telly, all we could hear was the children. It was horrible, Mika. I'm so glad you're back.*

So am I. And I'll introduce you to Ellie when she wakes up.

Good. Then I'll have two of you. Twice as much.

Three times, even. My sister's quite a character. I think you're going to like her.

Mika pulled her close and breathed in her hair. If Awen

smelled of butter cookies dipped in tea, Audrey smelled of flowers in the forest. It was good to have them both so close. Awen was so much more than a dog; Audrey was so much more than a partner in a Pod Fighter game.

After Gorman finished his breakfast, he considered his first lie of the morning. He usually sent the Northern Government a progress report at this time of day, but he didn't want the other ministers to know the army had just climbed out of bed and, of their own free will, tried to run away. It made him look like an idiot.

He summoned views from the new Houses of Parliament in the Golden Turrets. It was almost nine o'clock, but the ministers' offices were quiet. Nothing moved but the hands on the old-fashioned clocks on their walls.

I could get away with not telling anyone, Gorman thought, *if I threaten the fortress staff so they don't talk.*

For when this war was won, Mal Gorman didn't want any old mansion on the other side of The Wall. He wanted the mansion of Raphael Mose, the leader of the World Conservation Club. It wasn't the biggest or most expensive; it didn't have ten swimming pools and hundreds of rooms like some of the others; but this was the mansion Mal Gorman wanted. And if the government found out he'd almost lost the army, he'd probably end up in some rotting shack next to a swamp. This did not appeal to him. So he swept the empty offices away and wrote his nine o'clock report without mentioning the children's awakening.

When this was done, he spent a few happy minutes looking at curtain and carpet samples for Raphael Mose's mansion. Then he summoned his Chosen Ones for their meeting.

While he waited for them to arrive, he felt a bit excited and nervous, like a lion tamer with a new crop of lions. Ralph had replaced his breakfast with a bowl of Everlife pills. He crunched them and watched the door.

Men with guns arrived and formed a line against the wall. Mika and Ellie followed and stood before Gorman's desk.

This was the first time he'd seen them together in the flesh. For a moment they looked like part of the office, as still as the carpet, walls, and paintings. And their eyes had changed: Their black corneas had a mercurial gleam. In the light cast from his window, they looked very odd indeed. He'd never seen Ellie so quiet before, and the dark scowl that used to be a feature of her face had vanished. Mika looked put together in his new white uniform. Gorman decided, on balance, that he was pleased with them.

"Good morning," he said.

"Good morning, sir," Mika replied.

Audrey entered next. Mika's gunner, and what a gunner! Probably the best in the whole army. She'd been born without eyes, but the borg eyes that replaced them were better than any human's. Grass green and nuclear bright. Audrey was a radium fairy made by Irish and Russian blood and technology: weird, beautiful, and deadly. But she was also an optimistic child. She had none of Mika and Ellie's languor. Gorman liked her.

Audrey took her place at Mika's side and looked over her shoulder as the rest walked in.

Next entered Leo, the Lion Boy. He was born with a

skin-covered tail. His mix of Jamaican and Canadian bloods had bestowed on him gold skin, gold dreadlocks, and startling blue eyes. He walked toward Mal Gorman's desk with a sinuous grace that communicated all his newly awoken power. He was a perfect mutant specimen, with incredible leadership potential.

Leo wore a gold ring on one finger. Gorman looked at this. Leo had been told to take it off when he arrived at the fortress, but Gorman decided not to mention it. Everything else about the boy was perfect. This rebellious ring could be removed later.

"Good morning, Leo," Gorman said.

"Good morning, sir," the boy replied.

Next entered Iman, the ebony girl, with all the streamlined grace of a Pod Fighter. This child had been given up for adoption by her parents because she grew horns when she was four.

Their loss, my gain, Gorman thought.

This striking black girl was a brilliant strategist and another very good gunner.

Santos entered next. Santos, the Hawk Boy, with spurs that curved from his wrists. His eyes moved quickly as he took in the details of the office, and for a split second, Gorman felt dissected by his pointed stare. This boy's intelligence had a razor sharpness that made him an expert problem solver.

Last to come was Colette, the French girl who'd been born without hands and feet. She was a good example of a child who'd once been persecuted for her mutation but was now celebrated for it. Her new hands and feet were silver, and mimicked the mechanics of real bone, sinew, and muscle. They were expertly made and eerily beautiful. Since arriving in the fortress, she'd worn them without skin gloves. Long hair skimmed cheekbones of peaches and cream and hid the analytical mind of a chess champion. Colette was a shy one, but she was one to watch. Chosen from thousands and about to get a lot of money and time invested in her development.

Here were Mal Gorman's Chosen Ones, the most talented and useful children in the army.

"You look well," Gorman said.

He took an Everlife pill and crunched it contentedly. Then he looked at Iman. "Do your parents like their new home in the Golden Turrets?"

"Yes, sir," she replied. "They think it's beautiful."

"That's nice," Gorman said. "You're very special, Iman. Your parents deserve a beautiful home. And how are you, Audrey? What's it like living in your new enclosure?"

"It's nice, sir," Audrey replied.

"Excellent. So you're all ready to start work?"

They nodded and watched him take another Everlife pill. He put it in his mouth and crunched it with yellow teeth. So many tubes and wires punctured his skin, he looked like an accident in a spaghetti factory: swamped by his machines, frail, sitting among them. The golden light that radiated from his body ran weak into the blue of the machines. His mind was active, but the body that housed it was just barely alive.

He'll be dead within minutes if we take him without that life-support system, Mika thought.

Yeah, Ellie replied. *And he'll need medical treatment too.*

Maybe we should just take it all, Leo thought. *Life-support machine, doctors, and half a hospital unit.*

There has to be an easier way, Mika thought. *How are we going to hide him with all that equipment and medical staff?*

And what if something goes wrong? We don't want to risk killing him. The shock alone might do it. We have to keep him alive. He needs to know we're not like him. That we don't solve problems by killing things.

"I expect you want to know what I plan to do with you," Gorman continued, oblivious to the thought exchange. "You've got your crisp new uniforms now, and your new enclosure. You won't be bored, I can assure you of that. You start your new training today. You'll continue with exercises to develop your powers and you'll learn how to use the new equipment that will help you survive on the other side of The Wall. And if you're doing well next week, I'll send you all on your first mission. To the factories where they build the animal borgs. We don't understand the technology and we need more information about how they're made. However, Mika, Ellie, I'm sending you over tomorrow. I have a special mission for you."

Mika and Ellie looked at him, startled. They weren't expecting this. They'd hoped to escape before they were sent on one of Gorman's death missions.

"The rest of you can leave," Gorman said.

Mika and Ellie waited while Audrey, Leo, Iman, Santos, and Colette left the room, followed by most of the men with guns. Gorman told Ellie to shut the door behind them.

When she turned around to face him again, he said, "I'm pleased with you, Ellie. You look much calmer. Do you feel better now that Mika's here?"

"Yes," she replied cautiously.

"Good," Gorman said. He ate another Everlife pill.

"The mission I have for you is quite special," he began. "You could call it a warm-up, if you like. A special favor to me. And if you do well, I'll give your parents ten thousand credits to spend on furniture. I believe they moved into their new apartment with only the gray sofa they brought with them from Barford North. Is that right, Mika?"

"Yes," he replied.

"Do you think your parents would appreciate ten thousand credits?" Gorman prompted.

"Yes, sir," Mika answered.

"Good," Gorman said. "So I'll tell you how you can get it. I'm going to send you over The Wall to the home of Raphael Mose. Raphael Mose is the leader of the World Conservation Club. He's the most powerful man in the South and he lives in a mansion, a hundred miles from The Wall. When you get there, I want you to show it to me. I want you to walk around the grounds and the house so I can look at everything. You'll have com equipment and headsets, so everything you look at, I'll be able to see through my desk and we'll be able to talk to each other."

The twins felt confused. Gorman wasn't talking about killing anyone, which was good, but this didn't sound like a war mission. It sounded personal.

Ellie glanced at his desk and saw an open folder of . . . fabric samples?

I know what he's doing, she thought. *He's using us to go house hunting for him. We're taking him on a guided tour of the mansion he wants to live in!*

Perp, Mika thought.

At least we won't have to kill anyone, Ellie reasoned.

It was irritating. While they were off house hunting for Gorman on the other side of The Wall, the implanted army would be waiting. The twins had more important things to do. Like get rid of Mal Gorman and take his fortress away.

But then Gorman added a detail that would make their mission worthwhile.

"And when you've shown me the house," he said, "I want you to search for something in it and bring it back to me."

He looked a bit wild now, his eyes hot and his tubes twisting.

"What?" Mika asked bluntly.

"This," Gorman replied, picking up an Everlife pill. "But much, much better." He crunched it and his light brightened for a moment. "Everlife was invented by the scientists on the other side of The Wall, but they won't let us have the good stuff, only this, which is the first version, made forty years ago. It hardly does anything. I want you to find me Everlife-9. I know Raphael Mose will have some."

"What does it do?" Ellie asked.

"It doesn't just stop you from dying," he replied excitedly. "It reverses the aging process. There are people living on the other side of The Wall who look twenty-five but are older than me. Raphael Mose is a hundred and three years old and I bet he looks thirty. Everlife-9 is amazing."

"So if you take Everlife-9," Ellie continued, "you won't need that life-support system anymore? Or the doctors or anything?"

"Exactly," he said. "If you bring back Everlife-9, I'll never need this chair again. I'll be young, fit, and strong. So . . . what do you think of your mission? Think you can do it?"

"Yes," Ellie replied.

"You're not scared?" Gorman asked. "Of going over The Wall? It could be dangerous."

"We want to go," Mika said.

Gorman was impressed by the twins' resolve. "You'll get all the training you need, just quicker than the others. You'll spend the day learning how to use your new equipment and I'll send you over first thing tomorrow morning. Good luck."

"Thank you," Mika said.

Gorman watched them leave, thinking what a nice, polite boy Mika Smith was.

Mika followed Ellie into the elevator and they were taken by armed guards down the fortress to a training area, where they were left in a classroom. The men with guns settled at the back and leaned against the wall.

Ellie sat down and put her feet up on one of the desks. This was a familiar environment to her—she'd worked in classrooms like this for over a year—but it was not familiar to Mika. He milled around the desks, remembering their old classroom in Barford North. The bitter cold in winter, the unpainted concrete walls, the Plague posters, and Mrs. Fowler, who sat at the front wearing a pom-pom hat and mittens. The contrast between old and new was stark: This classroom was warm and bright, and full of expensive equipment.

And Ellie.

He glanced at her.

She smiled.

The door opened and a woman entered. She was dressed in white, with short gray hair, and she had the familiar sharp look of all the instructors they'd met. Jabbing a tablet with one finger, she hurried past them toward the desk at the front of the room.

"Find a place and sit down, Mika," she said. "My name is

Rona Strap. Hello, Ellie. Get your feet off the desk. Those screens cost several thousand credits."

Mika sat next to Ellie and they watched Rona Strap search for their lesson plan.

"I thought I was going to get a week before your first mission," she said, sounding flustered. "But we've only got one day, so we're going to have to get through everything quickly. It's going to be hard work."

Once she'd found their lesson plan, she looked at Ellie again. "Is there something wrong with your eyes?" she asked. "You look a bit . . . tired."

"I'm fine," Ellie said.

"OK," the woman replied. "But you must concentrate, both of you. Welcome, Mika."

"Hi," Mika said.

"OK, let's get on with it. Tomorrow, you'll be dropped on the other side of The Wall with equipment you've never used before. While you explore the mansion and search for Everlife-9, you'll be close to Raphael Mose and his family. You'll be breaking into his home and encountering the security systems that protect it, including animal borgs you may not have interacted with before. Raphael Mose is a very dangerous man, and a very important one at that, so if you want to survive, you're going to need to know your equipment well."

She paused. They were watching her steadily with those weird, mercurial eyes. She'd just told them they were facing danger and they hadn't blinked. She still doubted they were fully concentrating. She had planned to show them the drop capsules first, but she decided to save that lesson until later and show them something more interesting; something that would wake them up.

"Your biggest advantage on the other side of The Wall," she said, "will be that the borgs believe you're animal, not human. And we've designed something else that will offer protection from Mose's bodyguards."

She turned. On the wall behind her desk was a safe. She punched a sequence of numbers into the control panel, and the door swung open. Inside was a white case. She removed it and opened it and walked toward their desks to show them what was inside. The case contained eight silver orbs. She removed one and held it up. It was about the size of a golf ball, with a thin chain hanging off it.

"This," she said, "is an invisibility shield."

That woke them up. Their eyes were suddenly intense and curious.

"You wear it around your neck," she said. "And when you need it, you press the top."

She put it on. A small hole appeared and a cloud of tiny fragments puffed out like a swarm of shiny flies. They surrounded her, shimmering like millions of mirror fragments. Then they linked, flashed, and vanished—and she vanished with them.

"Each fragment of the shield is a tiny screen," she said. "And each screen has an even smaller camera lens right in the middle of it. The fragments work in pairs, transmitting an image to its counterpart on the opposite side. So whatever angle you look at my body, you see only what's behind it."

Her voice moved as she walked around their desks.

"The only fault with the shield is its fragility. The linked surface is not very strong. So if you bump into something, it will break apart for a few seconds, and you might be exposed. You must make sure this does not happen.

"Mika," she continued, "move your hand in front of you."

Mika swept his fingers, and the air stirred like water. They caught a glimpse of the woman's arm through the hole in the shield's surface.

"Do you want to try it?" she asked.

"Yes," he replied.

There was a whooshing sound as the silver orb sucked up the tiny screens, and Rona Strap appeared again. Then she took the chain from around her neck and passed it to Mika, letting Ellie take another one from the case. The twins stood up, put them on, pressed the tops, and vanished.

It happened so fast that Rona Strap felt a surge of panic, despite the presence of guards at every exit. As if guards could offer protection from mutants like these.

"That's enough, children," she announced nervously, her eyes scanning the room. "Turn them off."

The twins reappeared. She held out the case, and they put the silver orbs back.

"Right, that's your first piece of equipment," she said. "Now let's look at your headsets. They've got a navigation system different from the one you're accustomed to using in Pod Fighters."

Mika and Ellie watched her return the invisibility shields to the safe. She shut the heavy door and set the lock. Then her light pulsed with relief, as if she felt safer. As if such things as doors and codes offered protection from children like these.

7 No Time to Be Messing About

Audrey took Mika's hand and looked into it, at the golden light, at the way he was made. Skin, bone, muscle, blood — she could look atom-deep into his body now.

It was early morning. They were sitting on his bed again. In an hour he would be taken away and dropped over The Wall.

"What can you see?" he asked.

"The patterns in your veins," she whispered. "I was just thinking they're the same as those in leaves."

"And antlers," he said.

"Yes. Like leaves and antlers and branches and rivers."

She dropped his hand.

"I wish you were coming with us," he said.

"So do I," she replied, and he felt her try to suppress her thoughts, but she could not stop him from knowing them.

The first time Mika had flown over The Wall, Audrey had been with him and they'd nearly died. The Ghengis borgs on

The Wall had almost shot them down. Then they were attacked by an eagle borg and had fallen into a forest, where their Pod Fighter burned in the branches of a tree. It had been a very dangerous way to discover the truth about their world.

And now Mika was going again, without her.

And *she* was his game partner. *She* should be with him on the other side of The Wall. Audrey liked Ellie, but she couldn't help feeling . . . jealous. This was not a nice feeling. She didn't want to feel it and she tried hard to make it go away.

Mika took her hand again. Her fairy fingers were milk pale against his darker ones.

Ellie's my sister, he thought. *You don't get to choose sisters. I love her, but I didn't choose her. I chose you.*

Audrey, Leo, Iman, Colette, and Santos were taken away for a training session. Then the enclosure filled with adults who had come to help Mika and Ellie prepare for their mission. The children stood in the living area, feeling like dressmakers' dolls while these people rushed around them. They were given thermal suits to wear under their uniforms, and armor to wear over them. The armor was made of a strong, white material. Chest and back plates, shoulder pads, elbow protectors, lower arm guards, and knee-length boots.

Then they were given their headsets and equipment belts, and concentrated hard as the adults recapped the elements of their training. They wanted to survive and they wanted to find the Everlife-9 as much as Gorman wanted to take it. Everlife-9 would make him younger so he wouldn't need all those machines. Without realizing it, Mal Gorman was helping them get rid of him.

When they were dressed and checked, they were led out of the enclosure and down in an elevator to the hangar. Awen followed Mika with his nose glued to his leg.

In the hangar, they walked through the lines of shiny Pod Fighters toward a new craft called a Stealth Carrier. It had been designed specifically to carry them safely over The Wall. It had slim wings and a pale, metallic surface. It was about ten times the size of a Pod Fighter, but it had been built for the same kind of speed and agility. It was designed to get them over The Wall and back again as quickly as possible. The engine was silent. The surface was covered in tiny cameras and screens just like the invisibility shields that Rona Strap had demonstrated. While the craft rested on its launchpad, they could see it. The moment they boarded, it blinked and disappeared.

A drop capsule and several men joined them in the hold.

The Stealth Carrier rose silently. The children watched the fortress shrink until it was a black ring on the coastline. As they rose, the sun peeked up to the east, icing the lips of waves and the refugee towers. Then they shot toward The Wall and it all blurred into one gray streak.

They approached The Wall at high altitude. From this height it looked like a gray line drawn around the Earth just below the south coast of England and through the middle of France. The contrast between the landscapes was startling. Mika and Ellie pressed against the window, feeling rushes of anxiety and excitement.

"Pul on your headsets," someone said. "We'll be at the drop site in ten minutes."

The Stealth Carrier turned west, following the line of The

Wall across the Atlantic toward Canada. The children stood up and the men checked them over for the last time. When this was done, they activated their navigation systems. Suddenly, their visors were filled with green mesh light. When they looked down, they saw a string of red dots along the top of The Wall, showing the location of the Ghengis borgs.

They reached the east coast of Canada in just a few minutes.

"Climb into your capsule."

The capsule looked like a mirror ball until the door opened. Inside were two seats. Mika and Ellie climbed in, sat down and fastened their harnesses.

"Remember, the parachute will open automatically," someone said, "so you don't have to do anything until you land. Then make sure you roll the capsule out of sight, because you can't get back without the micro wings stored under your seats. Do you understand?"

They nodded.

The door closed, sealing them in.

"Have you dropped them yet?" Gorman asked.

"In thirty seconds, sir."

"Good," Gorman replied. "How long before they reach Raphael Mose's mansion?"

"Forty-five minutes, sir."

"OK," Gorman said. "I'm waiting. Tell me as soon as they reach the grounds and I'll join you."

Through the transparent wall of the drop capsule, Mika and Ellie watched the adults' lights pulse with relief as they were sealed inside. They felt a tug as the Stealth Carrier sprinted over The Wall, they saw hands press against the capsule, then they were hurtling toward Earth like an asteroid. The capsule was weighted to prevent it from spinning, but the g-force made them feel as if their innards were about to eject. The noise was intense, as if they were falling through a firestorm, and they could see the ground rushing up toward them. They heard a click and felt a sudden, violent jerk as the parachute opened. For a few seconds it dragged them back up, then the wind noise faded and they were falling again, more gently this time, and they watched through the floor of the capsule as the trees reached up to greet them.

They heard a crunch when the capsule hit the canopy. The scratch of small branches and leaves against it. Then it dropped again, hitting the ground with a soft thud. It rolled forward a short distance because it had landed on a slope, then it jerked to a halt as the lines of the parachute tangled in a tree.

It was dark inside the capsule. They could see nothing through its wall. They'd landed in North America, five hours behind Europe. It was still the middle of the night.

A voice spoke to them through their headsets.

"Are you down?"

"Yes," Ellie replied.

"Turn on your night vision."

They blinked at one of the icons on their visors and suddenly the trees beyond the capsule appeared as ghost-gray forms. They were different from those Mika had seen in northern France; these were Canadian redwoods, soft barked and colossal, their trunks rooted in the ground like mountains. As the children looked at the trees, they began to see their living light. Soon their new environment turned from gray to gold.

"What can you see?" the voice asked.

"Trees," Mika replied. "Giant trees. And a cluster of red dots. I think there's a pack of wolf borgs approaching us."

"They're coming to check you out," the voice replied. "Open the capsule so they can smell you or they might attack it."

They undid their harnesses, but as Mika reached toward the lock icon, he saw something move to their left. A huge body of gold light was shifting through the trees.

"There's something else here," Ellie said.

"What is it?" the voice asked.

"A big animal," Mika said. "Massive."

"I'll log into your visual so I can see with you," the voice told them.

"It's coming toward us," Ellie said.

A few seconds passed and they watched the red dots of the wolf borgs grow larger as they approached.

"Ignore the wolves for the moment," the voice said. "Look at the animal."

"We can't see it now," Mika replied. "It's dis—"

They heard a roar and a cracking thud as something hit the back of the capsule. It jerked forward, throwing them out of their seats.

"It's attacking us," Ellie cried.

"It must be a bear," the voice replied. "It's probably got cubs nearby."

"What should we do?" Mika asked. With the night vision and their special sight, they could see the bear standing on its back legs and throwing its full weight against the capsule as if it were trying to crack it like an egg. Its retinas glowed silver in a mass of angry, red-streaked light and its jaws yawned as it roared at them, its claws scraping down the wall of the capsule.

"Kill it," the voice said. "The wolf borgs have nearly reached you. You have to get out of there. If you don't kill the bear, they'll attack you as well and they'll damage the capsule. You know how. Just open the door and look at it."

"No," Ellie said.

"That's an order!" the voice shouted. "If you don't kill the bear, the wolf borgs will kill you!"

They looked to their right. They could see the giant silver wolves loping through the trees. They stood up, Mika hit the icon to open the door, and they both leaped out. The bear paused, startled by their sudden appearance.

You deal with the wolves, I'll deal with the bear, Mika thought.

Ellie ran toward the wolves, and Mika turned to face the bear, then pressed the top of the invisibility shield so it whooshed out around him. With a shimmering blink, he vanished and began to run, leading the bear with his scent and sound, away from the capsule. It bounded in his wake, roaring and swiping with an immense, clawed paw. He thought the shield would offer some protection, because the bear could not see exactly where he was, but he felt a blow on his shoulder and was hurled forward to smack against a tree. His headset flew off and he landed on his back with the bear almost upon him.

"Kill it!" the voice yelled. "What the frag are you doing?"

Mika fumbled with the shield, trying to get rid of it again. The technology wasn't helping. He heard a whoosh as it was sucked back in. He could smell sharp pine, hear the voice shouting through his headset, but it had rolled down the slope and was too far away to reach. He could see the giant silver wolves in his peripheral vision, running circles around Ellie. The bear rose on its back legs, ready to drop its weight on his chest, and Mika looked into its eyes, asserting his strength. It turned its head to the side as if Mika were leaning against its jaw, and after a few seconds, it dropped to all fours and lumbered away. Immediately the wolves ran in to inspect him, silver lips curling over daggered snarls and red borg eyes glowing in the darkness. He stood up and let them smell his face. They were immense, each one a ton of flex metal muscle, that towered over him.

He waited while they decided what he was.

Not human.

Animal.

Allowed.

The snarls subsided. For a while they walked around him, looking into the dark forest, then they loped off, leaving him and Ellie alone among the giant redwood trees. He walked forward and picked up his headset, brushed the dead pine off of it, and put it on.

"Hello," he said.

"Mika!" the voice yelled. "You *fragging* idiot! What happened?"

"Nothing," Mika replied. "The bear's gone. I'm fine."

"You do what you're told from now on!" the voice yelled. "Both of you. Do you hear me? If I tell you to kill an animal, you kill it. This is no time to be messing about."

"I didn't mess about," Mika replied calmly. "I didn't need to kill it."

"Go and hide your capsule. Cut the lines of the parachute, pull it out of the tree, and roll it somewhere it can't be seen."

"What are we waiting for?" Gorman asked angrily. "You said forty-five minutes an hour ago."

"They encountered a problem on landing," the voice replied. "The capsule was attacked by a bear. But they're approaching Raphael Mose's estate now. You'll be able to join them in about twenty minutes."

Ellie and Mika stood together while they looked at their maps. Raphael Mose's mansion was a mile away in the bottom of a valley. The forest sloped down toward it. Their feet slipped and crunched through a carpet of pine needles as they began their approach. They noticed the cold and turned up the heat of their thermal suits. But the rest of the gadgets they'd been given, they felt they could do without. The voice nagged them constantly, telling them to hurry up and watch out for bears. They turned down the volume so they could only just hear it, and turned off the night vision completely. They preferred their own method of seeing the trees: focusing on their trunks until they glowed with warm gold light, which was infinitely more beautiful than the gray ghosts of army night vision. Awen trotted before them, enjoying the walk, and for a few minutes, they marveled at the sheer beauty of it. They felt *right* here in this forest, calm and whole, as if *this* was home. The living light flowed through the ground and into their feet in the way it never did in the concrete towers on the other side of The Wall. This forest was part of them. They could see it. Feel it.

They were part of one great, complex organism.

And our parents don't know, Ellie thought. *They don't feel connected to each other or this. They've broken it somehow.*

But they could never see it like we do, Mika replied. *It's not really their fault. We'll find a way to show them.*

"Can you hear me?" the voice asked impatiently.

"Yes," Mika replied.

"Good," the voice said. "For a minute I thought you weren't listening to me. You should reach the perimeter fence of the grounds soon. Be careful you don't walk into it, because it's electric to keep out the bears."

They heard a bird clatter through the branches above and something scamper up a nearby tree. For a moment they wished they could sit down instead and watch the dawn arrive.

They heard the fence before they saw it, buzzing like a swarm of bees.

"We're there," Ellie said.

"OK," the voice replied. "Lift yourselves over it and wait. Mal Gorman wants to see everything from this point. I'll let you know when he's online."

They walked toward the fence and closed their eyes, focusing on their own inner light. Then they lifted themselves up and over it. Mika had never done this before. He was surprised how easy it was, but landed clumsily on the other side in the middle of a prickly bush. He stood up holding his shoulder, which still ached from the encounter with the bear.

"You need to work on those landings, Mika," the voice said. "Don't let yourself drop like that: Someone might hear you."

Mika stood up and joined Ellie at the edge of a shrub border. Here was nature shaped by humans: the bushes pruned, the trees spaced, tilled earth and bark chips beneath their feet.

"OK," the voice said. "Mal Gorman is online now. Use your invisibility shields and walk toward the house."

They activated their shields and moved quietly forward onto mown grass. It was cushion soft and damp. Beyond that they saw nothing but an expanse of darkness. The map told them to head southwest. As they walked, they heard Mal Gorman complaining because he couldn't see anything. Occasionally a tree loomed out of the darkness or a rabbit scarpered in front of them, but all they could really glean about the place was its vastness. The mown grass seemed to go on forever.

"Does Raphael Mose own all of this?" Mika whispered.

"Yes," the voice replied.

They saw a red and white pole sticking out of the ground, with a flag on the top of it. They walked forward and found themselves on a circle of closely cropped grass. It was flat and hard.

"What's this?" Mika asked.

"A golf hole," the voice replied. "Walk on."

The ground sloped suddenly and they found themselves in a copse of trees. Through the trunks they saw the faint glow of artificial light.

"You should see the house soon," the voice told them.

Just on the other side of the trees, they did. They stopped to look at it. The mansion was nestled in the bottom of the valley with its front bathed in light. It was immense, a colonial-style mansion with scores of shuttered windows and a grand pillared entrance. At the base were plinths, on which sat a pair of lions. It had a wide driveway lined with neatly spaced trees, a cluster of outbuildings, a pool and tennis courts and another garden to the rear, with lawns and flower beds that backed onto the forest. It was quite astonishing to imagine that one man owned all this.

It was quiet in their headsets.

Mal Gorman was absorbing it all. "I like it," he said.

The twins began to walk forward, but stopped abruptly. The giant lions on the plinths had begun to move, as if the stone were enchanted.

"They must be borgs," the voice said. "Just stay where you are and see what they do."

The lions dropped heavily from their plinths onto the drive. They were so huge, their heads reached the tops of the pillars. They had the sickle markings of mountain lions inlaid in their silver hides. They began to lope slowly up the lawn toward Ellie and Mika. The children felt the great weight of the metallic beasts rocking through the ground.

"Just stay there," the voice said.

The lions reached them and paced powerfully around them with their nostrils flaring, snorting hard. Patent flex metal muscles and titanium bones worked beneath silver skin. In the dense quiet, the children could hear all these mechanisms moving in complex coordination. The lions were the best that money could buy. They were a status symbol more potent than the mansion and its grounds.

The borgs took a while to decide what the children were. Low growls began to thunder in their throats.

"Stay calm," the voice said. "Don't move until they accept you. They're just confused because they can't see you."

At last the lions settled, but their immense size remained a threat. Mika moved just before one stood on his foot and it was a while before they left. They lay down on the grassy slope and gazed toward the house with their tails twitching. Long minutes passed, but eventually they rose and sauntered toward their plinths, their paws leaving a trail of deep dents in the lawn. The children followed at a safe distance and watched them settle.

"OK, that's them dealt with," the voice said. "It looks as if they're the only borgs inside the fence . . . not that they'd need any more. Walk past them toward the left side of the mansion. Mal Gorman wants to look at the outbuildings and the gardens. He'll guide you through this area."

The cluster of outbuildings was about the size of a small village. As they entered the area, they walked past a row of dark cottages.

"That must be the servant accommodation," Gorman said. "How many are there?"

"Eight," Mika whispered.

"What's that building ahead of you?" Gorman said. "It looks like a stable block "

The children entered a dark yard surrounded on three sides by long, thin buildings. For the first time in their lives, they saw the golden glow of horses through the half doors on the stables. The horses stirred, sensing them approach, and a couple stamped their straw.

"Show me them all," Gorman said. "I want to see what kind of stock he's got."

The children moved slowly around the yard, stopping by each door and stroking the long faces of the horses. Horse light was volatile. It warmed and softened as the children touched them, but as soon as they took their hands away, the horses jerked their heads back, their light jagged, fractious, as if they would run for miles if their stables were opened. The children showed Gorman every horse and he admired them as if he knew what he was talking about.

They heard human footsteps. A pair of solid boots on the gritty path. Then a woman appeared in the entrance to the yard, dressed in a black uniform with a gun on her belt.

"She's one of Raphael Mose's bodyguards," the voice said. "Don't move until she leaves."

She walked a few paces into the yard, then turned slowly and left. When they could no longer hear her, Mal Gorman made them walk on and show him the kitchen garden, full of fruit and vegetables. Then they looked at the pool, Plush Turf tennis courts, the terrace overlooking the rear garden, and a garage block. As well as several new pods, this contained some vintage gas-engine cars: a Rolls-Royce, a Porsche, and a Corvette Stingray. Gorman was quiet again while they walked around these, but they knew what he was thinking. His mind had already leapfrogged the war and he was imagining owning all this.

He's so stupid, Mika thought. *This mansion will be a heap of cinders after the war. And so will he.*

Next, Gorman told them to break into the mansion.

They saw another bodyguard as they left the garage, and had to wait several minutes before it was safe to approach the kitchen door. It was on the left side of the house, near the row of staff cottages. Ellie looked at the lock until it clicked, and they walked quietly into the kitchen. Then Mika looked at the alarm panel until a soft, green light appeared.

Now the hunt for Everlife-9 would begin, while Raphael Mose and his family slept on the floor above them.

8 The Goat Kid

Mika and Ellie walked quietly across Raphael Mose's kitchen.

They could smell a pie that had been left to cool on the kitchen table. It was a real cheese and vegetable pie, made with milk from cows and vegetables grown in soil. Food was the last thing on their minds, but they were drawn to it anyway. Food like this didn't exist on the other side of The Wall. The crust was glazed with butter and egg. They touched it curiously.

Next to the pie was another miracle: a jam jar full of wildflowers that glowed gold in their water. The tiny petals were closed, sleeping, but their colors were lovely, even in the darkness. Ellie touched these too, very gently.

Around the jam jar was a scatter of brightly colored pencils made from wood, and next to these, a child's drawing on real paper. Such ordinary things on this side of The Wall, but fascinating to children from the North. Ellie picked up the drawing. It was a bird in a tree, and the child had tried hard to capture the details under a warm, plump sun. It was a happy drawing.

Now they felt guilty. They hadn't realized there was a child in the house.

Gorman was bored. He couldn't smell the pie or care about flowers or drawings. He was more interested in looking at the size of the rooms and finding the Everlife-9.

"What are you doing?" he said. "Put that down and get on with it."

Ellie returned the drawing to the table.

They walked around the kitchen so Gorman could admire the massive cooking range and fridge. Then they explored the rest of the ground-floor rooms, showing Gorman the furniture and searching for Everlife-9. The rooms at the front of the house were large and the furnishings were a mixture of antique and modern. They smelled of polish and perfume. The children touched wood, stone, and silk and gazed into everything, even the walls, hunting for Everlife-9. They saw the smallest things normal eyes would never see, like the tiny gold lights of insects moving in the floorboards. But they did not find the drug.

In a study at the back of the house, they did find something that interested them. Behind a horse painting above the fireplace was a brushed-metal control panel with three red buttons.

What's this? Mika thought.

"I wish you would stop fiddling," Gorman said impatiently. "Get a move on."

He made them open the drawers in Raphael Mose's desk,

then look at the holopics on the mantelpiece. He spent a long time looking at these, and the children wondered why.

Do you think Gorman knows Raphael Mose? Ellie thought.

Maybe, Mika replied. *Or perhaps he's just imagining himself doing those things.*

The holopics showed Raphael Mose's family and friends living the high life. They lounged around on yachts, feasted in ski lodges, and gathered at weddings, wearing diamonds and silk. The man in the holopics appeared to be Raphael Mose. He looked young, strong, and healthy. He had a full head of dark hair and a muscular body, but he was not attractive. There was a hard edge to his smile and no emotion in his eyes. They decided it must be Raphael Mose. He looked exactly like the kind of man who could ruin billions of lives without feeling any remorse.

"OK," Gorman said. "I've seen enough. Go upstairs now."

They found the staircase in the great hall. It had a grand, shallow sweep and a carpeted tread.

"Nice," Gorman said. "I like it."

They climbed the staircase and took the last few steps cautiously. Now they were mere steps away from Raphael Mose, and after seeing pictures of him, they did not want to meet him.

They found themselves facing a wide landing and a long line of doors. They turned right and looked through each one without opening it. These were guest bedrooms with en suite bathrooms. The children looked at the beds and furniture in lines of blue light but moved quickly on from one to the next because there were no small objects in these rooms, no boxes or bottles that might contain Everlife-9.

At the end of the landing, they found themselves facing an

ornate oak door. It was significantly larger than the others, and the frame was carved with a beautiful pattern of wildflowers and butterflies. On the main panel was a goat kid, standing in a meadow of grass. It was beautiful. Mika touched the warm wood, admiring the carving, and Awen sniffed along the gap at the bottom of the door.

They got a shock when they looked through it. Sitting up in bed was a child, alert, scared, and listening.

Frag, Mika thought. *She's a mutant. She can see us through the door.*

They backed away.

"What are you doing?" Gorman said. "What's in there?"

"Nothing," Ellie whispered.

Their hearts pounded. They knew there was a child in the house, but they hadn't expected a mutant child, especially one so young and powerful. She was surrounded by plush toys and dolls. She couldn't have been more than seven years old and yet she'd seen them, easily. And if she decided to wake up her parents, they'd be in serious trouble. But they couldn't tell Mal Gorman. They remembered what happened when they encountered the bear; they were pretty sure he'd tell them to kill the girl just because she'd seen them.

We have to get out of here as quickly as possible, Mika thought.

Awen remained by the oak door, wagging his tail. As Mika and Ellie walked quickly away from it, his tail dropped and he followed.

At the other end of the landing, they found themselves facing another oak door. This one had a mulberry tree carved on the main panel. Through it they saw Raphael Mose and his wife sleeping in a four-poster bed. There were many objects around them, including a collection of bottles.

Gorman was talking at them impatiently, but they ignored him. They didn't have time to listen. The door swung open quietly and they crept into the bedroom and began to search frantically, with Raphael Mose and his wife sleeping right next to them. Although the children couldn't be seen, they knew they could be heard and that the slightest sound would wake Mose and his wife. It was a very tense search and every vessel they looked at contained beauty products, nothing more.

"Where is it?" Gorman said with urgency. "It must be there. You're not trying hard enough. Find it! Find it!"

They opened doors and drawers with their eyes. They searched every corner of the room. Awen began to circle nervously, sensing impending doom. Now there was only one place to look—the en suite bathroom. They gazed through the door and saw an old-fashioned bathtub and a pair of sinks, a mirror, and a cabinet.

Immediately their eyes fixed on the cabinet. Inside they could see three rows of small bottles filled with clear fluid.

That's it, Ellie thought.

They entered quietly and closed the door. The cabinet looked sharp and modern compared to the other fixtures. Mika opened it and a bright white light blinked on inside. The bottles were made of clear glass. Each had a silver cap and a white label on which was printed: Everlife-9 and an expiration date.

"How much should we take?" Mika whispered.

"Take three bottles from each row," Gorman replied greedily, then thought better of it. "No, actually, take two. They'll miss three."

The children removed the bottles as quickly as possible and put them in the pockets on their belts. Then they spread out those remaining to hide the gaps. All they could think about was getting out of there.

But just as they turned, the bathroom door opened and they found themselves facing the child.

They both jumped with shock, not just because she'd crept up on them so quietly but because they'd never seen such a startling mutant before.

She was dressed in a hand-embroidered nightgown. She had the look of those raised on real food and sunlight. She was cute, with wide dark eyes and coils of curly brown hair. In her arms she held a big brown teddy bear. But it was not these things that startled them. It was her legs. She had the hind legs of a goat, reverse jointed, with little hooves covered in coils of fine brown hair. She was a satyr from Greek myth. The most striking mutant child they'd ever seen. She tightened the grip on her teddy bear and a hoof clicked on the hard floor.

In a paroxysm of panic, Ellie lunged for her arm and dragged her in and shut the door.

"Kill her," Gorman yelled. "Kill her now!"

The child pulled against Ellie's grip with a frightened sob. She was powerful enough to hear through their minds what Mal Gorman had said. Mika and Ellie deactivated their invisibility shields, yanked off their headsets to get rid of him, and crouched down.

"Don't kill me!" she sobbed.

"We're not going to kill you," Ellie whispered desperately. "We're not here to hurt you. Please don't tell your parents we're here. Please be really quiet and let us explain who we are and why we've come."

But it had all happened too quickly. The teddy bear the child held was a borg as sophisticated as the lions guarding the house. As soon at it sensed her fear, it began to cry out in a teddy bear voice, "Help! Help! Grace is scared! Someone help her!"

"Frag!" Mika hissed. "Frag!"

He jumped up and locked the bathroom door, but within seconds, Raphael Mose and his wife were on the other side, banging and shouting.

The child didn't seem to hear them. Now she gazed at Ellie and Mika with intense curiosity. She could sense they were like her. For the first time in her life, she was with her own kind.

Can you hear us? Mika thought.

The child nodded.

Do you believe we're not going to hurt you?

The child considered this and nodded again.

I hear in your mind, she thought.

And we hear in yours. We're not going to hurt you. Look at our light. Just take a deep breath and look at us.

She gazed between them, deep into them, as her parents continued to bang on the door.

We were sent to your house by a bad man, Ellie thought. *The man who told us to kill you. He took us away from our parents because we're mutants and he's trying to use us to hurt people. But we don't like the man. We don't want him to use us to hurt people. We've taken Everlife-9 from the bathroom cabinet and we're going to use it to get rid of the bad man. Do you understand? We want to get rid of him. We don't want to hurt anyone.*

The child listened and calmed down. When Ellie had finished, Grace felt the rush of The Whisper pour through her mind. Somewhere out there were more children . . . like her!

You come from the other side of The Wall? she thought.

Yes.

But it's dust on the other side of The Wall.

We were told the same thing, Mika thought. *And look, here we are, talking to you. You can hear The Whisper, can't you? There are thousands of us on the other side of The Wall, and you're one of us. Help us.*

The child took a deep breath. Mika and Ellie watched her, admiring her. "Grace?" her mother yelled through the door. "What are you doing? Let us in!"

Mika and Ellie activated their shields and vanished. The child opened the door and faced her angry parents.

The twins stood behind Grace, praying their shields didn't fail them.

"Oh, Grace!" the woman gushed. "What were you doing in here?"

"I had a bad dream," Grace replied.

"Then why did Teddy start to shout?" Mose asked, concerned.

"I woke up in here," she replied. "And I was frightened, so Teddy got frightened."

"She must have been sleepwalking," her mother said wearily. She took Grace's hand. "Come on, let's get you back to bed."

Grace and her mother left, but Raphael Mose stayed and looked sharply around the bathroom. As he walked forward, the twins were forced back until they were squashed against the edge of the tub. He opened the cabinet and looked at his bottles of Everlife-9. As he did so, the twins saw cold aggression in his eyes. Here was a man more broken than Mal Gorman. And they would have to deal with him soon. If they were to stop this war, Raphael Mose was a man they would need to fix.

He closed the cabinet door, admired his young reflection, and left.

When they were sure he was back in bed, Ellie and Mika walked quietly past him and out of the bedroom. On the landing, they paused and watched his wife close Grace's door. Then they walked quickly down the stairs and through the house toward the kitchen. Mika primed the house alarm and they left, locking the kitchen door behind them.

Awen ran ahead up the sloping lawn, and the twins followed quickly. When they reached the copse of trees, they looked back and saw a gold light in Grace's window. She was watching them leave.

I feel sorry for her, Ellie thought. *Her father's Raphael Mose. She's going to get mixed up in this.*

We'll look after her, Mika replied. *If she needs looking after. I get the feeling she can look after herself.*

9 Dangerous Friends

Kobi's first night in The Shadows was cold. He'd forgotten how cold it could be. The damp permeated everything, and nothing ever dried. Clothes rotted in drawers, carpets rotted on the floor, and curtains blackened and fell to bits at the windows. The platform was to blame, and the burst river, and ultimately, the adults who had made this mess.

A couple of hours after they arrived, his father decided to go and find John, who'd moved his old pub in Soho to the eleventh floor of the Future Communication Building. He invited Kobi to join him, but Kobi didn't feel like it. He felt strange, a little sick, and he didn't understand what was wrong with him. So he said he felt ill and stayed behind.

But although he tried to sleep, he couldn't. His clothes and the bed were damp, and through the walls he could hear all the people around him. Children fretting, adults talking, doors opening and closing, and people walking up and down the passage. The room had no window, so it felt like a cardboard box left in the middle of somebody else's house.

He tossed and turned in the bed, unable to get comfortable and vaguely aware that he was missing out on something. He was also starting to feel guilty. He was in a safe place, but where were his friends? What had happened to Mika and Audrey . . . and Tom? Tom had been left without a game partner when Kobi stopped playing the game. Kobi hadn't cared at the time, but he was starting to care now.

He tried to call Mika but got no reply. Mika's companion had been taken away by Mal Gorman, but Kobi didn't know this.

He lay in the darkness feeling stifled and restless. Wondering if coming to this place had been a mistake.

His father returned after a few hours, looking warmed by beer and good company. He brought the bustle of the building with him. He talked loudly and filled the small room with movement. He didn't seem to care that everyone around them could hear what he was saying through the walls.

Kobi lay with his hands behind his head, watching his father change into his pajamas.

"John's really landed on his feet here," Abe said. "The bar was packed. He's got the old pub sign on the wall and they even salvaged his chairs and tables. Real wood. Two hundred years old. It's good in there . . . a really good atmosphere. You should come next time."

"I'm not old enough to drink beer," Kobi said.

"True," his father replied. "But you're old enough to be sociable. They let kids in."

"They're all younger than me."

His father looked at him, with one leg in his pajamas. "Do you still feel ill?" he asked.

"Sort of," Kobi replied. "And guilty," he admitted. "All my friends are gone."

His father finished putting his pajamas on and sat on the bed, next to his son. "Have you spoken to any of them? Have you tried calling Mika?"

"Yes. His companion's switched off."

"They've probably taken it away," his father said.

"That's what I thought," Kobi replied.

"We were talking about it in the bar," his father said. "You mustn't feel guilty. Everyone believes you did the right thing. They're all saying what a smart boy you are. You're a hero, Kobi."

"No, I'm not," Kobi replied.

"You are," his father insisted. "You were smart enough to realize that the government was lying to you, and you refused to let it exploit you. They tricked you into playing a game that was training you for war! They can't get away with that, Kobi. I don't regret coming here for one moment."

Kobi was quiet.

His father tried to see his son's eyes through his hair. "Are you regretting coming here?"

"Maybe," Kobi admitted. He felt compelled to admit it now that the feeling was so strong. "I feel weird. Like I'm in the wrong place."

"Try to sleep. You'll feel better in the morning. We've had a really difficult day. This situation will be much easier to cope with after a good night's sleep. I'm proud of you, Kobi. Really proud. And so are the SLF. There are some of them living in this building. I met them in the bar."

Kobi sat up.

"The SLF are terrorists, Dad."

"They fight for liberation, Kobi. They're the voice of The Shadows' people."

"Since when were you a supporter of the SLF?" Kobi asked sharply. "You hate politics."

"I'm not a supporter, I just happened to meet some in the bar, that's all. One of them bought me a beer and we talked about you. They're good people. They're your friends, Kobi. They're offering you protection."

"My friends are somewhere else," Kobi said. "I don't even know where my friends are."

"Look, just try to get some sleep. You're very tired."

His father climbed into bed and turned off the light. Kobi listened to him trying to settle in the damp bed. A few minutes later he began to snore softly, and Kobi lay in the darkness, alone and longing for morning so he could get up and work and think about something else.

But Kobi wouldn't have to wait until morning to have something else to think about. A couple of hours before dawn, he heard people stirring in the rooms around them, doors opening and low voices in the passage. A baby woke up and started to cry.

Kobi sat up and turned on the light.

"What's going on?" his father asked sleepily.

"I don't know. Will you go and ask them?"

"You go."

"I don't want to, I don't know them."

His father sat up slowly and groped around at the end of the bed for his sweater. But before he found it, there was a hard knock on the door that made them both jump. His father clambered hurriedly out of bed and opened it. A man stood beyond, panting as if he'd just run up the stairs. "You're an industrial robot engineer, aren't you?" he said quickly.

"Yes," Abe replied. "What's wrong?"

"We need you," the man panted. "Have you got any tools with you?"

"Yes," Abe said, pointing to his bag on the desk.

"Then follow me."

Abe grabbed his bag, Kobi jumped out of bed, and they both followed the man out of the room.

The passage beyond was empty. Everyone had beat them downstairs.

"What's happening?" Abe asked.

"I'll have to show you," the man panted. "I've never seen anything like it. I can't even describe it, but you could save a boy's life."

"Really?" Abe said, looking scared. They ran hard down the stairs. When they reached the eleventh floor, they followed the man into an area near the buffer zone. A large crowd had gathered there. It parted to let them through and they saw a strange black mass lying on the floor.

"Oh my odd," Abe said. "What is it?"

"We don't know. But you've got to get it off him or he'll die."

It looked like a giant dead spider with its legs contracted around the body of its last kill. A big black cocoon. There was some kind of web stretched between the legs, encasing the body within, and a pair of bloody feet stuck out one end of it.

Abe and Kobi crouched down next to the dark mass. Through the net they saw a pale face. The face of a boy with short red hair and a small silver disc in the middle of his forehead. One of the black legs was clamped over the bridge of his nose and he was coated in a viscous orange slime. His breath was shallow, as if he was struggling to breathe. The spider cocoon was locked fast around the child. Abe felt over a leg and tried to pull it back and cut his fingers on the barbs.

"Get more light," he demanded. "Get some lamps so I can see what I'm doing. Where did he come from?"

"Sandwood Seven," a woman replied. "It's a town on the north coast of Scotland. We think he was trying to escape from the fortress in Cape Wrath."

"So he's one of our children? One they took from the arcades?"

"He must be. But he was found in a Tank Meat factory. He fell though a skylight in the roof. The security guards heard the glass break, but by the time they got there, this thing was around him and they couldn't get it off. Apparently, the streets of the town were crawling with soldiers, probably searching for him. He must have escaped from the fortress. When the soldiers left, the security guards sent the boy to us. One of them had a daughter who was taken. He was very upset."

"Oh my odd," Abe said through gritted teeth. "And you feel guilty, Kobi? Because you're free? Because you didn't let them do *this* to you?"

Kobi dropped his head and hid in his hair, feeling as if he was about to vomit. Crouched next to the cocooned boy, he felt more guilty, not less.

The lamps arrived and his father started to work. Kobi shook out his father's bag of tools and laid them on the floor so he could take what he needed. Abe lay down, first on one side, then the other, so he could look at the Creeper Net from all angles, and when he found the processor unit connected to the legs, he began to burn a hole through it with a blowtorch. But the blood from his cut fingers made it slip in his hand.

"I can't do it," he said. "You're going to have to do it, Kobi."

Abe held out the blowtorch. Kobi tied back his hair, took the torch, wiped the blood off on his sweater, and began to work. The crowd loomed over him, watching. Spooked children pushing through the adults' legs. It felt as if the whole building was crammed in that room. This would have freaked out Kobi on a normal day, but he didn't even notice now: The only person who mattered was the boy. As he burned a hole through the hard, black case on the processor unit, he whispered, "I'm your friend. You're going to be OK."

When there was a large hole in the case, he took smaller tools and began to disassemble the processor inside. Suddenly, the legs relaxed and the Creeper Net opened like a black flower. The boy in the filthy white gown looked like its crushed stamen inside. Immediately, everyone rushed forward and many gentle hands picked him up. He was carried away and the crowd followed, leaving Kobi and his father alone, still crouched by the broken Creeper Net.

Kobi began to put the tools away.

He felt his father's hand press gently on his shoulder. "Well done. I'm really proud of you," he said.

"That could have been me," Kobi replied.

"Exactly. So don't you dare feel guilty that it wasn't."

10 A Strange Task

Ellie and Mika didn't talk to Mal Gorman until the mansion was far behind them. He'd told them to kill a young girl, and this made them so angry, The Roar crackled at the back of their heads, threatening to start more fires. It was not a good idea to talk to Mal Gorman while they felt this way.

Gorman became frantic with worry. After a quarter of an hour, he was convinced he'd lost his two best mutants *and* the Everlife-9. He sat at his desk, grinding his teeth. When he heard their voices again, his relief was intense. They blamed the loss of contact on signal failure, but he wasn't interested. He hurried them over the fence as quickly as possible. Mal Gorman was addicted to Everlife-9 before he'd even touched it.

On the other side of the fence, the children climbed the slope in the forest and searched for their capsule. But when they found it, they discovered the bear had gotten there first and crushed it. It had found their ration packs inside and there was a scatter of food packaging through the trees. Gorman ranted at them while they picked this up, telling them they should have killed the bear when they landed.

I hate him so much I could puke, Ellie thought.

Ignore him, Mika replied. *Just concentrate on getting back.*

They pulled the micro wings from underneath the seats and found they were damaged. But at least this meant Mal Gorman had to go so an engineer could talk to them. They sat at the base of a giant redwood tree and listened while they made their repairs. Ellie had to mend her engine. Mika had to fix one of his wings. Luckily, their tool kit had not been damaged.

The forest was peaceful. Gold light coursed through roots and earth and through the leaves and into them. That magic calm, that feeling of being part of something beautiful made their work enjoyable. By the time their micro wings were fixed, they knew they could face Mal Gorman again.

They placed the micro wings on the ground. They were sparse structures, just a skeletal frame with an engine attached. Just enough to get them over The Wall where the Stealth Carrier would be waiting for them. As the micro wings touched the ground, they sprang to life, standing up with their wings unfolding. Then the children backed into them and let the metal arms wrap around their bodies.

The wolf borgs returned to watch them leave.

The micro-wing engines were silent. The twins flew up through the trees as quietly as fish rising to the surface of a lake. As they cleared the forest canopy, they were spotted by a pair of eagle hawk borgs that rose up and followed them to The Wall. Great silver wings *whomped* the night air. Red eyes glowed in the darkness.

The forest ended abruptly and they crossed no-man's-land. This was a half-mile-wide strip of concrete scattered with dead leaves. The giant birds turned for home, and the children flew up and over The Wall. Then the Ghengis borgs watched them from their concrete plinths, with more pairs of red eyes. If the children had tried to cross from North to South, rather than South to North, they would have been shot down by their massive guns. The door over The Wall opened only one way.

Then the children crossed another strip of no-man's-land, this one scattered with concrete rubble and litter, and the North stretched out before them, concrete towers and people as far as their eyes could see. Plague sirens, factories, traffic trunks, and pylons that were denser than the forests on the other side of The Wall. Even so far above it, the children could smell the mold.

Just as they passed the first rows of towers, the Stealth Carrier appeared, hovering in the air like a lump of molten silver.

An hour later, they were standing in front of Mal Gorman with the bottles of Everlife-9.

"Give it to me," he said.

They placed six bottles on his desktop and watched him pull them toward him with bony fingers.

"Well done," he said. "You can go now. There's a mail pack for you by the door."

"From home?" Mika asked.

"Yes," Gorman replied.

Mika and Ellie turned quickly. It was sitting on a shelf, a bulging, white mail pack full of gifts from home. They walked toward it and Mika picked it up.

From Mum and Dad, Ellie thought.

Yeah, and I bet there's something in there for you.

Mal Gorman felt happy.

After Mika and Ellie left, he watched his fortress through his desktop, with a bottle of Everlife-9 in his hand.

His implanted army was sleeping. His engineers were working on Pod Fighters in the hangar. His Chosen Ones were resting in their enclosure after a hard day of a mission and training. Gorman watched them for a few minutes, curious to know what mutant children did when they were alone. Not much, it seemed. They were slouched across the white sofas in their living area. Leo was reading. Iman was stretched out like a black cat with her head in Leo's lap. Colette was oiling her silver hands. Santos was gazing at a screen that played a loop of old cartoons. Audrey leaned against Mika's legs, watching him open his mail pack. At his side sat Ellie, with her hot, black eyes fixed on it.

They looked so ordinary.

Mika pulled things out of the mail pack—a letter, candy bars, and a handful of holopics—and handed them to Ellie to look at. The only gift he kept himself was a packet of biscuits, which he put to one side.

Boring, Gorman thought. *But good.*

Everything was just as he wanted it to be: quiet and uneventful.

This was the perfect time to take Everlife-9.

He swept the images of his children away and summoned Ralph to his dressing room.

*   *   *

Ralph had been required to perform many strange tasks in the time he'd worked for Mal Gorman, but none as peculiar as filming his master while he took Everlife-9. Gorman sat before the fire in his dressing room, holding the small bottle in his hand. The butler felt as if he were about to make a horror movie.

"Hurry up," Gorman said.

The butler felt confused by all the buttons on the camera. He'd never used one before.

"Sorry, sir."

He found a child's tutorial in the menu and began to follow the instructions. Gorman waited, with a vision of his younger self walking through his mind.

"I think I'm ready now," Ralph said.

Gorman pressed the Everlife-9 to his lips and drank.

He felt something happen immediately. ·

"I feel hot," he muttered. A warmth built in his mouth that escalated rapidly to a blistering heat as if he were chewing a mouthful of Scotch bonnet chili peppers. His eyes began to water, he coughed violently, and the machines on the frame around his chair began to blink and beep. Ralph's hands trembled on the camera as the veins on Gorman's forehead began to throb.

"Do you still want me to film this, sir?" Ralph asked. "Or do you want me to help you?"

"Film!" Gorman rasped, clutching his throat. "Something's happening!"

Ralph had no doubt something was happening, but he wasn't sure it was what Mal Gorman wanted to happen. The life-support system was now in full panic mode as if Gorman were about to explode. There was a quiet knock on the dressing room door as a doctor from the hospital unit arrived to find out what was happening.

"Keep them out!" Gorman rasped. "I don't want anyone to see me until I'm young!"

Five awful minutes passed, and Ralph continued to film. But the spectacular event they were waiting for did not happen. The heat subsided in Gorman's mouth, and the machines fell calm again. The old man sat rasping in his chair, looking frailer and freakier than ever, with his last few strands of parched gray hair standing up like lightning rods.

"Give me the mirror," he choked. "But don't stop filming."

Ralph placed a mirror in his master's hand, and Gorman raised it to look at his reflection.

"I look worse!" Gorman yelled. "Look at me! Look at the state of my hair! I'm bright red! I look like a freak!"

"Perhaps it needs more time, sir."

"For what? To make me redder and older?"

"Do you want me to stop filming now, sir?" Ralph asked.

"Of course I do, you idiot!" Gorman yelled. "Turn it off and get it out of here!"

Ralph unlocked the door and hurried out with the camera, hearing the crack and smash of the mirror as Gorman hurled it into the fire.

In sleep Gorman twisted, tangling in his tubes.

At two o'clock in the morning, a shrill scream tossed Ralph out of bed. He pulled on his dressing gown and ran to Gorman's room. In the darkness, his master looked hideous, eyes white and mouth wide in a horror-film howl. Ralph grabbed him by the shoulders and shook him.

"Wake up, sir," he urged. "You're having a nightmare."

Gorman stopped howling and panted heavily, his eyes hazed with interlight.

"The vines," he muttered. "They won't let me go. . . ."

He trailed off and pushed Ralph away. "Light!" he shouted. "Light!"

The bedroom light blinked on, and Gorman looked up to see Ralph gazing at him strangely.

"What?" he snapped. "Why are you staring at me?"

"I'm going to get you another mirror, sir," Ralph replied. "You need to look at your reflection."

Ralph hurried out of the room and returned a minute later to find Mal Gorman staring at his hands.

"I can't see the bones," he whispered.

"Look at your face," Ralph said eagerly, handing him the mirror.

Gorman gazed at his reflection and saw a . . . boy.

He was quiet for a long time, touching his face and turning it from one side to the other.

"I took too much," he whispered. "I wanted to be thirty, like Raphael Mose. But I feel GREAT!"

Gorman dropped the mirror on the bed and began to yank out the tubes and wires attached to his body.

"Get the camera, Ralph!" he shouted. "Film me now! This is fragging brilliant!"

"Is there anything else you'd like, sir?" Ralph asked, looking startled.

"Yeah!" Gorman shouted enthusiastically. "Get me the biggest pizza you can find! A fragging enormous pizza! I'm starving!"

11 A New Sound

After rescuing Luc from the Creeper Net, Kobi slept the rest of the day and through the next night. He awoke to find his father leaning over him, looking worried.

He was lying on his back with his companion in his hand. He hadn't moved for twenty hours.

"How's the boy?" Kobi asked immediately.

"Still the same," Abe replied. "Asleep. I was beginning to wonder if you'd caught some kind of sleeping sickness off him."

Kobi sat up and looked at the screen of his companion, hoping he'd received a message from one of his friends. His companion was a girl called Anais; he'd won her in the game before he stopped playing. She had long black hair similar to his, but she washed and brushed hers. "Sorry," she said. "No messages."

Kobi sighed and leaned his head against the wall.

"You're not still tired?" Abe asked.

"A bit," Kobi replied. "But I'll get up in a minute."

"Come and have breakfast with us. Everyone's looking forward to seeing you."

Kobi almost refused, then realized how hollow he felt. The last meal he'd eaten was cold noodles outside the pub in Greek Street. He got up and changed and followed his father downstairs.

They entered the kitchen to find a dozen people sitting around the table, eating Fab egg and toast. They greeted them warmly and insisted father and son sit down while their breakfast was being prepared. Kobi sat between a woman and a young boy with blond hair who let his Fab egg go cold while he stared at him.

"Eat your breakfast, Oliver," the woman said.

The child ate, but kept his eyes on Kobi.

"My name's Oliver," he said. "I live here."

"Hi," Kobi replied.

Kobi was determined to eat and leave as quickly as possible. He felt self-conscious sitting there with so many people he didn't know. He wondered which ones were SLF, but they all looked the same: pale and drawn, with faces lined by worry.

When Kobi had a plate of food in front of him, they left him alone and began to talk.

"The government has to tell us about this war soon. They promised days ago and still, nothing. We deserve to know who our children have been taken to fight!"

"They won't tell us. They don't talk to us about anything else. I bet as far as they're concerned, this war is none of our business."

A man slammed his fist on the table, making Kobi's plate jump.

"How can it be none of our business when our children have been taken to fight it? We have the right to know what this war is about! They have to tell us!"

"Then we'll make them tell us."

"The boy might know."

"That's true."

"We ought to talk to him."

"He still hasn't woken up. The doctor suspects he's got a lung infection from breathing the fluid around the Tank Meat."

"But he's not in a coma, we know that. He's bound to wake up, even if he's sick."

"But when? It could take days, and we need to know what's happening now. Either that boy tells us what's going on or we'll have to make the government tell us."

This tension around the table was too much for Kobi. He couldn't eat while the adults were stabbing their breakfasts. He pushed back his chair and stood up.

Everyone looked at him.

"Sorry," he said. "I'm not very hungry."

"It's OK, Kobi," someone said. "This must be horrible for you."

"Yes," Kobi replied. "It is. I miss my friends. Can I see the boy?"

A man rose immediately.

"Of course you can," he said. "If it wasn't for you, he might have died. I'll show you where he is."

"Thanks."

"The doctor's with him at the moment, but I'm sure she won't mind."

Kobi followed the man toward the buffer zone. The boy had been put in a small room quite close to where he'd lain on the floor inside the Creeper Net.

The man tapped gently on a door and it opened. It was almost dark inside. The doctor was just rising, with her bag in one hand.

It was a small room. Along one wall were bookshelves. Against the opposite wall was a bed, with a table and a lamp and two chairs for visitors nearby. The boy lay under piles of blankets with two tubes running into the back of his hand, one delivering saline, the other, antibiotics. A bandage covered the place where the needles entered his veins. The adults talked quietly for a moment, then the doctor left.

"I'll leave you with him," the man said to Kobi. "Let us know if he wakes up."

"OK," Kobi replied.

He closed the door quietly and Kobi sat on the chair next to the bed and watched the boy's face. The skin around his implant was angry and swollen, but his features were calm, almost content.

Kobi wondered why.

It was quiet. The boy breathed softly and Kobi gazed at him.

After a few silent minutes, he heard a sound like a rush of wind, right inside his head. He was so startled, he panicked and it faded away. But for the next hour he sat there, wishing it would come back and learning how to hear it.

12 Return to the Arcade

Ralph took a deep breath before knocking on Mal Gorman's dressing room door.

"Come in," Gorman yelled.

The butler entered. The twelve-year-old Minister for Youth Development was lying on the rug before the fire, wearing a gold dressing gown, with pizza crusts and mirrors scattered around him. The hover chair, with its machines, tubes, and wires, had been pushed into the corner. He leaned up on one elbow and looked indolently at the pile of clothes hanging over the butler's arm.

"Where have you been?" he asked. "You took ages."

"I'm sorry, sir," Ralph replied, picking his way through the rubble. "I had to go all the way down to the storerooms near the implanted children's dormitories, and most of the clothes I found there were full of holes." He placed the pile on Gorman's gold chair. "But I selected the best, sir," he said. "I think these will fit."

"Show me," Gorman said.

The butler held up a freshly ironed blue T-shirt.

"Boring," Gorman said.

Ralph held up a white T-shirt with a small hole on the hem.

"Yuck," Gorman said.

Ralph held up a green T-shirt with a picture of a Pod Fighter on the front and the word *PLAY* on the back.

Gorman reached up and snatched it from his hand.

Then they went through the same process with jeans and sneakers. A few minutes later, Gorman was admiring his reflection in the full-length mirror on his bedroom wardrobe. The only old garments he wore were his brown socks and his gray underpants.

"Do you want me to call the doctors, sir?" Ralph asked. "So you can tell them what you've done? Perhaps the Prime Minister would like to know about Everlife-9."

Gorman jerked around and glared at him. "No," he said. "You're not to tell anyone. I want a few hours of fun before I have to think about work. I'm going out for a bit. Order me a pod."

"But you have meetings all morning, sir," Ralph replied. "There are people waiting in your office."

"Tell them to come back tomorrow," Gorman said.

"But where are you going, sir?"

"Out," Gorman said. "What is this? You're not my dad. If anyone asks, just tell them I'm at a meeting in the Golden Turrets and I'll be back tomorrow."

"Yes, sir," Ralph replied. "I'll do it now."

* * * *

Audrey lay on her stomach on Mika's bed. Her feet kicked against the wall and she held her chin in her hands. Mika was pulling on his white armored boots. Awen was sitting by the door, chewing at his tail as if he had a flea.

How can we be sure Gorman's taken the Everlife-9? Audrey thought. *If we go for him and he's still attached to those machines, it will be a nightmare trying to move him. It might go wrong. He might die.*

He will have taken it, Mika replied. *You should have seen his face when we gave him the bottles. I bet he took it the first chance he got.*

So he's above us now, a young man again.

I think so.

She rolled onto her back, stared at the ceiling, and tried to imagine what Gorman looked like.

I bet he's still creepy, she thought.

Yeah, Mika agreed. *I bet he is.*

He looked in the mirror above his desk, rubbed his hair, and turned to face her.

"Ready?" she said, grinning.

"Yes."

She jumped up as if the bed were full of springs rather than rock hard. Awen got to his feet and wagged his tail. In the dormitories far below them, the children stirred as if the wind had picked up.

It was time to get rid of Mal Gorman.

Gorman's pod sat waiting for him on his private landing strip at the top of the fortress. For a moment he stood next to it and watched the sea pound against the rocks of Cape Wrath. The wind buffeted him, almost blowing him off his feet, but he liked it. He closed his eyes and took deep breaths of sea air. His body was buzzing with an energy he hadn't felt for a hundred years.

When he'd had enough, he jumped into the pilot seat of the pod and looked over the controls. He hadn't flown one for such a long time, he wasn't quite sure what to do, but he felt invincible with all that young blood pumping through his veins, so he took off clumsily and flew with reasonable skill toward Sandwood Seven.

When he reached the town, he dropped the pod, messily, in the town square. A crowd of shoppers flapped about in a panic. It was illegal to park there, but Gorman knew he was above the law, and anyway, he had only one thing on his mind. He climbed out of the pod and walked purposefully toward the arcade. Once there he slid a key card by the glass doors and they swung open.

It was dark inside the arcade. The entrance mall with its rows of shops was veiled in shadows and as silent as a crypt. But Gorman could still smell the excitement, the shakes, the kebabs, and the perfume. He walked around the empty shops, imagining the thrill of coming there while the game was still a game. That he had ended it and turned dreams into nightmares did not make him feel any guilt. After admiring his twelve-year-old reflection in one of the shop mirrors, he headed toward the game room.

The game room was darker and oppressively quiet. As he walked down the red carpet, the simulators loomed around him and he felt the first pang of nerves since taking the Everlife-9.

He walked quickly toward the back, where there was a hidden door leading into the control room. Then he used the key card again and it slid open.

In the control room, he turned on the lights so he could see the simulators through the secret window. There were hundreds of them in long, straight lines, illuminated by soft red light. Each had four feet attached to the ceiling and four feet attached to the floor, with a round black body suspended in the middle. Gorman ran his hands over the control panels, entering key codes and touching icons to wake them up. Then he returned to the game room and chose a simulator near the back, where the cool kids used to play.

"Bet you're not feeling so cool now that you've got lumps of metal in your heads," he said.

Seven children and an invisible dog left the Chosen Ones' enclosure. They traveled down the fortress in the elevator, surrounded by men with guns. The men were beginning to relax in their company because they were being so quiet and obedient. These were strange children, but there was something likable about them, particularly Audrey, with her contagious enthusiasm, and Colette, with her shy smiles. The men leaned against the wall of the elevator, thinking about other things.

When they reached the training area, the children were left in a changing room. It was lined with metal lockers and had a long bench down the middle. There were seven piles of armor laid out on the bench. The men watched through the door cam as Ellie helped the others put it on. They'd been told to dress carefully. They were about to play a game called Swerve Ball to help develop control of their power, and it was dangerous.

When they were dressed and their armor had been checked, they were taken to an armor-plated gym with cage grilles over the lights. Two trainers were waiting for them, also dressed in armor with cage grilles on their helmets to protect their faces.

The children were told to stand in a line against the wall and put their helmets on. The men with guns retreated to the observation room. They would watch the game on a screen, out of range of the swerve balls. They put their guns on the floor and gathered to watch. Ellie was about to give the others a demonstration, and they were eager to see it.

Ellie walked to the corner of the gym and crouched down. When she stood up again, she had a silver ball in her hands about the size of a fastball and the weight of a bowling ball. Everyone watched her carry it to the middle of the gym and place it with a clunk on the armor-plated floor. Then she waited, watching the trainers through the bars on the front of her helmet.

One nodded.

Ellie pressed two icons, one on the top of the ball and the other in the middle of her chest plate. Then with quick, light steps she retreated from the ball until she was standing ten feet away from it. For a few moments it did nothing, and everyone watched in anticipation. Then it began to rise into the air until it was hovering level with her chest. Suddenly, it clicked and spikes shot out of it, covering the surface like the spines of a puffer fish. It began to roll in the air, as if it was charging up.

The men watched, entranced.

Ellie sidestepped, slowly, facing the ball as she would an angry bull. There was a flash of movement when the ball shot toward her, and the men almost gasped before she stopped it dead, an arm's length from her ribs. It vibrated in the air as if fighting against her control and determined to smash her to pieces.

"Break," the trainer shouted.

Ellie broke eye contact and the ball shot toward her chest. With a quick, practiced movement, she ducked, spun, and punched toward it, forcing it away without touching it. It looped quickly to come back, aiming for her head. She fixed it with her eyes again, then jumped and kicked powerfully, sending it away. Then the trainer activated another ball and threw it into the game. It spiked midair, and hurtled toward her head. She was now fighting two. The men in the room next door watched, captivated.

Then something happened they didn't understand.

They heard a loud bang, and the gym vanished from the screen.

For a few seconds, they were so startled, they stared at it. Then one tapped it, hoping the image would reappear. It did, slowly, but it was not the image they were expecting to see. Out of a gray cloud of litter fragments they saw the gym, but no children and no trainers.

"Get in there!" one yelled.

They fumbled around on the floor for their guns and ran as fast as they could to the gym. They swung the door open and blustered in to find the gym silent and empty. Their feet crunched over fragments of swerve balls. For a moment they thought there'd been a horrible accident and were prepared to see blood on the walls. But there was no blood and no children, only a huge, ragged hole in the armor-plated wall at the back of the gym. They raced to it and peered through.

On the other side was the classroom Ellie and Mika had used to prepare for their mission.

The men still didn't understand. They climbed through the hole, and on the other side they found the trainers lying on the floor and the door to the safe open. They ran to it and looked in. The white case was open, and seven of the invisibility shields were missing. Only one remained.

"NO! They've taken their invisibility shields!"

"We have to find them, quickly."

They tugged on the classroom door but found it had been melted into its frame. They climbed back through the hole into the gym and ran to the other door, only to find this melted too. They waved at the security cameras, to find them blind. Soon they realized even their guns had been deactivated, their innards melted by mutant eyes while they were traveling down in the elevator. The children had outwitted them and escaped.

Mal Gorman stood by the legs of the simulator, trying to remember how to bring the body down. He had known, once, but he'd forgotten, and this game had been designed so the children had to solve problems like this. For ten minutes he walked around it, racking his brain, then he lost his temper and kicked it.

"Stupid fragging machine!" he yelled, twisting his young face so it looked like his old one. "Drop down and let me in!"

While he was having his tantrum, he accidentally stood on the floor plate. Immediately the lower legs contracted and the body of the simulator dropped.

119

Now he had to figure out how to open the door. This took another ten minutes. By the time he climbed into the pilot seat, he was wondering why he was bothering. But when the seat gripped the sides of his body and the door slid shut, he felt a rush of excitement.

Now he remembered. For weeks he'd watched the children have all the fun while he was trapped in that parched old body at his desk. Now it was his turn.

Five minutes later, he'd figured out how to activate the control panels. Suddenly, he was surrounded by brightly lit icons that covered every surface of the cockpit.

Then he put on the headset and fiddled again until he could see through the Pod Fighter windshield. Now he was ready to take off.

His Pod Fighter sat on the deck of a virtual aircraft carrier with its nose pointed at the sea.

He gripped the hand controls and pulled back.

The powerful engines began to roar.

He felt another rush of excitement that made his new hair stand on end, and he pulled back again. The Pod Fighter shot forward.

The sudden drag in his gut was electrifying and he felt the urge to whoop for joy, but instead of flying up, the Pod Fighter flew down and crashed into the sea. It plunged with bubbles running up the windshield, and two words appeared in his visor.

Game Over.

"Frag!" Gorman yelled. "Fragging stupid game!"

While Ralph tidied up the pizza crusts and mirrors, he wondered what to do. The Everlife-9 had transformed Mal

Gorman into an obnoxious twelve-year-old boy who was still in control of a fortress full of weapons. He knew he ought to tell someone about this, but he was too scared. He'd spent forty years ironing Gorman's underpants, tolerating his abuse, and telling him he was right about everything. These were not easy habits to break.

Was Mal Gorman mad? Ralph wondered.

His master slept with a carving knife clutched to his chest.

Only a few days ago he'd awoken, screaming, with his arms cut to pieces.

But maybe this was normal behavior for men in positions of power.

They all lived in a broken world.

Ralph made Gorman's bed and polished the mirrors on the front of the wardrobe. They were covered in fingerprints where Gorman had been touching his new reflection. When this was done, Ralph dusted the bedside cabinets. As he stood back to admire his work, something moved.

He jumped so hard, he bounced back against the wardrobe. Then he clutched his duster to his chest while he tried to determine what he'd just seen.

Gorman's bedspread was the antiquated sort: thick, gold, and quilted. Four small dents, each about the size of an old-fashioned coin, were running across the surface. For a moment they paused, then they changed direction and headed toward the pillows; then a larger dent appeared. Ralph heard a weird whooshing noise . . . saw a metallic flash . . . and a *monkey* materialized on the pillow. The butler was so startled, he bounced back again and almost broke the mirror. But the monkey didn't notice. Puck was far more interested in the silver ball he held in his hands. With a whoosh he vanished, then reappeared and disappeared several times.

Then Ellie appeared next to the bed.

Ellie Smith with no men or guns!

Ralph wouldn't have been more astonished if a puffin and a unicorn had appeared in Gorman's bedroom.

He watched, aghast, as she leaned across the bed and grabbed the monkey, who continued to flash on and off in her hands. "Puck, stop it," she said. "Or I'll take it away."

"Where are the men?" Ralph stammered. "Why are you here?"

"I'm looking for Gorman," Ellie replied. "He's not in his office."

The butler began to tremble.

"Don't be scared, Ralph," Ellie said. "I'm not going to hurt you. We've always got along OK, haven't we?"

"Yes, miss," Ralph replied. "But I'm not sure Mal Gorman would like you in his bedroom, with Puck . . . and no men."

"Do you really care what Mal Gorman thinks?" Ellie asked. "He's horrible to you, Ralph. He was horrible to both of us."

She looked at him with penetrating directness and he remembered she could see what he was feeling. He would have felt uncomfortable if this were anyone else. He would have felt ashamed and vulnerable. After all, he was a grown man, Mal Gorman's butler, and he wasn't supposed to fear his master or question his judgment. But no one understood what it felt like to be bullied by Mal Gorman better than Ellie did. Ralph had watched Ellie suffer Gorman's abuse and she'd watched him suffer it. Perhaps he didn't mind that she knew how he felt. Their shared experience had bound them together a long time ago.

He closed the bedroom door.

The time for truth had begun.

"Why are you here?" he whispered.

"Because he's mad," Ellie said. "And he's about to turn our planet into a heap of orbiting ash. You know this, don't you? Better than anyone."

The butler looked at his duster for a moment, then put it down. "Yes, miss," he said. "I do."

"Has he taken the Everlife-9?" Ellie asked.

"Yes."

"So how old is he now?"

"The same age as you, miss. He took too much."

Ellie raised her eyebrows. "Really?" She tried to imagine a twelve-year-old Mal Gorman. It wasn't a pretty picture. But a boy would be a lot easier to remove than a corpse attached to a machine. "So where is he?" she asked.

Now the butler felt uneasy. He'd felt empathy for Ellie's suffering since the day she was taken, but she was still a mutant, a very powerful mutant, and she was hunting for Gorman. Ralph knew his master was power-mad and about to start a terrible war, but he did not want to be responsible for his death.

"We're not going to hurt him," Ellie said. "We just want to stop him. Please help us."

"You promise you're not going to hurt him."

"I promise. Gorman doesn't understand us. Just because we can kill doesn't mean we want to. It's like a side effect of what we can do. Do you understand? We want to stop the killing. We want to make people happier, not sadder. And we've got a plan. First we're going to remove Mal Gorman, then we're going to take control of the North and The Wall, and then we're going to negotiate with the South and try to sort out this mess without fighting a war. We want our parents to see the forests, Ralph. *You* should see them. It makes you happy just looking at them. I want you to see them."

"But who's helping you?" Ralph asked, confused.

"Nobody," Ellie replied. "It's just us, the children."

"You and the Chosen Ones?"

"And the implanted army," Ellie said. "There are twenty-seven thousand of us."

"But Gorman controls the implanted army."

"No, he doesn't. We've discovered a new trick, Ralph. We've been talking to it. Those children look as if they're sleeping, but they're not—they're waiting for us to get rid of Mal Gorman and take control of the fortress. The implants don't work. Those children came back to the fortress to help us."

Ralph was quiet while he absorbed this information. That the children had returned because they wanted to, not because the implants had started working again, frightened him. He looked at the floor, imagining the army waiting to wake up and wreak vengeance on the government that had lied to it.

"We don't feel vengeful," Ellie said. "Honestly, we don't. We're not going to hurt anyone. We're just going to take over and sort out this mess our own way."

"Children . . ." he muttered. "Take over . . ."

"Yeah. You look pale, Ralph. Are you OK?"

"Yes," he said. "I'm just getting used to the idea."

"We're not just children," she told him.

"I know," he said, looking at her. "I knew that the day I met you."

"Then please help us. Tell me where Gorman is."

Ellie watched him and waited. Fear, doubt, and guilt pulsed through his light. This was a difficult decision. But then something deep inside him rose, something that had been stifled for a long, long time: his own beliefs, his own sense of right and wrong, and a desperate craving to be on the good side, the truthful side, the kind side.

He wanted to help them.

He took a deep breath and spoke.

"Actually, I don't know where Gorman is," he said. "He was supposed to be in meetings this morning, but he went out without telling me where he was going."

"Where could he be?" Ellie said. "What was he wearing when he left?"

"Some of your clothes," the butler said. "Jeans, sneakers, and a Pod Fighter T-shirt."

"A Pod Fighter T-shirt?" Ellie looked at him sharply.

"Yes, miss, a Pod Fighter T-shirt. A green one with *PLAY* on the back."

She grinned.

"I know where he is," she said. "He's playing the game."

She stood up quickly, holding Puck to her chest with one hand. "Thank you, Ralph. I always knew you were a good person." She kissed him lightly on the cheek, startling him, and opened the bedroom door. Beyond it, Mika and Audrey were waiting by the dressing room fire. When they saw Ellie, they began to move.

Ralph watched them walk toward the door, feeling vulnerable now. He was about to be left behind, after betraying his master.

Ellie stopped and turned.

"Do you want to come with us?" she asked.

"Yes," he replied immediately. "I do."

"Oh, good!" she cried. "You'll be really helpful, Ralph! Really helpful!"

"Thank you, miss."

"Do you know where our companions are?" Mika asked. "Gorman took them away from us."

"Yes, I do, sir," Ralph said. "They're in the bottom drawer of his desk."

13 Game Over

An hour after Gorman climbed into the Pod Fighter simulator, he was still trying to take off without crashing. He'd seen the words *Game Over* so many times, they seemed permanently glued to his visor.

But on his forty-seventh attempt, he succeeded. The Pod Fighter shot off the aircraft carrier, he pulled back with just the right amount of power, and the fighter shot up into the sky instead of diving into the sea. For a moment he could hardly believe he'd done it, and his hands were frozen to the controls because he was so scared of making it go wrong again. But the Pod Fighter continued to shoot up through clouds, which whooshed like smoke around him. Then he could enjoy the power in his hands. This game really was amazing. Like every child who'd played it before, he'd already forgotten it wasn't real.

On the other side of the clouds, the sun and the sky

dissolved in inky space. Up, up, he flew until he hit the planet atmosphere.

"Yeah!" he yelled.

Then he remembered he was flying without a gunner and that the Red Star Fleet would attack him. He let the Pod Fighter drop until he skimmed the snowy landscape of the clouds. For a second he wished he'd made Ralph come with him as his gunner, then he laughed at the idea.

A green dot appeared on his visor.

He ignored it for a few seconds because he didn't know what it meant. It was difficult enough keeping the Pod Fighter steady without trying to figure out all the other stuff. But soon the green dot grew larger and he began to realize it was something moving toward him. He pulled back, wanting more speed, but got too much and lost control. The Pod Fighter roared into a messy corkscrew and by the time he pulled out of it, he was gasping with fright and the pitted orb of the moon was looping around him like a ball on a length of elastic. He steadied the craft and managed to drop again until he was just above the clouds, but within seconds, the dot reappeared, closer this time and beginning to take the form of another Pod Fighter.

It roared toward him.

He cursed and tried to throw his Pod Fighter out of its path, but it anticipated this move and looped around him in a fluid weave.

Then it turned and came back.

Now he was very scared. He tried to outwit it by dropping, but it passed overhead, looped, and shot toward him like an arrow. His hands failed. The Pod Fighter stuttered like a shot bird, plunged into free fall through the clouds, and hurtled toward Earth. And the other Pod Fighter was still chasing him.

Land rushed up to greet him, a poisoned wasteland of dust and skeletal trees. Somehow he managed to control his spin and pull up a few seconds before impact. But the other Pod Fighter was still there, harrying him like a hyena, and he couldn't get up enough speed to outrun it.

Over deserts and dead cities it chased him, until he crashed into the dust.

He saw a flash of light as the Pod Fighter exploded, then the words *Game Over*.

He removed his headset.

He panted in the darkness.

Wiped the sweat from his face.

He'd had enough for one day.

This game was really difficult and scary.

He decided to go back to the fortress and have Ralph serve him a nice lunch. He opened the door, dropped out on shaky legs, and saw Ellie Smith standing in the darkness. Ellie Smith with no men with guns, and that monkey sitting on her shoulder.

14 A Wistful Oliver

K obi leaned against the wall outside the boys' room, waiting for the adults to leave. Every hour or so, the doctor came and made him wait outside.

The passage had a distinctive smell of old office, cooking, and people. Sometimes they walked past him, going about their business. Some greeted him and others didn't. He felt better if they ignored him.

After a while he sensed someone watching him and glanced down the passage, to feel a pair of eyes vanish as his head turned. When this game had continued for a few minutes, the blond boy, Oliver, stepped out and stood where he could be seen.

"Hi," Kobi said.

"Hello," Oliver replied.

The child walked toward him, swaying his arms. He was

wearing a Pod Fighter T-shirt borrowed from an older child. It came down to his knees. Kobi grinned through his hair.

"What are you doing?" Oliver asked, kicking the wall.

"Waiting for the doctor to leave," Kobi said. "So I can go back in and sit with the boy."

"Can I see him?"

"You could ask," Kobi replied.

"OK," Oliver said.

He leaned against the wall next to Kobi, with his hands behind his back. They were quiet for a while, listening to the drone of adult voices talking inside the room. It took ages for them to leave.

"What was the game like?" Oliver asked.

"It wasn't a game," Kobi replied.

"Yeah, I know. I didn't mean it like that. I mean, what was it like when you thought it was a game?"

"Amazing," Kobi said. "I used to love flying."

"So you were a pilot?"

"Yeah."

"I wanted to be a pilot," the child said enviously. "But I wasn't old enough."

"You're lucky, then," Kobi said.

"I know," Oliver said. "But I wish it had been a game. I don't have anything to look forward to now."

"What else do you like doing?"

"Drawing," Oliver said.

"Then do that instead," Kobi replied. "Much safer. You won't end up with a lump of metal in your head, drawing pictures."

"I suppose so," replied Oliver wistfully. "I could draw a Pod Fighter."

He stretched out his T-shirt and looked at the picture on the front.

"Yes," Kobi said. "Do that. Draw a Pod Fighter and show it to me."

"OK," Oliver replied happily.

The voices inside the room grew louder as the adults prepared to leave. Kobi and Oliver moved away as the door opened. The doctor left first.

"Still here?" she said to Kobi, with raised eyebrows.

"Yes," Kobi said, feeling offended. Of course he was.

"It's OK," she told him. "I just thought you might get bored sitting with him while he sleeps."

"No," Kobi said.

"Can I go in too?" Oliver asked.

"No, not you," the doctor said. "The boy's sick. He's got a lung infection and we need to be really careful that he doesn't get The Shadows sickness. He doesn't need small children messing about in his room."

Oliver's face clouded with humiliation.

"He won't mess about," Kobi said.

"No, I won't," Oliver agreed moodily.

The doctor looked at him, weighing him up. "OK," she said at last. "But only you, Oliver. Not all your friends. And do what Kobi says. That boy needs peace and quiet."

"I will," Oliver replied earnestly. "I'll be really quiet."

15 Mika Offers Gorman a Biscuit

orman's eyes met Ellie's and his young heart stopped as if she'd clamped his aorta. In that half-light, after dying so horribly in the game, he wasn't even sure she was real. For a split second her eyes flooded black and it was a look of such distilled power, he felt as if she could blink and vaporize him. Then it passed and she looked almost normal again.

"What are you doing here?" he asked. He looked beyond her for men with guns. But there were no men, no guns, just Ellie and that monkey. She didn't move or reply. She held Puck firmly with one hand as a simulator dropped behind her.

The door opened, and Mika and Audrey climbed out. Now nuclear eyes met his, and he began to understand.

It had been *them* in the other Pod Fighter.

They'd chased him down and killed him in the game!

They walked toward him, slowly. This was their place, their

arcade, and he'd just made a complete idiot of himself. He began to shake with fear. He knew what he'd do in their position.

"Don't kill me," he begged, putting his hands up to protect his face. "Please don't kill me."

They surrounded him. He sank to his knees and clung to the arcade floor like a baby.

"Get up," Mika said, nudging him with the toe of his white armored boot. "We're not going to kill you."

Gorman looked up. "You're not?"

"No," Mika said. "We're not like you. We don't believe killing solves problems."

"So what are you going to do to me?"

"Take you away."

"What?"

"We're going to put you somewhere out of the way, and then we're going to take your fortress. We don't want to fight your war."

"No . . ." Gorman muttered, frozen by shock. "You can't. . . . I'm the Minister for Youth Development! And that fortress is government property!"

"Not for much longer," Mika said. "As soon as you're out of the way, it's ours."

"Don't be ridiculous," Gorman spluttered. "Three children and a monkey can't take over a fortress. Even ones like you . . ."

"Watch us. And anyway, there are more than three of us. There are twenty-seven thousand of us. The implanted army came back to the fortress because we asked them to. Not to fight your war."

"But they're obeying *my* order. They're sleeping."

"No," Mika said. "They're waiting. They're waiting for us to get rid of you. And I have a message from them. They say, 'Thanks,' for teaching them how to fly. They really appreciate it.

"Stand up."

In a shocked stupor, Gorman rose and followed them to the door at the back of the game room. As they began to climb the stairs, he realized they were taking him to the roof and that they were going to fly him away. Then he began to panic. They were taking him away from his fortress! They were refusing to fight the war! What could he do? How could he stop this from happening? Raphael Mose's mansion filled his mind. The house, the golf course, all those beautiful cars, the horses and terrace and pool . . . He *loved* those things. He already felt as if he owned them; he'd already picked out the curtains and the carpets and his favorite car. And to feel them slip through his fingers made him lose his mind for a moment. He stopped on the stairs and turned, determined to break free and run. But immediately, Mika's eyes met his and he felt a sharp pain in his head. He gasped and fell back against the wall with his hands over his face. But it was just a warning. The pain lasted a moment, then it was gone.

"You can't escape," Mika told him. "Just accept that we're stronger than you and keep walking."

Gorman plodded up the stairs.

When they reached the roof, he blinked in the bright light, then saw the Stealth Carrier perched on the pod strip. His Stealth Carrier. The craft he'd spent billions of credits developing to fly these children over The Wall. And worse than that, Ralph, *his butler*, was standing by the door.

His light burned red with rage.

"You!" he yelled at the butler. "What are *you* doing here?"

"Helping, sir," Ralph replied politely. "Mind your step as you climb aboard."

Gorman took a seat in the Stealth Carrier, and his Chosen Ones filled those around him.

"You traitor," Gorman snarled, picking on Ralph because he was the only one who couldn't hurt him.

"It's for your own good, sir," Ralph replied. "I still serve your best interest."

"Don't get funny with me," Gorman threatened. "You just wait—"

"Leave him alone," Ellie said. "I won't let you bully Ralph anymore."

Gorman looked at Ellie and fell quiet.

The Stealth Carrier rose.

Leo and Iman were flying.

Gorman watched through the window as his fortress shrank. He was still determined to get out of this somehow. He was young and powerful. This couldn't be happening to him.

"You can have mansions," he told them tentatively. "Have you forgotten? If you fight the war, you can have first pick after mine."

"We don't want mansions," Ellie replied. "While people starve and suffer. We want just enough, like it ought to be. Enough food, space, light, and nature around us. There's enough for everyone."

"Really?" he mocked. "I wonder if your parents will agree. They haven't seen you for a year and a half. Do you plan to go home and tell them they were cheated out of their land but they can't have it back because you like trees and flowers? I don't think they'll like that."

"We're going to make them understand," Ellie said.

"Good luck," he sneered. "You'll need it."

Ellie looked away and blinked.

"Leave her alone," Ralph said.

Ignore him, Mika told his sister. *He's just trying to upset you.*

I know, she replied. *I'm OK.*

Gorman smiled nastily, knowing he'd scored a point, but his satisfaction didn't last long. He suddenly realized that nobody knew where he was. That he'd gone out that morning having told his staff he'd be in the Golden Turrets until the next day. He'd taken Everlife-9, so only Ralph and these children recognized him. The Stealth Carrier had vanished, the children had vanished, and he had vanished with them.

Then it occurred to him that they'd stolen a craft that was designed to fly over The Wall.

"Where are you taking me?" he asked.

"To a safe place," Mika replied.

"Over The Wall?"

"Yes."

"It's not safe over The Wall!" he cried. "Not for me! I'm not like you! I'll be ripped to pieces by the animal borgs!"

"We're going to protect you," Mika said.

"No! Please! I don't want to go over The Wall! Please don't take me over The Wall!"

"I thought you couldn't wait to go over The Wall," Ellie said sharply.

"Not yet," Gorman said. "Not now, you stupid children. I don't understand. Why over The Wall?"

Mika leaned across the seat and picked up a packet of biscuits. Gorman recognized it immediately. It was the one he'd watched Mika remove from his mail pack.

"What's a packet of biscuits got to do with anything?" he said impatiently. "I don't want a biscuit. Just tell me why you're taking me over The Wall."

Mika opened the biscuits and pulled out a small piece of paper that had been slipped down the side. He gave it to Gorman, who squinted at it. There was a set of numbers scrawled across it in inky black handwriting, with a kiss at the end.

"What's this?" he said. "I don't understand."

"Map coordinates," Mika replied.

"What?" Gorman said. "Where have they come from? How did you get them?"

"They were sent to me by my friend Helen," Mika said. "In the biscuits. First to our old apartment in Barford North, then to our new apartment in the Golden Turrets, then our parents put them in our mail pack. My friend Helen is on the other side of The Wall and we're taking you there because we know you'll never be found by your men."

Gorman's face turned white with rage.

"You'll never get away with this," he said, throwing the map coordinates onto the floor. "You children are mad."

"I disagree, sir," Ralph said, picking them up again. "I think there's a general consensus that *you're* the mad one."

16 Helen's Hat Falls Off

Mika thought about Helen as they flew toward The Wall, and Helen thought about Mika. He was hoping she wouldn't be too shocked when he turned up with six children, a monkey, a butler, and the Minister for Youth Development. She was hoping he was still alive. They'd both known there was something wrong with the game but that Mika had to play it to find Ellie, but Helen hadn't spoken to him since he was taken. She'd known there was something special about him, though, long before anyone else had.

She waited for him in a woodman's hut buried deep in the forest of Brittany. It stood in a clearing of wildflowers. A winding path led up to its door. Its walls were made of whole polished trunks, and a pretty coil of smoke rose from its stone chimney. All it needed were a few sweets stuck to the roof and it would have looked good enough to eat.

Inside were just three rooms: a large one downstairs with a kitchen, wooden table, fireplace, and armchairs; and two smaller rooms upstairs, a bedroom with a brass bed and a hygiene room containing an old-fashioned bath with claw feet. All technology—the cleaning borgs, air-conditioning, TVs, security systems—had been hidden so as not to spoil the hut's rustic charm. It looked one thing, but it was quite another.

A woodman had lived in the hut many years ago, but it was Helen's home now. Her yellow Wellington rain boots stood by the door, her strawberry sunglasses lay on the kitchen table, and she could be seen through one of the crooked windows, washing up her breakfast dishes and frowning at the birds. She had just removed her rubber gloves and was walking to the door with a handful of crusts to feed them when her companion said, "You have a message from Mika."

Her heart leaped.

She hobbled to the table, dumped the crusts, wiped her hands on her dress, and read it.

I'm coming now and I'm bringing friends.

Quickly, she sent one back:

Land in the meadow near the hut, but don't leave your craft until I arrive. It's dangerous here.

After so long waiting, she was in a state. Mika, *with friends*. Probably more children, to a forest riddled with wolf borgs.

She dropped her companion and hobbled quickly to the kitchen. Her arthritis was better on this side of The Wall, where she had access to new drugs. In the cupboard under the sink, she found a box of borg tags. She put this in a flowery shopping bag, then hobbled to the fireplace, where she pressed an icon hidden among the stones.

Several stones slid back to reveal a screen. On this she summoned a map of the forest and checked the location of the wolf borgs. There were two packs within running distance. Panic-stricken, she grabbed her sun hat and rammed her feet into her yellow wellies. Then she left the hut and walked as quickly as she could into the forest, with the bag of borg tags over her arm.

It was a beautiful morning. A winding path carried her through the forest to a bridge. The stream below tumbled over smooth rocks. The shallow banks were covered in moss. She usually stopped there to watch, but today there was no time.

On the other side of the bridge, she could see the meadow through the trees. It was a small meadow, once used to graze horses. But now the horses were gone and spring grass swooshed around her knees. As she dropped into the dip surrounding the meadow, she saw a flash in the sky. The Stealth Carrier appeared, hovering like an alien ornament. It descended slowly, causing a frenzy in the forest. Birds rose from the canopy, their wings cracking the morning air. Then several eagle hawk borgs appeared, their wings *whomping* over the trees.

"Oh dear," Helen muttered. The borgs were twice the size of the Stealth Carrier; their talons could crush it like a bean can. They circled above the craft, metallically screeching. Now Helen was limping so fast, her hat kept falling off.

How she wished she had a remote control for moments like this.

Then she saw Mika climbing out of a door on the side of the Stealth Carrier.

"NO!" she yelled.

He stood on the ledge and pulled himself up onto the roof.

"Mika!" she bellowed. "Wait! I told you to stay inside! It's dangerous!" She rushed on, waving her shopping bag in the air like a flag. Wolf borgs were slipping through the trees, snarling and running at the carrier. Then the first eagle dropped with its talons reaching down.

Helen couldn't bear to look.

She closed her eyes.

But the bloodcurdling scream she expected didn't come. She opened her eyes to see the eagles rising and the wolves quietly gathering around the carrier. Mika slid down the wing and landed softly in the grass. He put out his hand, and the wolves sniffed his fingers. Then he looked at Helen with a big grin.

"Are you trying to give me a heart attack?" she said, with her hands on her hips.

He laughed. He was so pleased to see her and she looked as kooky as ever. Her gray hair had been cut short, but it still stuck out around her head as if she were a witch. She was wearing a flowery dress, mismatched earrings, and her old yellow rain boots from Barford North.

"Sorry," Mika said. "I should have said in my message, I've been here twice before."

"Really?" she said, astonished. "But why don't the borgs attack you?"

"They think I'm an animal." His words came breathlessly. "Because I'm a mutant." He had so many things to tell her, about the game, the war, and himself. So much had happened since they'd last met. Mika could see her own questions fluttering around her like butterflies. But the others were waiting.

"So who have you brought with you?" Helen asked. "Are you all mutants? I have some borg tags with me." She opened her shopping bag and showed him.

"I've brought Ellie," he told her.

"Ellie!"

"Yes."

"Oh, Mika," she gasped. "I hoped you would. Well done!"

"And my best friend, Audrey," Mika told her enthusiastically. "You'll like Audrey; she's really cool. She's got borg eyes. And I've brought the others who won the competition. There are seven of us, including Ellie, all mutants."

"Lovely," Helen said. "I'll make you all a nice cup of tea."

"And someone else . . ." Mika added nervously. "I've brought someone else. We need your help, Helen . . . to hide someone."

"Who?" she asked, her eyes sharpening.

"The Minister for Youth Development."

"The Minister for Youth Development? The Northern Government Minister for Youth Development?"

"Yes," Mika replied. "Mal Gorman. The man who invented the game. We've sort of *removed* him. We let him take Everlife-9 and he's made himself twelve. You'll see. The government wants a war, Helen. The game was recruitment for an army. They want to use us to bomb the forests so they can live in the mansions, but we plan to take over, sort it out another way. So we've kidnapped him and we need to hide him somewhere. Actually, we need to lock him up, because we can't trust him."

He looked at her anxiously. This had all come out in a mad gush and he hoped she understood. She was once the only person who understood him. . . .

"OK," she replied, reaching into her shopping bag. "So you *will* need one of my borg tags."

"Two, actually," Mika said. "We brought his butler as well."

"Ah, of course you did," Helen said, rummaging. "Are we locking them both up, then?"

"No, Ralph's nice. He's come to help."

When Mika slipped back into the carrier, the wolf borgs smelled Mal Gorman and Ralph and exploded in a frenzy of bloodlust. Gorman could see them through the windows, leaping, twisting, barking, and snarling, their claws dragging down the hull, leaving deep scars in the shiny metal. While the children fitted his borg tag, he froze like a shop mannequin. Puck hooted nervously on Ellie's shoulder. Outside, Helen clutched her hat and watched from a safe distance.

"Do it quickly," Gorman said. "Make me safe!"

The borg tags were made of thick gray plastic. They fit onto Ralph's and Gorman's wrists with a neat *click*. Thirty seconds later, a band of green light blinked below the surface and immediately the wolves dropped back.

Gorman panted with relief and clutched his tag with one hand as if he was afraid it might fall off. Ralph pulled down his sleeve to cover his.

"OK," Mika said. "Let's go."

The door opened. The wolves gathered, licking their metal lips.

"Make them go away," Gorman said.

"They'll leave soon," Mika told him. "They're just curious. Let them sniff you and try to stay calm."

Mika jumped down into the meadow, and the wolves

parted as if he were a member of the pack. But the children had to push Mal Gorman out of the carrier, and the wolves weren't so sure about him. They ran at him, heads down and snarling as if preparing to attack. The children surrounded him to keep them back. It felt like a precarious situation.

Helen looked at Gorman shrewdly from beneath the rim of her hat. "Mmmm," she said, pursing her lips. "Follow me."

By the time they'd reached the trees, Gorman had peed his pants with fright, and only Ralph and Puck had a chance to absorb their beautiful surroundings. Puck gazed up at the trees and chattered in amazed monkey dialogue and tried to leap from Ellie's shoulder onto a branch, but she held him firmly.

"Yeah, I know," she whispered. "You want to play in the trees. But let's deal with Gorman first, before the wolf borgs try to eat him."

Helen marched ahead. Her yellow boots flashed like beacons through the trees. She led them over the stream and past the hut into deeper forest.

It was dark and cool there, mysterious, quiet. Mal Gorman's fear cranked up another level. The wolves slunk through the trees around him, their red eyes glowing in the deep forest light. They waded through bracken and brambles that slowed them down and snagged at their legs. Puck stopped trying to jump from Ellie's shoulder, and Mika walked with Awen by his side. Leo, Iman, Colette, and Santos followed in a state of distracted shock. This was the first time they'd seen a forest.

"Not long now!" Helen shouted, with the plastic fruit bobbing on her hat.

Eventually, the path cleared.

"Look," Audrey said. "A house."

Helen marched on as if it were perfectly normal. The children, Ralph, and Gorman stopped at the edge of the lawn.

The path that led up to the front door was lined with overgrown columns of topiary. The house was hundreds of years old . . . and silent. The quiet of it throbbed as the forest loomed over it. Three rows of windows peeked through a tangle of vines. Ivy had grown right up the walls and over the roof to poke pale fronds at the sky. Its great front door stood ajar, among a litter of leaves from past autumns.

"Does this belong to Helen?" Ellie asked. The house was neglected and overgrown, but it was clearly worth billions of credits, and when they thought about all the land it was on, it became money they couldn't imagine.

"I don't know," Mika replied uncomfortably. "I don't even know what's she's doing on this side of The Wall. When I met her, she was living in a fold-down, like us. She was my counselor. Mum and Dad paid her to make me forget you, but she helped me remember instead. She could hardly walk, her arthritis was so bad. I don't understand."

Helen had vanished after their last conversation in Barford North. He'd gone to her apartment to find it full of Magpie Men picking through her things, knocking her precious books to the floor. But how had she ended up here, on the other side of The Wall, stomping through a forest as if it were all hers? If Helen belonged here, if she owned this mansion, she was one of the people who'd lied to their parents. That wasn't a nice thought.

Gorman hadn't expected this either. The topiary needed trimming and the ivy cutting back, but he quite fancied staying here. It wasn't as alluring as Raphael Mose's mansion, but it was a mansion. He was first to set off up the path, and the children, wolf borgs, and butler followed.

Helen was waiting at the front of the house. Before Gorman reached her, she began walking again, around the side of it. Mika ran ahead and caught up with her.

"I see what you mean," she muttered. "Gorman's a sly one."

"Yeah," Mika replied. "He's the Knife Sharpener."

"Really?" Helen said with raised eyebrows. "That was a terrible nightmare. Is he as horrid in reality?"

"Yes," Mika replied. "He was the one who took Ellie. I didn't see him while I was awake until the prize-giving dinner."

"I bet that killed your appetite," she said. "Well, he won't be able to scare anyone where I'm going to put him."

"He doesn't scare me anymore," Mika said. "I know what he is now."

"You do seem different," Helen observed.

"I am."

They were quiet for a moment. He was about to ask her how she came to be on this side of The Wall, when they reached a long concrete building. He decided to leave the questions until later. The building was right at the forest's edge, surrounded by bushes and trees. It had a large, heavily fenced enclosure attached to it. Mika looked through the wire. He saw a landscaped area with smaller trees and a muddy hollow. Helen rooted around in her shopping bag for a key card, and Gorman and the others caught up with them.

"Why are we here?" Gorman asked, looking back down the path toward the mansion.

"Because this is where you're staying," Helen replied.

"You're joking," he said. "It's a concrete shed."

"It's not a concrete shed," she countered. "It's an animal

enclosure with an electric fence. You won't be able to escape. After The Wall was built, we used enclosures like these to breed wild boar to repopulate the forest. The babies look like mint humbugs, you know. With their brown and cream stripes."

"I don't care," Gorman said furiously.

"It's warm and dry," she continued. "All you'll need is a sleeping bag and a porta-potty. I've got them in the house."

Gorman gave her his coldest, most evil look. "You're not serious," he said. "You're *not* going to put *me* in a *pig house.*"

"Why not?" Helen replied.

"You wouldn't dare!" Gorman ranted. "I'm the Minister for Youth Development! You can't expect me to use a porta-potty!"

His shouting aggravated the wolf borgs and one ran at him, snarling. He cowered against the wall while the children shooed it away, and as soon as Helen unlocked the door, he shoved rudely past her. Now he was in the building, but he didn't want to be, so he cursed and stomped while the children closed the door against the wolves.

Inside there was a long trestle table against one wall, and three doors to the right lead into spacious pigsties. The children looked through the windows of the sty doors. On the floors old straw glowed gold in natural light. At the far end of each sty was another, smaller door that led out to the grassy enclosure. The sties looked comfortable. The children could still smell the animals that had lived there.

Helen unlocked one of the sties. "The only thing that won't work," she said, "is the water trough. I'll just pop up to the house to fetch some bottled water. You might as well lock him in there now."

She left.

The children faced Mal Gorman.

"No," Gorman said. "I'm not living in a pigsty."

"You shut me in a coffin," Ellie said. "And Puck. You cut my hair. You made me spend weeks blind."

Gorman's light withered, but he stomped into the sty and turned to glare at her. She shut the door and watched him through the window. Then he exploded, unleashing his fury in a frenzy of flailing arms and legs.

The children realized this was an important moment. Ellie had locked up the man who'd done the same to her.

She felt relieved. Not malicious or bitter or hateful. Just relieved she was free and Mal Gorman couldn't hurt anyone.

Mika put his arm around her.

He looks like a total perp, he thought. *Flailing around like that.*

Ellie grinned. *Yeah, he does.*

Then Mika started thinking about Helen again and considered following her up to the house.

Go, Ellie thought. *You need to talk to her. We'll stay here and watch Gorman.*

Mika walked along the path alone.

The mansion was silent.

He felt nervous.

He wanted to talk to Helen, but he wasn't sure if he wanted to know the answers to his questions.

The stone steps up to the front door were covered in moss. As he entered, he called out to her, "Helen?"

"Up here!" she bellowed from one of the bedrooms.

He was in a wide, wood-paneled hall, and it surprised him. Although the house looked deserted from the outside, the inside was littered with dusty family things, as if the people had walked out one day and never returned. Near the door was a table covered in letters and keys. On the wall was a screen with a faded shopping list stuck to it. It was Helen's writing. Mika would have recognized it anywhere. So she had lived here once.

The floor was covered in leaves that had blown in through the door. As he walked toward the stairs, a rabbit hopped past. Mika stopped and watched it, entranced by its beauty, startled by its nonchalance.

At the top of the stairs, Helen's head poked out of a door. "There you are," she said breathlessly. "Come up here and give me a hand."

He climbed the stairs and followed her into a dusty bedroom.

There was a surfboard hanging over the bed. The floor was covered with heaps of sports gear and game consoles. Helen had emptied out all the closets. Awen sniffed at an old pair of sneakers while Mika lingered in the doorway.

"I think the sleeping bag is on the top shelf," Helen said. "I can't reach."

Their eyes met.

There was an awkward silence.

"You're wondering who I am," she said quietly.

He nodded.

She took a deep breath and sat on the end of the bed. Mika sat next to her, hoping she'd be able to explain all this away. But he felt dread.

"Who are you?" he asked.

"Helen Gelt," she replied. "I called myself Helen Green in Barford North, but on this side of The Wall, I'm Helen Gelt."

"So Gelt is your real name," Mika said.

"Yes," she replied.

He nodded again and looked at his hands.

"I was married on this side of The Wall," she said, "and I have a son here. My husband was Victor Gelt, who owned Unistore, the food corporation that ran the supermarkets before The Wall was built. This room is my son's room. His name is William. He's grown up now, but he spent his childhood in this house."

Mika tried to imagine Helen's son, but he could feel no warmth for William Gelt.

"So you're one of them," Mika said.

"Yes."

"And your husband was Victor Gelt of Unistore." He sat silent for almost a minute, then stood up and moved away from her.

"This is difficult," he said.

"I know," she replied.

"You should have told me," he said. "You should have told me before. I told you everything about me. You knew exactly who I was. This isn't fair."

"You know why I couldn't tell you before," she replied. "I couldn't tell you who I was without telling you The Secret. When I realized what you were seeing in your dreams, I was so excited, Mika. I wanted you to know you were right and I wanted to help you find Ellie, but telling you The Secret would have been a death sentence then. I wouldn't have been much of a friend if I'd put your life in danger, would I?"

"No."

"So I tried to help you without putting you in harm's way. And that meant I couldn't tell you the truth of who I was."

He closed his eyes and pressed his eyelids, trying to ease

the pressure behind them. "OK," he said. "I'm just trying to get my head around it. Victor Gelt . . . Unistore . . . It just doesn't seem very *you.*"

"That's because it's not very *me,*" she replied.

"But" —he cast his hand around the room— "you own all this?"

"I own the whole of Brittany, in what was once France," she said. "I'm the ninth richest person in the world—or at least Helen *Gelt* is the ninth richest person in the world. Helen Green knows none of it belongs to her."

Mika had faced many difficult challenges over the past few weeks while he was searching for Ellie, but this had to be one of the worst, because it made him feel so torn. One of his best friends had been responsible for The Wall, and now he had to decide whether she was guilty. The evidence stated YES, but her light and her eyes said NO. He thought of his parents. He remembered how tired and unhappy they were. All that suffering on the other side of The Wall had been caused by people like Helen Gelt.

He looked her straight in the eyes. "You need to tell me how Gelt became Green," he said. "Because I don't want to feel this way about you."

"I know," she said. "I don't like Helen Gelt any more than you do. We were *all* broken back then, Mika. Every single one of us. Come downstairs. And then I'll explain how I changed."

He followed her, Awen trotting ahead, nudging the hem of her skirt. She led them down to a large room with three long windows overlooking the garden. It was bursting with books. Newspapers and magazines fell like stuffing out of the shelves and lay in piles on the floor. Mika wandered through them, touching paper warmed by sunlight.

"I was born rich," Helen said, watching him. "And I grew up rich, surrounded by rich people and expensive things. I was given every privilege a child could wish for and I can't remember a single day when I felt like you did in Barford North—cramped and cold and hungry. Do you wish you had a childhood like mine? Instead of yours?"

He shook his head.

"Of course you don't," she said. "Because you understand what sort of person it made me. I had no idea what it felt like to suffer, because I had never suffered. I did not feel empathy for those who did, and I never questioned the justice of our world. During my childhood I believed what my parents believed. And when I married I believed what my husband believed. I grew up being told I was better than most people, and I was surrounded by people who believed they were better."

Mika walked toward the window and looked out at the overgrown garden. "So when The Wall was built . . ." he said.

"I had no idea what we were doing to people like you. I wasn't . . . myself. My best self."

"Did you think The Wall was a good idea?" he asked.

"Not exactly," Helen replied. "But I did think it was necessary, because that was what everyone around me was saying. It seemed a fact plain as day that there were too many people, and that if they kept on using up and fighting over resources, the natural world would die. And it would have. Yes, The Wall felt necessary, necessary to save nature. I believed we were building a Brave New World. Containing the overpopulation in the North, planting forests and breeding animals in the South to replace all those that had been killed. Even the fold-down apartments looked nice on the plans I saw. But I had no idea how much greed was involved. I believed what our politicians told us and I didn't understand how the people on the other side of The Wall would suffer. Helen Gelt was very naïve, Mika."

"Tell me what made you change," he said.

"My husband died," she answered. "That's what started it. He died of cancer caused by the drug Everlife-5. There I was, living in this Brave New World, breeding boar for the forest and raising my son, and then that happened."

Mika knew it would be polite to say he was sorry her husband had died of cancer, but he couldn't.

"It's OK," Helen said. "I'm not expecting you to be sorry."

Mika just looked at her.

"Victor was a lot older than me," Helen continued, "and he took Everlife-5 to stay young. But Everlife-5 was a terrible mistake. It killed lots of people on this side of The Wall. And as I stood by my husband's grave, watching clods of earth land on his coffin, I saw the first crack in my Brave New World. And then, because I was suffering, I began to ask questions. I wondered how such a thing could have happened when we were supposed to be so perfect. And the more I found out, the more cracks appeared. After I took control of Victor's business affairs, I realized his company, Unistore, had been selling this stuff called Fab Food to the people on the other side of The Wall. I'd never heard of it before, Mika. So I asked for some and I discovered just what we'd been feeding you. I will never forget my first mouthful of Fab peas — my tongue was green for days!"

She began to stomp through the piles of magazines.

"Imagine!" she snorted. "Finding out the man I'd lived with half my life, the father of my child, was the stinking rogue responsible for that monstrous muck Fab Food! And making a profit out of it! I was furious, Mika! Absolutely furious!"

Mika watched as she knocked over a heap of magazines, then crouched down to tidy them up. Red light fizzed around her.

"The cheap scoundrel!" she raged on, making a worse mess in her fury. Mika crouched beside her and helped straighten the stacks of paper.

"Then guess what I found out," she said.

"What?" Mika asked.

"That the directors of Unistore were stealing money from him. Stealing from him on his deathbed! So Victor was swindling the poor people in the North, and the directors of Unistore were swindling Victor. Suddenly I realized I was surrounded by scoundrels and liars. And how *stupid* I'd been . . . and how awful life was for you . . . for you poor people in the North . . ."

She stood up creakily. "The next day I packed a bag and moved to Barford North. I wanted to see what life was like there. And I wanted to figure out how we'd all gotten so broken. And that was the first sensible thing I ever did in my life. I took books with me. Lots of books: For years I'd had this library and never used it. I thought of books as decoration, until I started asking that question—how did we all get so broken?—and I couldn't find the answer. I suddenly realized how much knowledge I had all around me, all along."

Mika ran his fingers along the books' spines. "How many have you read?"

"Most," Helen said. "Some were boring. That's the boring pile over there where the ducks have been nesting. I read for years. First novels and biographies, then the heavy stuff: history, philosophy, science. And all these magazines."

"And did you find an answer to your question?" Mika asked.

"I may have," she said cautiously. "I don't want to say 'I did' because that would be incredibly arrogant, but I've got an idea what broke us."

"Tell me."

"We forgot what we are. We forgot we are animals and that our feelings are controlled by instincts. Instincts were useful in ancient times, when we were living as hunter-gatherers, trying to find food for ourselves and avoid becoming food for other animals, but in the age of science we don't need these instincts so much. We battled so hard against nature, inventing things to keep ourselves alive, that we forgot we were part of nature." She looked at him. "Does that make sense?"

He nodded.

"And I think it's dangerous to forget we are controlled by instincts," she said. "It makes us do things without understanding why. It makes us destructive, angry, and cruel."

She picked up a magazine about kitchen gadgets and handed it to Mika.

"I'll give you an example," she said. "Humans like to collect things, don't they? Like squirrels collect nuts."

Mika flicked through the pages. It was full of strange devices invented during the twentieth century to cut vegetables.

"In ancient times," she continued, "the instinct to hoard was useful, because it meant we were able to survive through the winter. But since we invented cans and freezers, we didn't need to hoard loads of stuff. But we continued to do it anyway: We'd forgotten why we did it, but we still followed our instinct to do it. Like broken squirrel borgs that couldn't stop squirreling, we filled our houses with things we didn't need."

Mika was looking at a picture of a food processor that

boasted over a hundred ways to slice and dice potatoes.

"We almost turned the natural world into one gigantic junk pile," Helen said. "By the time every home owned a chocolate fountain, there were almost no trees left. And," she went on, "one of the most painful things I realized was that it wasn't the fault of the poor, like your parents, who were forced to pay for this mistake. It was the fault of the rich who ran the corporations like Unistore. Because these corporations understood human instincts and took advantage of them. We actually encouraged people to buy things they didn't need. I felt so guilty when I realized that. I can't tell you how sorry I am."

Helen sighed deeply and hung her head.

"Most humans," she said after a long pause, "live only for love. To love and be loved. That's what novels taught me. All the rest, all the food processors and leaf blowers and chocolate fountains, are just the scenery for love."

Their eyes met. Hers were searching; his were calm and steady.

"Can you forgive me for what I once was?" she asked.

"Yes," he replied. He could understand now how her life of privilege had shielded her from the truth. But she had learned to think for herself, and she had changed her ways. He felt immensely relieved.

"And can you forgive me for leaving you in Barford North?" Helen continued. "I didn't want to. I wanted to stay and help."

"I know you did," Mika said. "I saw Gorman's men in your apartment. It was too dangerous for you to stay. But what happened when you came back here, to the other side of The Wall?"

"My son locked me up in his house," she said. "And hired dementia nurses to look after me. He thinks I'm senile because

I refuse to take Everlife-9 or live in this mansion. Can you believe it? It's not easy being different in this world, as you know . . ."

"At least you weren't born with webbed feet," Mika said.

"So we're still friends?" she ventured.

"Yes," he replied.

She smiled. It made her happy to see him in her library, looking at her books. Somehow he had survived all the training and mind games without losing his independent thought.

"You mutants are different from us, aren't you?" she said. "Us old, broken humans."

"I think so," Mika replied. "We know what we are."

"So what now? What next?"

"Take over the North," Mika stated. "Negotiate freedom with the South. Help people fix themselves so they can live in a natural world without destroying it."

She gulped. These children weren't messing about.

"We hear things you can't hear," he told her. "We call them The Roar and The Whisper. The Roar is the sound of emotion and The Whisper is the sound of thought. We mutants see a light too. I see what you're feeling in your light. And I see what the forests mean. We see us all, atom-deep, as one being, connected. Your answer makes perfect sense to me."

"Does it?" Helen said.

"Yes," he replied. "Can I use you for an experiment?"

"Of course," she said, a little nervously.

"It won't hurt," Mika told her.

He opened a window and helped her climb out into the garden.

"Well, this is interesting," she said, her yellow wellies deep in the green uncut grass. "What do you want me to do?"

"Touch one of the vines covering the house," Mika said.

There were plenty to choose from. They could hear the birds nesting in them, tweeting and rustling among the leaves. Helen grasped a length of wisteria and looked at him.

Mika stood behind her and put his hand on her arm.

"Your eyes have gone weird," she said. "They're all black and oily."

"Don't look at me," Mika said. "Look at the house. And relax."

"I can see the swallows have come back this year," Helen said. "That's their nest up there in the eaves."

"Stop thinking about swallows and concentrate," Mika said. "Or it won't work. Let your mind relax."

Another minute passed.

"I think I feel something," she said tentatively. "But I'm not sure. My fingers are a bit tingly."

"That's it," Mika said. "Relax."

The feeling intensified. Soon her fingertips buzzed where they touched the bark of the wisteria.

"I can see it," she whispered. "Yes, I can see it!"

Gold light grew in her fingertips and coursed into the bark. It ran like fluid up the vine and into all the other vines, until the whole house was covered in a twisted mass of golden light.

"Look at your feet," Mika said.

Helen looked down and saw the light running through the grass. It was coursing through her like electricity. Showing her that she was connected to all living things.

"What does it feel like?" he asked.

"Amazing!" she said, almost crying. "Absolutely amazing!"

17 The Wrong Place

The boy Luc breathed steadily.

His face was calm.

His arms were out of the blankets, hands open and relaxed at his sides.

Oliver sat on the chair by the lamp, and Kobi sat at the end of the bed. He tilted his chair back so he could lean against the wall and huddled down in his coat with his hands in his pockets. They were both silent. Oliver stared at the implant, as if he was trying to understand the adults who'd done such a thing. Kobi listened to The Whisper, which now flowed through his mind like a story. After sitting with the boy for a couple of hours, he knew everything the army knew: where they were, why they were taken, and what they were trying to do.

Then he had to pass through all the emotions they'd felt while he sat there in silence, with Oliver. The shocking truth about The Wall hit him like ice. The outrage that followed made him want to punch something.

His mother had been killed by the rich living on the other side of The Wall, and by a corrupt government that knew the truth but still left them to rot in darkness!

Kobi burned in his black coat, waiting for his anger to pass. For that implanted boy wasn't sleeping so peacefully for nothing. The army of children was about to rise and set this mess straight.

When his rage passed, he began to feel the more subtle emotions, the wonderment that forests still existed and the fear that they would burn before he saw them. And he felt a sense of alignment too. He'd come from a similar mold to Mika's; he'd always felt there was something wrong with his world, and now he knew he was right. That he could trust his instincts and stop wondering if there was something wrong with him. Beyond The Wall were forests and rich people.

It made sense. Perfect sense.

Then something else occurred to him. This boy was waiting to wake up in the wrong place.

In the *worst* place.

If he woke up here, in The Shadows, alone, the adults would pounce on him and pump him for information.

He must not wake up here, Kobi thought.

Now he was desperate to speak to Mika.

He felt in his pocket and realized he'd left his companion upstairs on his bed.

"Oliver?" he said.

"Yeah?"

"I've got to go back to my room for a minute. Will you stay here and watch the boy?"

"OK," Oliver replied.

"If he wakes up, run as fast as you can and find me. But don't tell any grown-ups, just me. Do you understand? It's really important."

"OK," Oliver said gravely. "I won't tell anyone, I promise."

Kobi sprinted up the stairs to his room and grabbed his companion.

"Call Mika again," he told her. "It's really urgent now, Anais. I have to speak to him."

He paced up and down while he waited.

"I still can't get through," she said. "I'm sorry."

"Frag it!" Kobi cursed.

18 A Sad Supper

Mika stared thoughtfully at the screen of his companion. Lilian's battery had gone flat. She'd been lying in Gorman's desk for several days and he didn't have her charger.

Now he wished The Whisper was a more precise form of communication, that he could connect with individuals, like through a com network, but it didn't work like that. All those thoughts and feelings were woven together with no names or places attached. He sensed he and Ellie had the strongest threads, but all the rest were as fine as gossamer. And he was stuck with the unsettling feeling that something was happening they needed to know about. He heard it in The Whisper, but he couldn't grasp it and didn't know where it was coming from.

It was dark now.

They'd left Ralph at the mansion to keep an eye on Mal Gorman and returned to Helen's hut to eat before they left.

Their mood had changed. Their thoughts had shifted. Now that Gorman was out of the way, they had to take over the fortress. Helen busied around them, lighting a fire and making tea, but the children were quiet. They would eat one meal together and then . . . they wouldn't see Helen again unless they succeeded. And if anything went wrong, they might return to find a wasteland of blackened bones and trees. Or never return . . .

After pacing the cabin for a few minutes, Colette and Santos went out to check on the Stealth Carrier. Leo and Iman sat by the fire and stared into the flames as if they were making them. Ellie, Mika, and Audrey sat at the table with Puck clambering between them. The monkey was behaving badly, grabbing things and running around the hut.

"It's like having a toddler around again," Helen said, as Puck stuck his fingers in the sugar bowl.

"Sorry," Ellie said. "He senses my mood."

"I'm not complaining," Helen replied, placing it out of reach. "I feel sorry for him. It's not surprising he wants to stretch his legs and fiddle with things after being locked up for most of his life. What do you fancy eating? You could do with packing a feast if you're going to take over a fortress tonight."

"What have you got?" Mika asked, putting Lilian down.

"Not much in the hut," she replied. "But you can order anything and it'll arrive in ten minutes. It's good like that over here."

When Colette and Santos returned, she opened a cupboard in the kitchen. There was a screen on the inside of the door. The children told her what they wanted and she ordered it.

While they waited for the food to arrive, Audrey helped set

the table. Helen noticed how she looked at the plates, as if she'd never seen them before. They were different, of course, from those used by people in the North. They were bone china with a gold rim and had been in Helen's family for a hundred years. But Audrey's fascination seemed to go beyond that. When she'd laid the plates on the table, she stared at them.

"What can you see?" Helen asked.

They were decorated with a leaf pattern.

"I was just noticing," Audrey replied, "that when humans copy nature, they get the pattern wrong. Real leaves don't look like this. Every leaf on a tree is different, but these are all the same."

Helen looked at the plates. Audrey was right. All the leaves were the same size and shape and placed at regular intervals. "I see what you mean," she said.

"I think humans want nature's pattern to be the same," Audrey said. "So they can understand it."

"That sounds about right," Helen replied. "Humans spent a long time trying to survive nature and it wasn't easy."

"And now they've forgotten they're part of a pattern."

"Yes." Helen looked at Audrey shrewdly. "Gosh," she said. "I can't remember what I was doing when I was twelve, but it wasn't observing chaos theory on dinner plates."

"What's chaos theory?" Audrey asked.

"Never mind," Helen replied. "Don't worry about it now. You've got enough to think about."

"Tell me another day," Audrey said. "I want to know."

"OK," Helen agreed. "I get the feeling you do already, but I will tell you."

The food arrived in a small, unmanned pod. It settled on

the porch like a wingless bee and beeped to announce its arrival. The children had asked for bread, cheese, grapes, and apples. They helped set it out and ate quietly. It was a necessary meal. They'd eaten ones like this before. Puck walked on all fours across the table, pinching food from their plates, but they hardly noticed.

"Do your parents know where you are?" Helen asked.

"No," Mika replied. "We can't tell them the truth yet or they'll start the war themselves."

"Oh yes," Helen said. "Of course. I must admit I am a bit worried about you. This is all very precarious."

"I know," Mika said. "But don't worry."

When they'd eaten as much as they could, they cut more bread and cheese to take with them. As they left, Mika promised to call Helen soon. She watched him walk down the path into the forest, with a tight feeling in her heart, and closed the door with a sigh.

The hut was not so warm without them. She sat in her chair by the fire, put a blanket over her knees, and called Ralph to make sure he was comfortable in the mansion, and that Gorman had settled in the boar house. Then she began the long, worrying wait for the children's return. She'd read about wars and she'd read about stopping wars. Stopping a war could be like trying to stop a boulder rolling down a mountain. However smart or strong these children were, they still ran the risk of being flattened by it.

Kobi returned to the sick room and sat with Oliver. He now felt as if he was guarding the boy, rather than watching him. Oliver left for a few minutes and returned with coloring pens and paper.

They were not like Grace Mose's. The paper was gray and rough because it was made of recycled food packing. The pens were the cheapest kind and he had to scrub to make a mark. Kobi listened to this sound and to The Whisper. Oliver drew a Pod Fighter. It was good, Kobi thought, and told him so.

They spent an hour like this. The child focused on impressing Kobi, and Kobi focused on learning more. He picked quietly through the threads of The Whisper, listening as hard as he could. The more he learned, the more afraid he became that this boy would wake up. No amount of strategy or skill would stop the war if their parents found out.

When the door opened, both boys startled. Suddenly, the small room was full of adults and noise. A woman waved Oliver off his chair.

"Come on, Oliver, your mum wants you to go back to your room and do your homework."

"But I've done all my homework," Oliver told her. "I want to stay here."

"No, that's enough now. The doctor's going to give the boy a drug to wake him up. He's not going to want a crowd of strangers around him when he opens his eyes."

"I'm not a stranger," Oliver argued. "I'm his friend."

"Don't be silly, Oliver," she said. "You can't make friends with someone who's fast asleep."

"Well, I did," Oliver argued.

"Out," the woman said, pushing him toward the door. "And no more of that sass or I'll tell your mum."

When Oliver had bumped furiously past the adults, the woman turned to Kobi.

He was sitting at the end of the bed, panicking.

They were trying to wake the boy up.

He tried to think of a way to stop this happening, but couldn't.

"Hi, Kobi," she said in a more respectful tone. "You'd better go as well. We've got a job for you and your father that will utilize your engineering skills. He'll explain."

"What's the drug you're giving the boy?" Kobi asked.

"It's a drug used in hospitals to bring people out of comas," the woman replied.

"But he's not in a coma," Kobi said.

"We know. Don't worry. The doctor knows what she's doing. You go and find your dad. Go on."

She waved him out. For a moment, Kobi considered refusing to leave. Then he looked at the boy in the bed and remembered he was sleeping because he wanted to; that he wouldn't wake up until his friends in the fortress did. And, if he was strong enough to defy a government implant, that coma drug wouldn't touch him.

Kobi clung to this hope and left, determined to get back in that room as soon as possible.

19 Bolt Borgs

Kobi returned to his own room to find Abe sitting on his bed with his head in his hands. Nevermore was perched on the edge of the desk, watching him.

"What's up?" Kobi asked.

Nevermore *craarked* and his feet clicked as he walked across the desk.

"They want us to do something strange," his father replied.

"What? Some woman downstairs said they have a job for us."

"They want to take us to the underside of the platform to fix some bolt borgs. Apparently, they were used during the construction of the Golden Turrets. They tightened the bolts that hold them onto the platform."

"Why do they want us to fix bolt borgs?" Kobi asked.

"Well, that's it," his father replied. "They didn't say. But I'm worried that the SLF are involved and that they're planning to *undo* the bolts. If the bolts are undone, the turrets will fall over. When I was in the bar earlier, they were talking again about threatening the government and forcing it to tell us what this war's about. They're coming to collect us in a few minutes."

"Oh no," Kobi said. "I told you the SLF were dangerous! You don't want to get involved with that, Dad; there are thousands of people living in the Golden Turrets, not just the government."

"I know," Abe said.

"If you don't want to do it," Kobi said, "tell them. You're not a terrorist."

"How can I?" he replied desperately. "They're helping us. They're hiding you. They're providing us with a home and food, and every time I go to the bar, one of them buys me a drink. They haven't let me buy a drink since we got here, and they talk about you all the time. You're a hero twice over for escaping from the game and saving the boy. We've got to at least go up there with them and find out what they want. Perhaps I'm wrong."

"I don't think you are," Kobi said. "From the way you describe it, there are only two things bolt borgs do: tighten bolts and undo bolts."

"Let's just go and see, Kobi. Please, don't make this more difficult. I'll find a way to get out of it if necessary. We can't fall out with these people. We have nowhere else to go."

"OK," Kobi said. "But I'm only going to look. I'm not fixing anything. They're also trying to wake up the boy by giving him a coma drug. But he's not in a coma."

"They're angry. They've run out of patience."

"I know and I don't like it."

Kobi lay on his bed and waited. A few minutes later, a man

and a woman arrived, and Kobi and Abe followed them down to the eleventh floor. In the buffer zone, they were given wading suits that covered the lower halves of their bodies. Outside the door, a cold wind gusted up the stairs, carrying the stench of slime. In the foyer, they found the tide rising and the water waist-deep. It would have made sense to fly from such a place, but civilian pods were banned in The Shadows because of all the pillars holding up the Golden Turrets. So Kobi waded after his father, feeling uncomfortable and annoyed and hoping to get this over with as quickly as possible.

They waded through deserted, flooded streets, east along the river through the old financial heart of the city. The water rushed around them, tugging with the tide. It coiled through the doors of the buildings as if searching for things to wash away. Sometimes it was difficult to stand up and they had to stop, swaying unsteadily, as the water wound around their legs.

Then they saw a pillar in the road ahead. When they reached it, they waded around it until they found steps leading up to a damp, black door. Through this they found themselves in a cold, dark space facing another door, to an elevator that was bubbled with rust. It opened creakily and they squashed inside. The walls were streaked with black mold.

"Don't worry, it's safe," the man said. "These elevators were built for the engineers working on the Golden Turrets. They haven't been used for years, but we've fixed this one."

Kobi did not feel reassured by this statement. As they rose in that old, dark elevator, he could hear the chains creaking and the wind beyond the pillar wall. He had to close his eyes and tell himself that he would be out of it soon; that he was doing this for his father.

The elevator stopped and the door opened again. Now they were right at the top of the pillar, just beneath the huge, black metal platform supporting the Golden Turrets. Kobi followed the strangers and his father onto a steel mesh walkway that was suspended only a few feet below it. Kobi looked down and felt a surge of vertigo. He could see through the mesh as if it weren't there. The River Thames twisted below them, dark and deadly.

"Don't look down," the woman said.

They began walking. The mesh creaked and Kobi began to wonder if he could do this at all. The walkway didn't feel safe and here he was with his father, when neither of them even wanted to come. Eventually, they paused and the man and woman pointed toward a shadowy hulk above them. It clung to the underside of the platform like a giant cockroach.

"That's one," the man said. "They left several hundred bolt borgs behind when construction of the turrets ended. I suppose it was easier than getting rid of them. They have rotating jaws inside their heads, but because they haven't been used for so long, they've seized up."

"Why do you want us to fix them?" Abe asked. "I don't understand."

The man moved closer and his eyes filled with hatred. "The government took our children," he said. "And put lumps of metal in their heads. The days go by and they still haven't told us what this war is about. Do you know what the government ministers are doing while we wait for them to talk to us?"

"No," Abe replied uncomfortably.

"They party," said the man. "Every night, while we worry about our children, they gorge themselves on fine food and wine. Our people wait at their tables; we've seen it with our own eyes. Now it's time for the party to end. We want to know why our children were taken. We're going to undo the bolts on one of the Golden Turrets so it falls over, and then, if they still refuse to talk to us, we'll undo the bolts on them all."

It was several seconds before Abe was able to speak.

"Let me have a look at it," he said quietly. "Then I'll need to go back to our room and get the right tools."

"I thought you brought tools," the woman said. "We were hoping you could start now."

"I brought some," Abe replied. "But I won't know exactly what I need until I've looked at the bolt borg. I've never worked on one before."

Kobi watched his father climb a metal ladder. In the dark space beneath the platform, he watched the beam of the flashlight dance as Abe removed a section of the bolt borg's shell and looked inside it. After several minutes, he replaced it again and climbed down.

"We have to go back," he said. "There are several tools I need."

"OK," the man replied, and they began the tiresome journey back to the Future Communication Building.

"You should have told them you don't want to do it," Kobi whispered furiously, as they waded away from the pillar.

"I didn't know what to say to them," Abe replied. "They looked so angry. I'm trying to buy us more time. We can go back for tools, pretend to try and fix it, then say that we can't, that it's broken beyond repair."

"Great," Kobi said irritably. "That will take hours."

"I can't just tell them," his father said. "They're scary."

"I know," Kobi said. "But I'm not coming back. I want to stay with the boy."

"What has the boy got to do with this?" his father whispered. "I need you more than he does."

"I'm not coming back," Kobi insisted. "I don't want anything to do with terrorists."

His father looked sad. "This is crazy," he said. "How did we end up living like this?"

20 Tank Meat Surprise

The fortress looked quiet as the invisible Stealth Carrier approached Cape Wrath. Leo and Iman paused the craft over Sandwood Seven and they waited for a few minutes while a freighter dropped in and left again, having delivered a load of supplies. When they were sure the path was clear, they followed, dropping down into the hole through the middle of the fortress.

They landed the carrier in the hangar on its launchpad, then the children waited for another few minutes, observing the activity there. Delivery borgs droned around, moving palettes of supplies. The only human they saw was a woman with a battered tablet who sauntered past, yawning with boredom. She would not be doing that if anyone had realized Mal Gorman and his Chosen Ones were missing.

"Good," Mika said, tugging Awen's ears. "Let's go."

The children activated their invisibility shields.

The carrier door opened and Awen blazed a trail to the elevator.

When they reached the top of the fortress, they had a difficult moment when the door opened again. Two of Mal Gorman's officers were waiting to get in it, and the children had to creep around their sides. Shaken by this close encounter, the children walked quickly away, with their blood rushing.

They reached Mal Gorman's office to find the door locked. They stood against the wall as more staff meandered past, then Ellie opened it and they crept in. When it was locked again, she appeared with a flash, leaning against it. Then the others appeared, dotted around the office.

"That was close," she said.

Puck dropped from her shoulder and scampered across the floor. The children worked quickly, looking into the walls for hidden cameras and melting the lenses with their eyes. Soon Mal Gorman's office was theirs.

It was quite different without him in it, seething and glaring at everyone. Ellie pulled a chair up to the desk. Mika watched. He'd never imagined seeing his sister do this. It pleased him.

She touched the screen gently with her fingertips and it woke up, casting her in light.

"He's still logged in," she said. "Ha-ha. I wonder if he's realized. I bet he's regretting taking that Everlife-9 now."

"I bet he's regretting lots of things now that he's sitting on a pile of straw," Mika said.

They gathered around the desk and watched Ellie summon views from around the fortress and explore Gorman's security clearance and software. She had access to everything: all the security systems, communication networks, and weapons. One chain of feeds even monitored the *Queen of the North*, the space station in orbit around Earth, where she'd once been imprisoned.

For a while they just looked at areas of the fortress, figuring out where everything was stored and what the staff were doing. The men they'd locked in the gym were sitting on the floor, looking bored and anxious.

Then they explored the control panels for the alarm systems and the fence. When this was done, they focused on the children. The implanted army was sleeping peacefully. The other mutants, like them, who'd not been chosen by Mal Gorman, were stored in another enclosure, halfway up the fortress. These mutants were not implanted, but they knew what was happening and they were waiting too. They paced their enclosure, looking quiet and thoughtful.

"Good," Ellie said. "We're ready. Does everyone agree?"

They nodded.

"OK, let's take over a fortress."

She opened the alarm and security systems. Then she summoned views from around the fortress, so they could watch Mal Gorman's staff in some of the larger areas: the dormitories, offices, and refectories. Next she searched through the alarm panel for the loudest alarm she could find. It was labeled DEATH SIREN.

"That'll do," she said.

Then she wrote a security alert that would appear on every screen around the fortress.

Tank Meat Surprise was on the menu that night. Gorman's staff walked away from the serving machines with white trays that held a brown lump, a green heap, and a yellow blob. The staff looked half asleep. It was mid evening, almost the end of the second shift, and nothing interesting had happened for hours . . . at least not that they knew about. They walked through the rows of tables and sat down to eat. On the screens around them a game show played and they stared at this blankly, unaware that they were about to get more surprise than they were expecting with their meal.

In Mal Gorman's office, Ellie bit her lip and pressed Send.

Immediately, the Death Siren began to wail, the game show disappeared, and her message began to flash against a red background.

INCOMING MEGABOMB
FIRST-LEVEL ATTACK
ALL STAFF EVACUATE

The children held their breath and waited. They expected an immediate response, for this was a top-level alert. But for a good thirty seconds, all the staff did was look around and ask each other what was happening. The fortress was full of shrugging shoulders and raised eyebrows. Some even continued to eat, as if they were trying to finish their meal before they were forced to leave it.

"What are they doing?" Audrey said. "We've just told them the fortress is about to be hit by a megabomb."

"Perhaps they think it's a drill," Ellie said. "Like the fire alarm drills we used to have in school. They probably don't believe it's real and they don't want to go outside because it's cold. We'll have to scare them a bit."

She found the control panel for the light network and turned them off. For a moment the whole fortress was plunged into darkness. Then the emergency lighting system came on and every room was lit by a bloodred glow. This seemed to make a difference. The people in the refectories stood up and began to walk toward the doors. But it was still like trying to start a stampede of sleepy buffalo. In the dormitories the nurses lingered around the beds, looking at the rows of children as if they weren't sure what to do about them.

"Send the nurses a message," Mika said. "Tell them to leave the children behind."

It took a while, but eventually panic ignited and Gorman's staff began to pour down to ground level like water running out of a punctured vessel, leaving all the children behind.

"Some officers are coming this way," Leo said.

"They're his chief officers," Ellie observed. "We have to get rid of them."

She moved her hands quickly over the desktop and added another alarm on the top floor. It was so piercing, it made them wince. Immediately, the officers turned and ran in the other direction.

"Nice," Leo said.

Then Ellie summoned a view from above the fortress and they watched the staff pour out over the rocks and toward the electric fence. Thousands of soldiers, nurses, engineers, and maintenance staff, some still in their pajamas. The wind buffeted them. Their light was a mass of fear and panic.

"Keep going, keep going," Ellie whispered.

She pressed an icon, and the giant electric fence began to sink into the ground. The staff ran over it, heading toward the town. They were really scared now and running for their lives.

Eventually, the evacuation slowed down to a trickle. When Ellie was sure they were all gone, she made the fence rise again. The only adults left inside the perimeter were the seven men locked in the gym.

"That was tense," Mika said. "I thought we were going to have to go out there and prod them with sticks."

For a minute they watched the darkness on the other side of the fence, wondering if the staff would realize they'd been tricked and come back. But the darkness remained solid.

"Good," Ellie said. "Now let's deal with the *Queen of the North*."

She set up a distress signal and sent it to the space station. Then they paced Gorman's office while they waited for it to arrive.

Kobi and his father followed the man and woman through the metal door and into the buffer zone. After undressing clumsily because their hands were so cold, they left them and walked up the stairs to their room. They opened the door to find Oliver sitting on Kobi's bed.

"Hello," Oliver said. "Where have you been?"

"Just out for a bit," Kobi replied.

The child fell quiet, sensing the strained atmosphere. He and Kobi watched Abe pack more tools in his bag, do it up, and sling it over his shoulder.

"I'll see you later," Abe said.

"OK, Dad," Kobi replied. "Good luck."

When Abe had left, Kobi immediately turned to Oliver. "Is the boy awake?" he asked.

"No!" Oliver whispered excitedly. "The medicine didn't work! He's still asleep! All the grown-ups are talking about it. I stood outside the kitchen and listened. They don't understand why it didn't work."

"They wouldn't," Kobi replied.

"What do you mean?" Oliver asked. "I don't understand either."

"Nothing," Kobi said.

He felt immense relief that he'd guessed right; that the boy would sleep until the others awoke, but he also felt the walls of the room closing in on him. He was trapped in a box in a building, with the weight of the Golden Turrets pressed down on his head and all these angry adults around him. And although he was glad the boy had not awoken, he knew he would awake, soon, in the wrong place. He needed help.

If Oliver had been older, Kobi would have told him everything at that moment. But Oliver was too young to understand how precarious this situation was. Kobi could not expect a seven-year-old child to keep his mouth shut if he knew the children of the North were about to stage the biggest rebellion in human history. And that there were forests and rich people on the other side of The Wall.

No, Oliver couldn't be told that. But he looked upset. He knew Kobi was keeping something from him.

"I'm hungry," Kobi said. "I could really do with something to eat. Do you think you can help me?"

"Yes," Oliver said, immediately distracted. "I'll show you where to make a sandwich. You don't have to ask, you can just go to the kitchens and make it yourself. That's what I do."

He stood up and straightened his Pod Fighter T-shirt.

"Thanks," Kobi said. "I'm glad I've got you to show me around."

Then he followed the child down the stairs, with his head full of the sleeping boy.

"Here it comes," Ellie said.

The *Queen of the North* descended slowly, its engines vibrating through the fortress, the coastline, the town, and the sea. Mal Gorman's Chosen Ones stood at his window and watched the clouds part and a few megatons of metal and light fill the sky.

"Frag!" Mika said. "It's huge! Are you sure we can take control of that?"

"Yeah," Ellie replied. "Its weapons systems are rubbish compared to the fortress. It's a research station, not a warship. But our main advantage will be surprise."

They heard a beep from the desk as a message arrived. It was from the Commander of the *Queen of the North*, asking Mal Gorman if the distress signal was a drill.

Ellie replied:

Yes, this is a drill.

Testing evacuation procedure in advance of war.

Follow guidelines.

Evacuate the *Queen of the North*.

The children watched the screen with their hearts thumping. A minute passed before the Commander replied.

Requesting authorization code

"Oh," Ellie said. "I was hoping they wouldn't ask for one of those."

"Search the desktop," Audrey suggested, chewing her nails. "Perhaps Gorman keeps it in a file somewhere."

Ellie searched quickly, but all she found was a folder of wallpaper samples. She dragged it into the bin. "OK," she said. "We don't have an authorization code, so we're going to have to invent one."

"Quickly," Mika said. "We don't want to give them time to start wondering what's happening."

Awen paced the office with the whites of his eyes showing.

Ellie summoned a side view of the fortress, so they could see the space station hanging above it. Then she opened the weapons panel.

"I've heard Gorman boasting about his cannons," she said. "They're supposed to be huge. Perhaps they'll work as an authorization code."

"Try it," Mika said. "Quickly."

They watched Ellie sweep her hands over the desk. After a

few seconds, they heard a great, grinding noise in the bones of the fortress. They leaned over the screen and watched as the cannons rose out of the top.

"Frag!" Audrey said, grinning. "Gorman wasn't exaggerating."

The cannons rose to form a ring, transforming the fortress into a huge weapon powerful enough to blow a hole in the moon. When they'd risen to their full height, Ellie sent another message to the Commander of the *Queen of the North*:

> **Authorization Code:**
> **Look out the window.**

They waited several agonizing minutes. The *Queen of the North* hung above them, a dark silent hulk, and nothing appeared to happen for ages. Sometimes they watched it through the window, sometimes they watched it through the desktop, urgently wanting to see signs of movement. But when things started to happen, they happened quickly. Openings appeared on the undercarriage of the space station and bright yellow evacuation pods began to fly out. It started with twos and threes, but soon there were so many, it was like watching popcorn explode from the ship. The pods puffed out in yellow clouds, then swarmed away from the fortress. The children watched, feeling rushes of excitement, until it slowed down and stopped.

"It's ours," Ellie said. "The *Queen of the North* is ours."

"Can we control it from here?" Audrey asked enthusiastically.

"Yes," Ellie replied.

"Can you move it a bit?" Audrey said. "So it's not hanging over our heads."

"I think so."

Ellie fiddled for a few minutes until the enormous space station began to rumble toward the sea. Ellie stopped it a mile away, where they could keep an eye on it.

"You just parked a space station," Audrey said mischievously.

"I'm tempted to drop it in the sea," Ellie said. "I was forced to live on that thing for a year and a half."

"Don't do that," Mika said immediately. "You'll cause a giant wave."

"I know," Ellie replied. "I'm not actually going to do it. I was just joking."

"Well, it wasn't funny."

They looked at each other.

"Why are you in such a crappy mood?" she said.

"Because we haven't got time for jokes," Mika replied. "Now that we've taken the fortress and the *Queen of the North*, we have to move quickly. We've got to wake up the army, take control of The Wall, tell our government what we've done, and then negotiate with the South. And as fast as possible so our parents don't realize what's going on. I feel like there's something happening we need to know about. I want Lilian's charger. Now."

They watched as he searched the drawers in Gorman's desk. Ellie scowled.

"I don't understand," Audrey said. "What do we need to know about?"

"Well, that's it, I dunno," Mika said. "I just feel it. I wish we could hear more in The Whisper. There's something in it I want to hear louder. Frag! I can't find my charger! Where did Gorman put it? I need it!"

"Don't worry," Audrey said. "We'll find one. Calm down, Mika. You know we won't be able to do this if we get all stressed."

Seven children, a monkey, and a dream dog had taken control of a fortress and a space station. This was an auspicious act, but it was also a catalyst. Taking over from the Northern Government would be like tipping out a box of marbles and trying to catch them all again before they rolled off the table. They'd started something that couldn't be stopped, they'd never done anything like it before, and they were aware that if even one marble fell, the consequences would be devastating. Their world could end up more of a mess than it had ever been before.

For half an hour they remained in Mal Gorman's office, trying to think of everything that could go wrong and securing the fortress through his desk. They turned off the security borgs that patrolled the passages. They deactivated the children's implants, so they no longer had to fight the Northern Government commands. Then they spent a few minutes trying to figure out how to transport the Pod Fighters up to the hangar. There were thousands of them stored underground, but it was a complicated process. When this was done, they searched for clothing for the implanted army. They couldn't fly out of that fortress in white gowns and bare feet. And they would need food, water, medical supplies. There was so much to think about, with marbles skidding across the table.

While all this was going on, the communication network crashed under a sudden deluge of messages. The fortress staff were not completely stupid. As they ran through the streets of Sandwood Seven, they waited for the megabomb to fall, but instead, after several quiet minutes, they saw the *Queen of the North* arrive.

Why would Mal Gorman summon the *Queen of the North* when a megabomb was just about to hit the fortress?

This did not make sense.

Gorman's precious space station had no weapons to defend it against the might of a megabomb and now it was perched right above the fortress, where it would get hit.

As evacuation pods began to fly out of it, the staff clicked that there was something fishy going on. They turned and began to run toward the fortress, sending messages, demanding to know what was happening.

"Look at them," Audrey said, as they began to appear on the other side of the fence. "They're really angry."

"They can't get back in," Ellie said. "They're the least of our worries. Try to ignore them."

She swiped them away, turned off the communication network, and stood up. "Right," she said. "That's everything we can do here. Let's find Mika a charger and collect the army."

They quickly explored the rooms around Mal Gorman's office. They found companion chargers in the drawer of another desk belonging to one of his commanders. Mika connected Lilian and left her in a heap with the rest, then they set off down the fortress toward the mutants' enclosure.

The fortress felt cavernous with the adults gone, like a lost ship drifting through space. Security borgs slept in the silent passages, and computers dozed in their desks. Now and then a cleaner borg droned past, looking a bit lost and lonely. The children hurried toward the mutants, knowing they'd feel more in control when they were all together again. They'd met many of these mutants during the game. They had competed against each other then, but now they were a team. The mutants were the elite, the best pilots and gunners. Working together, leading squadrons of Pod Fighters, they would be very useful.

The mutants paced their enclosure, watching the door. As Ellie and Mika and the others walked through it, they came together in a rush of risk fueled adrenaline. They wore a similar white uniform, without the black stripe down the side. Standing together, they looked exactly what they were: young, talented, and dangerous.

When they'd talked for a few minutes and most of them had marveled and smooched over Puck, they prepared to move down the fortress again, to wake up the implanted army. But as Mika moved toward the door, he had a sudden, horrible thought. He'd forgotten about someone. Someone who ought to be there but wasn't.

"Audrey, stop," he said. "Where's Ruben? Where's that nasty little perp, Ruben Snaith?"

Audrey turned and scanned the crowd with her green eyes. "I don't know. I haven't seen him."

"Who's Ruben?" Ellie asked.

"You know him," Mika said. "He was in our class in Barford North. That rat boy who bullied mutants."

"Yeah, I remember him," she scowled. "That's one person I didn't miss when I was taken."

"And he's a mutant," Mika said. "Can you believe it? He made our lives hell during the game and he didn't get chosen because he's such a psycho. We have to find him. Does anyone know where he is?"

The question traveled, but nobody knew. Ruben had wanted Audrey as his gunner when the game first began, but she'd chosen Mika instead. Ruben had never forgiven him for this and made a dangerous game miserable too. Ruben wasn't like them; he used his power to cause pain. He fed his jealousy and hatred instead of trying to control bad feelings. No one had seen him since the prize-giving dinner when he'd transformed the table into a whirlwind of knives and broken glass. He'd been shot by Gorman's men and dragged away. . . .

But to where?

"We have to look for him," Mika said. "We can't leave here until we know where he is."

They began searching the rooms around the enclosure. After a few minutes, a boy came running to find them and they were taken to an area just along the passage on the same floor. They walked through a pair of two-feet-thick security doors into a suite of rooms.

"Oh no," Mika said, looking around.

Despite the heavy security, it looked like a luxury hotel suite, fitted with everything a psycho boy like Ruben could wish for. A king-size bed; a sea view; a fridge full of real food; a cinema-size screen on one wall; a large, illuminated mirror to preen himself in. Most of the furnishings looked as if they'd come from Mal Gorman's private apartment. There was even one of his oil paintings hanging over the bed. Soft towels, silk curtains, an antique vase, and hanging in the wardrobe, a row of uniforms similar to theirs . . . but black . . .

"Gorman's been treating him like a prince," Audrey said. "He must be crazy!"

"We already knew that," Mika said. "Frag it! Where is that rat boy? We let him escape when we opened the doors."

"He'll be long gone," Audrey said, closing the wardrobe. "He's not going to hang around to help us stop a war. He's not one of us."

"We have to go," Ellie said urgently. "We could spend hours searching for him when we're supposed to be waking up the army and flying out of here. We need to concentrate on what we're doing."

She began to walk toward the door.

"But I want to know where he is," Mika said.

"We haven't got time," Ellie said. "Come on, we have to go. Please. If he follows us, we'll deal with him then. Forget him for now. Come on."

They moved down the fortress toward the implanted army, and Ruben was shelved. There really were more important things to worry about. They all knew this. They were about to fly again, most of them for the first time in reality. Now they'd taken the fortress and the *Queen of the North*, they would have to take control of The Wall. They would stand on The Wall that divided their world and talk to the adults who'd broken it.

The mutants stood among the implanted army, watching them sleep in their beds.

It was thrilling to be among them like this. There were so very many, and the second awakening would not be like the first. There would be no pain or confusion or anger, just haste to climb into their Pod Fighters.

Ellie, Mika, and Audrey stood among the rows of beds. They waited in the silence until they sensed everyone was ready, then they took a deep breath.

Wake up.
Wake up.
It's time to fly.

22 The Second Awakening

Kobi sat at the desk between the beds, working on the borg kittens. They were nearly finished. He was attaching their silver whiskers and the tiny pads on each paw. Nevermore watched him intently, with beady silver eyes. He watched the kittens glint in the light of the lamp as if he understood how precious they were and as if he'd quite like to thieve them before they were finished. Kobi knew this was an illusion and that Nevermore didn't really know what he was doing. But it made him feel a bit better. His father was still out, pretending to fix the bolt borg. Kobi was working on the kittens because the boy's room was still out of bounds, and he was sure he'd go crazy if he didn't force himself to think about something else.

The Whisper had been quiet for a while. It was pensive, as if it was waiting for a coin to land, heads up or down. . . . Kobi realized something was happening.

He couldn't concentrate on the kittens. He got up and paced. Then he felt a bit better and sat down again and managed to focus for ten minutes. Then he started feeling something else, a feeling he recognized from his days in the arcade: the anticipation of flight; the nervous excitement and the lust for speed as he slid into the pilot seat and put his headset on.

Was the army waking up?

His put down his tools and stared at the wall behind the desk, listening carefully.

Nevermore pecked at the kittens.

Then he heard it.

Wake up.
Wake up.
It's time to fly.

His heart began to pound.

He burst out of the room and ran down the stairs, determined to be with that boy even if he had to kick the door down and wrestle the adults out of the way.

But when he reached the boy's room, he found the door open and the bed empty. For a moment he stood and stared at it, confused. Then he noticed the thin plastic tubes that had been attached to the boy's arm were dripping drugs and saline on the floor. And there were patches of blood on the sheets where the needles had been yanked out. The boy must have done this himself. He'd awoken already . . . and run. . . .

Kobi turned, panic-stricken, wondering which way he'd gone. It could only have happened moments ago. He found his path blocked by a startled woman.

"Where is he?" she cried, pushing past him. "I only left him alone for a minute and he was fast asleep. What happened?"

"I don't know," Kobi replied. "I've only just got here."

The woman began to shout for help, and suddenly, adults were running in from every direction.

Kobi thought fast.

Which way would *he* go if he'd awoken in the wrong place?

Out, he decided. Out of that building and away, to find the army.

But beyond that building was a stinking, broken river and it was high tide. And the boy was sick. He wasn't well enough to be out of bed; he'd never survive The Shadows. Kobi pushed through the adults and hurried toward the buffer zone, hoping they wouldn't notice him leave. But within moments, they were following and he had a mob on his tail. He half fell down eleven flights of stairs, throwing his coat off, taking three, four steps at a time, desperate that the boy would either drown or the adults would reach him first.

In the foyer he found the tide higher than he'd ever seen it before. It was almost up to his chest and it heaved around the stricken walls. He leaped into it and gasped as the cold hit his chest. Then he half swam, half waded to the doors. Just beyond them he saw the boy about a hundred feet away, struggling west through the water. His pale arms flailed as it dragged him toward the corner of a building. Kobi swam with all his might, using every bit of strength Fit Camp had given him and reached the boy as he slammed against the wall and turned facedown.

The pull of the water was so strong, it was difficult to turn him over. Kobi pushed him against the wall, gripped him under the arms, and yanked him up. He could hear the adults behind him, shouting. He cut them out, refusing to listen to them.

"What's your name?" he asked the boy frantically. "I'm one of you, talk to me."

But the boy lolled in Kobi's arms, his red hair plastered to his head, and his skin tinged blue by the cold. He wasn't asleep, he was unconscious.

"You mustn't tell," Kobi whispered urgently. "Can you hear me? Please don't talk. Don't tell these people anything."

Then Kobi was surrounded by adults grabbing at the boy's arms. He would not let go.

"Let me do it!" he shouted. "He needs to be with me!"

The adults looked at him with a mixture of surprise and pity.

"It's all right, Kobi," someone said. "We know this is upsetting for you, but the boy needs medical care. Let go of him."

It became a tug of war. The adults pulling one way and Kobi pulling the other, with the boy limp between them, and the black water rushing all around.

"What are you doing?" someone said. "Let go!"

Now they were angry. Kobi wanted to yell at them. He wanted to tell them exactly what he thought of them, but he knew if he pushed this too far, he might never be allowed near the boy again. He let go of his arms and they pulled him away as if he were a sack of gold. Then Kobi followed them back into the building.

The second awakening happened quickly. The children opened their eyes and gathered momentum. They visited the uniform stores and collected clothes — underwear, trousers, shirts, and boots — searching the metal shelves for their sizes and sitting on the floor to dress in a concentrated silence. They left their long white gowns behind, in heaps on the floor.

Then they collected water bottles and ration packs and returned to the dormitories to form the squadrons that would fly to The Wall.

"I need a gunner," Ellie said.

"I know a good one," Mika replied. "Find one of the nurses' tablets and we'll search for him."

Ellie found one under a bed, where a nurse had flung it as he ran from the megabomb. Stored in its memory were the locations of every child in the dormitories.

"What's his name?" Ellie asked.

"Frazer," Mika replied. "Tom Frazer. He was Kobi's gunner in the game. He's not a mutant, but he's still really good."

Ellie entered Tom's name, and a dormitory and bed number appeared. "He's in dormitory nineteen," she said.

"Let's go and find him."

Mika felt better now that the army was awake. They were moving quickly, proving how much they'd learned through the game, and he liked the idea of Ellie flying with Tom. Tom had been completely beguiled by Pod Fighter and refused to listen to Kobi's and Mika's warnings, but that wasn't his fault, and any gunner good enough to fly with Kobi Nenko was good enough to fly with his sister. It felt right and safe that Ellie flew with Tom. No mutant would try harder for her.

But when they found him, Tom started with shock. He hadn't seen anyone from Barford North since he lost Ana, and Mika reminded him what a fool he'd been.

"Mika," he said. "Audrey." Immediately, his face reddened with embarrassment. "You tried to warn me. . . . I'm really sorry."

"I know," Mika said. "Forget about that now. We've been looking for you. I have a special favor to ask."

"Anything," Tom said.

"I want you to gun for my sister. Meet Ellie . . . and Puck."

Tom blushed again, moved by Ellie's dark charisma and startled by her monkey friend. Then he felt a glow of gratitude and pride that they had searched for him, despite what had happened before. Pilot and gunner relationships were special. They chose each other carefully. "I'd love to," he said.

"Yaaay!" Audrey cried. "I'm excited now! We've got Tom back!"

"I wonder where Kobi is," Tom said.

"I dunno," Mika replied. "But I wish he was with us."

Each dormitory formed a squadron of a hundred pairs of pilots and gunners, with at least four mutants in each. The structures that Mal Gorman made, the children adapted and made their own. This was still Pod Fighter and this is what they were born to do. They'd known it in their hearts since the day the arcades opened. And the addiction they'd felt to this dangerous game, that had landed them in this mess, now seemed to have a reason instead of just being stupid. They would use the same skills to stop a war that their government would have used to start one.

When the squadrons were formed, they divided into two teams, one that would stay to protect the fortress, and one that would fly to The Wall. It was difficult to do this. They'd never craved to fly this much. But they had learned through the game that strategy was everything. That those who didn't fight were as important as those who did.

They were almost ready.

As the squadrons prepared to leave, Mika left Ellie with Tom and traveled up the fortress with Audrey to collect their companions. Once they'd taken The Wall, they would have to make two calls. One to the Northern Government and another to Raphael Mose.

In the elevator, Mika leaned against the wall, worrying about this.

"That's going to be the most dangerous time," he said. "When we're standing on The Wall and we've told both sides what we've done. They're going to be very angry."

"I know," Audrey replied. "It'll be a while before they calm down and listen to us. But we'll be standing on The Wall. We'll control all the weapons in the North. It doesn't matter how angry the Northern Government gets; they won't be able to do anything. They can't threaten us with sorting beads and detention collars anymore. And the South will be scared. When they calm down, they'll realize they have to take us seriously."

"Yeah," Mika said.

"And we're being reasonable," Audrey said. "We don't want to hurt anyone, we just want to talk."

She leaned against him and he put his arm around her, soothed by her simple optimism. Sometimes it seemed as if Audrey was "happiness," that all he had to do was talk to this girl and the way he felt changed.

The elevator reached Gorman's floor and stopped.

I love you, he thought, as the door opened.

And I love you. And we're going to fly!

He grinned in her hair.

That's all you care about, isn't it? Getting in a Pod Fighter again.

No, she thought. *But since I was thinking about things I love, I thought about that as well.*

He laughed and followed her out of the elevator. He was still feeling happy when they were traveling down in it again, with their charged companions in their pockets.

23 Doing It for Real

Mika and Audrey found Ellie in the hangar, watching the first squadron prepare to leave. Leo and Iman were flying with it. Mika watched Leo tie his dreadlocks at the nape of his neck, just as he'd done during the game. The gold ring glinted on his finger. He looked as calm as ever. Watching Leo like this, with Audrey and Ellie, made Mika feel that anything was possible. Anticipation ran through The Whisper like a fast, bright stream.

"See you on The Wall," Leo said, then Mika watched him follow Iman through the rows of Pod Fighters. They looked magnificent; their smooth black lines gleamed in the hangar light. Polished windshields slid back, and hundreds of children in blue and white uniforms jumped lightly onto the wings and dropped into the cockpits. Pilots at the front. Gunners at the back. As they slid down, their seats gripped the sides of their bodies. Then hands worked over headsets and controls.

Harnesses clicked, icons blinked on, and blood pumped hard as they prepared for takeoff.

The hangar roof opened like a giant retina and their engines began to roar. Leo and Iman's Pod Fighter was the first to rise. For a moment it hung above them, roaring like a thousand tigers, then it shot up like a black dart and vanished, pulling the first squadron after it as if they were all connected by string.

Ellie gripped Puck tightly as the noise made him convulse with panic.

"Our turn next," Audrey said.

The departed squadron left the hangar bare. Only the Stealth Carrier and a freighter remained. But the fortress was equipped with enough Pod Fighters to have the whole army in the air together. Immediately, hundreds more arrived, with loader borgs attached to their wheels. Then the second squadron gathered. When the hangar was filled with Pod Fighters, and all the loader borgs had scurried away, Ellie, Mika, Audrey, and Tom walked out with the others.

Ellie had to grip Puck with both hands. The last time he'd flown in a Pod Fighter, they'd almost drowned in the River Thames.

"It's OK," Ellie whispered. "Trust me and hold on tight." She dropped into the pilot seat and the animal clung to her chest. Then Tom dropped in the back and they put their headsets on.

Mika and Audrey took the Pod Fighter next to them. As they fastened their harnesses, Mika felt their minds synch. He was with Ellie, Tom, and Audrey, and he was with all the others. The windshield clicked down. Hundreds of colorful icons blinked on. Audrey felt over her gun controls and took a deep breath.

Are you ready?

Yeah.

Mika took off. The roar of the Pod Fighter shattered the air and he felt Audrey's adrenaline fuel it. He rose up through the fortress slowly, then when they were above it, they formed a cyclone around it, as the squadron gathered and prepared to fly south. Then, like a swarm of black flies, they unwound and shot toward The Wall.

It was a cloudy night, but the wind was moderate and there was only the odd spat of rain. They would have preferred moonlight, but these conditions were safe enough.

When they reached The Wall, they turned west and followed its line across the Atlantic. They flew in single file, high above the clouds, balanced on the knife edge between the two worlds.

When all the squadrons had arrived, they prepared for the first strike. They had 3,150 Pod Fighters, but they would need to destroy four hundred thousand Ghengis borgs. That meant 126 strikes, one strike per minute for over two hours. It would be the most dangerous game they'd ever played.

"My hands are sweaty," Audrey said.

"Wipe them," Mika replied.

Ellie was now a few miles ahead, leading the squadron with them at the rear. It was the farthest they'd been apart since they were reunited, and Mika felt that tug again, that need to be closer to her.

I'm OK, she thought.

Please stay alive, he replied.

I've been flying Pod Fighters for a year and a half. How long have you been doing it?

Eight weeks. OK, fair point.

See you on The Wall.

Each Pod Fighter indicated when it was ready to attack. A line of amber lights appeared above The Wall. They heard three beeps, then dove through the clouds, falling out of them in a dark shower. They came down five hundred yards south of The Wall because their laser fire was useless against the flex metal coating on the Ghengis borgs. They'd decided to use cunning rather than might; to sneak up behind them and blow out the concrete plinths on which they stood.

The Ghengis borgs felt the vibrations as the Pod Fighters fell out of the clouds, but they were programmed to attack northward, not south, so they did not know what to do. The Pod Fighters pulled up from their dive, and the air filled with streams of laser fire. Then tons of concrete exploded beneath the Ghengis borgs' feet. Over the roar of engines, the children heard the crack and boom of heavy metal hitting The Wall. Some borgs fell headfirst, red eyes following their guns into the sea. Others fell back, their guns hitting their chests as they cracked against The Wall. But in that first strike, almost half the Ghengis borgs were left hanging from their broken plinths with the warped roots of their guns still attached to The Wall.

The moment the children pulled up on the other side, the Ghengis borgs began to fire. The air filled with cannon balls of laser light that shot toward them like lumps of sun. And this fire was quicker than the Pod Fighters could fly, so the pilots had to dodge it without crashing into their friends. When they all made it through the clouds alive, they felt horribly shaken.

"We're going to have to do better than that," Ellie said. "That was awful. We need to aim for the base of the plinths so it completely blows out the roots of the guns."

They gathered for a second strike and dropped. This time they blew out the last twisted roots and pulled up safe.

"That's better," Ellie said. "Let's do them like that."

Kobi now hated the stairs up to the eleventh floor of the Future Communication Building. As he climbed them once more, with his clothes dripping, he wished he could do what the boy had done and try to run away. But his father was here, in a difficult situation, and the boy was back in this building. It was time to accept that this is where he belonged. That by trying to avoid conscription into the army, he'd landed the worst job in it: trying to stop The Secret from getting out before the army was ready.

He collected his coat on the way up. This was also wet. It had been trampled by the adults carrying the boy up the stairs. When he reached the buffer zone, he didn't bother to take his wet things off. There didn't seem any point, but he was stopped immediately by a woman walking past him.

"You're soaked, Kobi! Look at you. Go and change or you'll get ill."

"Where have they taken the boy?" Kobi asked.

"Into the big meeting room. He's semi-conscious now, and talking, and there's more space in there for people to listen. But forget about the boy. You're soaked. Go and get changed. If your father saw you like that, he'd be horrified."

"OK," Kobi said, but the moment the woman was out of sight, he walked in the opposite direction, searching for the meeting room. When he found it, the door was shut. When he tried the handle, he discovered it was locked. He knocked hard, determined to get in. The man who opened it didn't look pleased to see him.

"You're going to have to come back later, Kobi."

"What's the boy saying?" Kobi asked.

"It's difficult to tell; he's delirious. He thought he was in a forest a minute ago. It's not a good time for you to come in."

Kobi tried to see past the man. The boy was lying on a bed in the middle of the room, reattached to his drip and wrapped in silver thermal blankets. He writhed against them as if he was trying to fight them off and he was surrounded by a large crowd of adults, some asking him questions, others listening. More adults arrived and the man let them in, then he moved to block Kobi's view and began to close the door. "Come back later," he said. "Don't worry, if he says anything important, we'll let you know."

"Is my father in there?" Kobi asked.

"Yes."

"Please let me in, I won't get in the way," Kobi said, feeling as if he was being forced to beg, like Oliver. "I'll stand at the back."

"No, sorry, Kobi, come back later."

The door shut in his face.

"Frag!" Kobi cursed. He turned and ran up to his room to find his companion.

If he didn't get hold of Mika soon, he felt like he would explode.

The Pod Fighters followed the night around the world, shooting out the plinths beneath the Ghengis borgs. The more the children felled, the better they got at doing it. Most went down the first time. But there were always a few left clinging to the twisted roots of their guns, pumping balls of light. After an hour, thirty Pod Fighters had been hit. Most landed their damaged crafts on cleared sections of The Wall, but as the others flew on for the next strike, they never knew quite what horrors they left behind.

Borg sharks wove below the waves on the south side of The Wall.

"This isn't fun!" Audrey cried.

"Only you could hope it'd be fun," Mika said. "Hang in there. We've halfway there."

The second hour was worse. Each time they dropped to strike, it took more effort to concentrate; more willpower to stay alive; to drop, to level, to shoot, to pull up. On and on they fought until they were welded by sweat to their Pod Fighters. Eyes blinded by laser fire.

It was in this state Mika realized Lilian was yelling at him from his pocket.

"I'm busy!" he shouted, pulling up from a strike. "I can't talk to you now."

"But it's really, really important," she yelled. "Kobi's trying to call you! He says he has to talk to you! He won't stop bugging me! He's insisting it's really important!"

"Did you say Kobi?" Mika shouted. "Kobi Nenko?" It was difficult to hear her over the roar of the Pod Fighter, and she wasn't connected to its com system.

"Yes!" Lilian yelled. "Kobi Nenko!"

They were now above the clouds, and the rest of the squadron was forming to drop for another strike. Mika felt a shot of happiness that his friend Kobi was trying to call him, but he'd only heard half of what Lilian said.

"Tell him I'll call him back as soon as I can!" he shouted. "Tell him I can't wait to speak to him!"

"OK," Lilian yelled. "But he's not going to like it."

Mika didn't hear that last bit. They were dropping out of the sky, engines roaring, ready for the next strike.

The children felt numb when The Wall was theirs. They'd been flying for over two hours, facing death with every strike. They'd felt so many intense emotions, they were too exhausted to feel anything else.

They landed on The Wall in Germany. Mika helped Audrey climb out of the Pod Fighter. Her legs were trembling. She couldn't do it on her own.

It was dark. The wind blew drizzle in their faces. For a few minutes, Mika sat on the wing of the Pod Fighter with Audrey in his arms, shuddering against him. The wing was hot, almost too hot, but at least it was still attached.

"I thought we were going to die," Audrey said. "I didn't realize how difficult it would be."

"But we didn't," he replied. "And you were amazing."

"Imagine how our parents would feel if they knew we were doing that."

"Best not think about our parents at the moment," he advised. "Look where we are."

He stood up and led her away from the Pod Fighter. The top of The Wall was as wide as a traffic trunk—the air-roads that networked above the cramped cities of the North. They were high above their world, with towers on one side and forests on the other. They could smell wet earth on the wind. On each side were waist-height concrete barriers and rolls of razor wire.

When they looked south, they could see the light of the forests as a great gold mass. When they looked north, they could see more lights, the lights of millions of people sleeping in their beds or moving around their fold-down apartments.

"It's beautiful," Audrey said.

"We're on The Wall," Mika said. "We're standing on The Wall."

The other children were gathering, leaving their Pod Fighters and climbing over the broken Ghengis borg plinths to form small groups. Nearly fifty Pod Fighters had been shot down and they needed to find the lost pilots and gunners.

Ellie, Puck, and Tom arrived, then Leo and Iman, Colette and Santos. They made calls to the children in the fortress, and the Stealth Carrier was sent out to fly along The Wall and collect the stranded pilots and gunners. While this was happening, they heard stories of Pod Fighters hanging by the twisted guns that had shot them down. Children in the sea, glowing gold, as mutants hunted for them. Nobody talked about death, but they all worried about it. The Whisper was full of it. And when the last child was found, The Whisper was full of this too, a huge rush of relief coursed through it.

Then Awen mooched around Mika and his friends with his tail wagging.

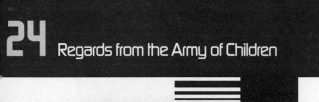

Now the children felt time pressing on them again. The seven Chosen Ones stood together with the windswept monkey and looked north toward the German city Mainz. The mile-wide strip of no-man's-land was covered in concrete rubble and litter that had blown there from the streets. Across this they could see the lights of the people, moving. Crowds were beginning to gather in the streets. Curiosity pulsed through their light. They'd heard the Pod Fighters. They could see heaps of Ghengis borgs and concrete lying at the base of The Wall.

Ellie explained what she could see to Tom, who saw only darkness on both sides, then this coursed through The Whisper too, so all the implanted children knew what she could see. Then it was agreed it was time to tell the Northern Government that they had taken over.

"Who's going to do it?" Ellie asked. "Mika? Do you want to do it?"

"No," Mika said immediately. "I'm too nervous and it has to be done right. Leo should do it."

Everyone turned to Leo, who was leaning against the north side barrier. He hadn't broken a sweat in the past few hours.

"I will if you want me to," he said.

"Yeah, you do it," Audrey enthused. "You'll do it best."

"OK," Leo said.

He got out his companion. They'd found the numbers for their own government ministers stored in Mal Gorman's desk. They waited for a few minutes as more children walked along The Wall to watch. When they had a group of several hundred around them, Leo took a deep breath and wrote a message:

We are the army of children.

We don't want to fight your war.

In the past few hours we've deposed the Minister for Youth Development, Mal Gorman, and taken control of the fortress at Cape Wrath, the *Queen of the North*, and The Wall. We now control all weapons in the North and we assert our control over you.

We are about to negotiate with the South for freedom for everyone, not just you, because we want our parents to be happy and we want to live in a world with trees and animals in it.

We want a future.

And as you told us during the game:

We are the future.

Regards from the army of children

"That's good," Ellie said, reading over Leo's shoulder.

"Send it!" Audrey said, biting her lip.

"Do you like it, Mika?" Leo asked.

"Yeah," Mika said. "It's good."

"OK," Leo said. "I'll send it to all the government ministers and I'll forward it to the fortress so it can be sent out to all the staff who've been asking what's going on. Then everyone will know."

For a few moments after he sent it, the children looked at each other, imagining the mayhem this message would cause. Then Audrey grinned with glee, then they were all grinning.

"I wonder what sort of messages you'll get back," Audrey said.

"We don't have to read them," Leo replied stoically. "We're not asking for permission to take control; we've just done it and there's nothing they can do. We have all the weapons and we're standing on The Wall. It's the South we need to worry about now. We do have to negotiate with them. It's time to call Raphael Mose."

Helen had given them Raphael Mose's private number. Leo searched for it and their mood changed. The children stopped grinning and stood in the rainy darkness, watching anxiously.

* * *

It was a long time since Raphael Mose had thought about the people in the North. Forty-three years had passed and that was plenty of time to forget what he'd done. Sometimes when he was out on his golf course, playing a few holes with his friends, the wind changed and he thought he could smell concrete and a kind of stuffy sadness. But it was easy to ignore this with acres of freshly mown grass and forests around him. And sometimes the sudden jolt of anxiety improved his game. He didn't care what was happening on the other side of The Wall. He didn't even want to look over it to see if all those people were still alive. Out of sight, out of mind. That was his philosophy.

He did wonder sometimes how his daughter, Grace, had been born so weird. Her goat legs had frightened him in the first few days after her birth and he didn't want to hold her. How could this have happened, when everything else in his life was perfect? But he quickly learned to look at the top half of his daughter and ignore the bottom bit he didn't understand. It had taken his wife many years to fall pregnant, so the top half of Grace was very precious to him.

It was morning in Oregon. A beautiful spring morning. Raphael Mose was in the kitchen making breakfast for Grace, who sat at the table drawing a picture of a cat. Although he had hundreds of staff at his disposal, including a chef and a nanny, who were among the lucky few given jobs in the South, he made breakfast for Grace every day before he started work. He enjoyed it. The top half of his child was very beautiful.

Sun poured through the kitchen windows. His wife rode past on one of her horses. He tipped porridge from a pan into two bowls and drizzled honey over it. He looked perfectly ordinary from a distance. A good father spending time with his child, but the eyes that watched the honey drizzle were cold and disconnected from the beauty around him.

The first time his companion called, he ignored it because he was just sitting down at the table with Grace to eat his porridge. The second time, he removed it from his pocket, but he didn't recognize the number, so he put it away again. But the third time it called, he felt annoyed and put down his spoon and stood up.

"Who is this?" he asked angrily.

For a while he heard nothing, as if the person on the other end was thinking, then they said, "We know what you did to us."

Mose was silent for a few seconds. It was so long since he'd thought about the North, he didn't know what this person was talking about.

"What?" he said at last. "Who is this? What do you mean?"

"I'm standing on The Wall," Leo said. "Looking at forests."

It still took Mose a while to understand. But when he did, the shock was so intense, he felt plunged into freezing darkness, as if he'd been thrown into the river in The Shadows.

"You're standing on The Wall?" he whispered.

Grace stopped eating her porridge and looked at him.

"Hang on a minute," Mose said. "I'm going to take this call in my study. Grace, I'm sorry, darling, but I've got to talk to a man about work. I'll be back in a minute." Then he ran from the kitchen to his study and slammed the door.

"Tell me who you are," he demanded.

"My name is Leo. I'm calling on behalf of the North. We know what you did to us, and our people are dying. We want to negotiate with you. We want you to let us out without fighting a war."

"No," Mose replied instantly. "You can't come out. Listen, what do you want? Let's strike a deal. What about a new telly for every fold-down apartment? A new telly and a sofa? And medicine. If your people are sick, we'll let you have better medicine."

"No, thanks," Leo said. "Our people need sunlight and nature, not tellies and sofas. You have to let us out. This is the starting point and we want to negotiate how it can be done. It's not as bad as you think. We won't let our people damage the forests like they did in the past. We know what we're doing."

"And who are you exactly?" Mose said. "You sound very young. How old are you?"

"Thirteen," Leo replied.

"Thirteen!" Mose laughed.

It was a crazy, relieved laugh. "Are you serious! This is a joke, isn't it? You're thirteen years old and you want to negotiate for freedom on behalf of the North?" Then his face set and his eyes chilled until he looked more evil than Mal Gorman had ever done. "Listen to me, Leo," he said. "Take the tellies and the sofas and medicine while the offer is open, because if your people take one step beyond The Wall, we'll destroy them. You stupid boy. Stop wasting my time."

Mose slammed his companion down.

"OK," Leo said. "So he tried to bribe us and then he threatened us. It's what we expected. Now we wait a few minutes until he calms down and then we try again. He'll realize soon he can't ignore us."

The children spent this time looking north. The people of Mainz were now venturing onto no-man's-land and there were thousands in the streets between the towers, looking toward

The Wall. It was the middle of the night, and drizzle soaked through their clothes, but nearly everyone was out.

"They worry me more than Raphael Mose," Mika said. "If they find out what's going on before we've negotiated a deal, we're in big trouble."

"They won't," Ellie said. "They've no idea what's going on. They're just curious. They can see us up here and they're wondering what's happening."

"Call Mose again," Mika told Leo.

"In a minute," Leo replied. "It's too soon yet."

Mika paced around him, knowing this was true and glad he was not the one holding the companion.

"OK," Leo said at last. "I'll call him again now."

The children gathered and watched.

Raphael Mose sat at the desk in his study, staring at his companion.

He'd had a horrible few minutes. He'd yelled at a maid who'd tried to come in, then sat there, frozen, struggling to absorb what had just happened. One minute he was eating porridge with Grace, the next he was talking to a thirteen-year-old boy who was standing on The Wall, trying to negotiate for freedom for billions of people. This meant all the Ghengis borgs were gone.

How had they gotten rid of the Ghengis borgs?

The thought that The Wall now stood unprotected made him feel sick, and he wished he hadn't ended the call. He needed to know more. He needed to know what was happening in the North so he could decide what to do about it. They clearly had weapons powerful enough to take down the Ghengis borgs and he already knew that if he attacked first, he could start a war that would come back at him like a boomerang. That he might die, his wife might die, his beautiful half of Grace might die. And that his house would burn. . . . These were sobering thoughts with the sun shining through the window. But through his blood pumped the cold, hard human instinct to protect his territory and tribe. In his heart he felt murderous.

Then Leo called again and Mose snatched up his companion to talk to him.

"OK, I'm listening," Mose said. "Explain to me who you are."

"I'm one of the firstborn children," Leo said. "There are twenty-seven thousand of us, aged twelve and thirteen. We were trained by the Northern Government to fight a war against you, because they wanted to take your land. But we don't want a war. We know what will happen if it starts, so we've taken control and deposed our government. We, the children, control the North now and we want to resolve this problem without fighting. We want a better life for our people and we don't want to destroy the forests."

"Really?" Mose said. He couldn't help being impressed by this statement. A bunch of children had deposed their government and taken over all the weapons. And they sounded sane. This boy Leo was talking sense, even if he didn't want to hear it. Then something occurred to him. "Do your parents know what you're doing?" he asked. "You've said you've deposed your government, but what do your parents think?"

"They don't know," Leo said. "We haven't told them yet."

"Ah," Mose replied with a nasty smile. "I thought not. And I know why you haven't told them, Leo. Because if you did, they'd go completely nuts. Do you think I'm crazy enough to negotiate with children whose parents don't know what they're doing?"

"We can control them," Leo said. "It was easy deposing the government. We took the Minister for Youth Development, Mal Gorman, as if he was a baby."

"Mal Gorman!" Mose repeated. "MAL GORMAN! Of course it was easy taking *Mal Gorman*. Do you know who Mal Gorman used to be?"

"No," Leo replied.

"My security guard," Mose sneered. "One day I came home and found him lying in my bed, eating a box of my wife's chocolates. Mal Gorman is so stupid he dared to do that, and got caught! Your whole government is a bunch of bumbling idiots."

"We know," Leo said. "But we can control our parents."

"How?" Mose mocked. "There's a flaw in your plan, isn't there? How are you going to stop your parents coming over here in a mad scrum to fight for the land they've lost?" He stood up and walked around his desk. "Your parents are a bunch of knuckle draggers, Leo! We built The Wall because there wouldn't be a tree left on the planet if they were left to carry on."

"We're different from them," Leo said. "We're going to fix them. We know how."

"Really?" Mose sneered. "You're just as crazy as they are if you believe that. I've had enough of this conversation now. You don't know what you're doing. Go away, little boy. Go home and play some safer games. And I will say again, that if your people take one step beyond The Wall, we'll kill every one of you. You'll either be eaten by wolves, crushed by berserker borgs, or poisoned like rats."

He slammed down his companion once more. Then he grasped one corner of the horse painting over the mantel and swung it out on a hinge. Behind this was the control panel Mika and Ellie had seen while they were searching for Everlife-9.

For a moment he looked at the three red buttons, then he pressed the first.

"Mal Gorman indeed," he snarled. "Those children are crazy if they think we're going to let people like that back over here."

"That didn't go well," Leo said. "Mose doesn't think much of Mal Gorman. He used to work as his security guard. He caught him eating his wife's chocolates in his bed. And he doesn't believe we can control our parents."

"What do we do now?" Audrey said. She was beginning to feel cold. It was still raining and they were soaked to the skin.

"Wait again," Leo said. "Next time I speak to him, I'll explain about the light and that we can help our parents see it."

"Yes, do that," Audrey said, brightening. "He doesn't know about that yet."

"We can do this," Leo said. "It's not going to be easy, but we can do it. He did listen to me for a minute."

They heard a noise; a faint rumble on the south side of The Wall. Startled, they walked across and looked down through the darkness at the strip of no-man's-land. On the south side, it was covered in dead leaves and the lights of small animals and insects. The rumbling noise was coming from beneath it.

"What is it?" Mika said.

They began to see movement.

Leaves slid, insects scattered, and a line of giant square

holes opened up in the ground, all along The Wall. They listened to the rumbling noise for a few moments more, then saw the tops of giant silver cubes rising up from the darkness.

"They must be some kind of weapon," Ellie said.

"Berserker borgs," Leo replied. "Mose said that if our people take one step beyond The Wall, they'd be eaten by wolves, crushed by berserker borgs, or poisoned like rats."

When the cubes had risen to their full height, they looked strange against their dark forest background. Their silver surfaces were ghostly pale, their edges hard and sharp, like a warning from the future to the victims of the past. They were immense, their bases as big as a tower and half the height of The Wall.

Suddenly they shifted, with one quick, synchronized movement, expanding and splitting into many more, smaller cubes that shuffled in the air and settled again, as if giving the children a demonstration.

"Oh, frag," Mika said. "I don't like the look of those. Santos, you've got the best head for engineering: Look into them and try to figure out what they do."

"OK," Santos said.

They left the Hawk Boy staring at the cubes and walked to the other side of The Wall. The people of Mainz had now ventured halfway across no-man's-land. It wouldn't be long before they covered it.

"It's OK," Mika said. "We just have to stay calm and wait until we can talk to Mose again."

"Yes," Audrey said. "We just have to stay calm and everything will be fine."

25 Shut Up and Do What You're Told

Kobi sat on his bed, waiting for Mika to call him back. He couldn't believe he was still waiting. He'd called his best friend, begging to talk to him, and had been told Mika was too busy. And because he was riddled with panic and crazy with impatience, he couldn't stay quiet enough to hear The Whisper, so he was cast out, with something terrible happening downstairs.

"Call me," he said, glaring through his hair at his companion. "Come on, Mika, call me back, you perp!"

Eventually, he couldn't sit still and ran down the stairs to the meeting room. There was a gathering of children outside the door, wondering what had happened to their parents. Some clutched badly made sandwiches. Others looked tired and confused. Oliver was holding a baby that was screaming its head off.

Kobi tried the door. It was still locked. He pressed his ear against it but because the baby was screaming, he couldn't hear anything.

"Oliver," he said. "Whose baby is that?"

"My baby," Oliver replied desperately. "It's my baby sister. My parents told me to look after her, then they went into the meeting room and haven't come out. I don't know what to do with her."

He was holding the baby under her arms, so she was almost dropping to the floor. Her diaper was sodden and hung between her legs as if it had a bucket of pee in it.

"Give her to me," Kobi said. "And go and find her a diaper."

Oliver ran off and returned a minute later, then Kobi laid the screaming baby on the floor and Oliver gave him the diaper. But when Kobi unfolded it, he had no idea how to put it on. He turned it over in his hands, mystified.

"If I can make kittens out of vacuumbot," he muttered. "I'm sure I can do this."

After several minutes of failed attempts and help from all the children, the diaper was on and the baby had stopped crying.

"Thank odd for that," Kobi said, handing her back to Oliver. "She screams louder than a Plague siren."

He stood up and pressed his ear against the door. Now he could hear what was happening.

"What are they saying?" Oliver whispered.

"Shhh," Kobi replied.

He could hear the boy muttering deliriously, unaware what was coming out of his mouth. Everyone else was listening. Occasionally an adult would ask a quiet question, then there would be a rush of incredulous whispers, then more muttering from the boy. A dreamlike jumble was pouring out of his head, but the adults were beginning to make sense of it.

Kobi realized that if he didn't stop it now, it would be too late.

"Stand back," he said to the children. They shuffled back with wide eyes. Then he began to kick the door, making them jump with fright.

But he was too late.

The voices grew louder on the other side of the door. Shouting began, then yelling. Kobi stood back and listened, wondering if they were yelling at him, then he realized they hadn't even heard him kick the door. They were so full of rage, they couldn't hear anything else.

He heard chairs clatter as they rose. Then the door burst open and they poured out like a pen of bailed bulls. The younger children shrank back, but Kobi lurched forward and tried to grab his father's arm. Abe shook him off as if he didn't recognize him.

"Dad," Kobi cried. "Stop!"

"No!" Abe yelled, his face contorted by rage. "Get out of my way."

He shoved Kobi aside and began to follow the others.

Kobi ran after him.

"Where are you going?" he said.

His father turned on him. "To find the parts to build a bomb!" he yelled. "So we can blow a hole through The Wall!"

"Dad, no!" Kobi pleaded. He tried to grab his father's arm again. "Please don't build a bomb! You'll start a war! You'll start a terrible war!"

His father shook him off again. "Good!" he yelled. "There are forests on the other side of The Wall! Beautiful forests, Kobi!

And a few thousand rich people living in mansions! They stole our land and left us to rot! They murdered your mother! They killed her with greed and lies! What do you think of that, Kobi?"

Kobi looked away.

"Do you know?" his father roared. "You don't look very surprised."

Kobi didn't reply.

"You do, don't you? You're doing that thing when you hide in your hair. Tell me, Kobi! Did the boy tell you?"

"Sort of," Kobi said.

"How long have you known?"

"Not long," Kobi replied. "A day maybe."

"You knew? YOU KNEW! AND YOU DIDN'T TELL US? HOW DARE YOU?"

"Because look at you!" Kobi yelled. "Look at the state of you! You're going to kill people now! That's why I didn't tell you! The army of children are out there, trying to solve this without fighting a war, and now you're going to ruin it all. You're going to start a war and make it ten times worse! Everyone will die! And those forests on the other side of The Wall will burn!"

"I am so ashamed of you!" his father yelled. "You stupid child! Now go and pack our bags! You're coming with me to The Wall!"

"Please, Dad, no! Calm down and think about what you're doing! I know Mum died, but killing loads of other people because of her doesn't make sense!"

"Shut up, Kobi! You're twelve years old. Just shut up and do what you're told! I'm building a bomb to blow a hole through The Wall and you're going to help me! That's our land on the other side of The Wall! OUR LAND THEY STOLE!"

Kobi watched his father rush off, then turned to find Oliver trembling behind him, with his baby sister crying in his arms.

He crouched down. "Listen to me," he said. "Don't be scared. Somewhere out there is an army of children. All those children who used to play Pod Fighter are trying to stop this war. We'll tell them what's happened and they'll help us."

"Do it quickly," Oliver cried. "I'm scared. I don't want to be in a war! I don't want everyone to die!"

"OK," Kobi said. Then he removed his companion from his pocket and tried to call Mika again.

Once The Secret was out, it spread like a fire in a hay barn in the middle of a hot summer drought. It began in the meeting room in the Future Communication Building, then the heat threw it up into the air to fall all over the North and start many more fires. It wouldn't be long before the whole northern hemisphere was burning.

On The Wall, Santos and Colette observed the giant cubes, while Mika, Ellie, Audrey, Leo, and Iman watched the crowd on the other side. Suddenly, they saw heat spots appear in the light.

"What's going on?" Mika said.

They watched for another minute as the red patches spread and began to join up. Each time they blinked, there were hundreds more. Soon it looked as if molten lava was pouring through the streets between the towers. The children looked at each other. They knew there was only one reason why so many people would behave this way.

"Do you think they know?" Audrey asked tentatively.

"Surely not," Mika replied. "It would be the worst possible thing that could happen. Our luck can't possibly be that bad."

They didn't want to believe it. They continued to watch for a while longer, trying to stay calm and hoping this was happening for another reason. But when the crowd reached The Wall, it attacked it in a frenzy of fists, roaring, raging, hands bleeding, feet kicking.

"Oh frag," Mika said.

They turned away and began to pace, breathing hard. All the other children were panicking around them and this was spreading through The Whisper, dousing it dead.

"We have to stay calm," Leo said. "All of us. If The Secret's out, we have no choice but to deal with it. This can't be stopped now. Everyone, try to calm down so we can hear each other and work out what to do."

They fought hard for quiet. The crowd was roaring below them and they could feel vibrations through The Wall as all the people pounded against it. They knew what this meant. These people would never listen to them while they felt this angry. The war was starting and Raphael Mose had been right. They couldn't control their parents. It was all going wrong.

This thought was too much. They started to break apart.

Audrey put her hands over her face. Awen shivered with his tail between his legs. Mika watched Ellie blink; she was doing that bad blinking thing again. Then her face darkened and she took a step away from him. Immediately, he realized what she was thinking. Their parents would be part of that raging mob.

"Ellie, no," he said.

She took another step back, as if to stop him from touching her.

"No, Ellie!"

"But they'll come here!" she cried. "Everyone will come here and so will Mum and Dad and they might get killed and I'll never see them again! I have to stop them!"

She turned and began to run toward her Pod Fighter.

"No!" Mika yelled, sprinting after her.

She reached it and leaped onto the wing, and Mika found himself fighting with her, grabbing at her legs, trying to stop her from getting in. He pulled her down and they slipped over the wet, black wing, with Puck perched on the windshield, screeching at them. In a mad frenzy, they both fell down and landed on The Wall. Then they were wrestling in the puddles as they'd done when they were toddlers.

"You can't do anything!" Mika yelled, trying to pin her down. "If Mum and Dad know The Secret, they'll be just as angry as the rest! You don't want to see them like that, Ellie. Stop it!"

"Get off me!" she screamed. "I have to find them!" She struggled against him, furiously, her wet hair plastered to her cheeks, but he would not let her go. He'd felt her break as she ran toward the Pod Fighter. In this state of mind, she'd kill herself. But then the fight got nasty. He felt a sharp pain in his eyes as hers locked on his, then he was gone for a moment, in agony, rolling over on the wet wall with his hands over his face. Then he saw flashes of white all around him. He opened his eyes to see Audrey, Leo, Iman, Santos, and Colette running in to help. But Ellie was now curled up in the puddles, weeping, with her hands over her eyes. She'd shocked herself back to sanity.

Mika stood up and pulled her to her feet. They were both sodden and filthy.

"I'm sorry," she wept.

"So you're not going to fly off like a perp on some kamikaze mission?"

"No," she replied.

He put his arms around her. "OK," he said. "But you can't do things like that, Ellie. The best way to help Mum and Dad is to control yourself. Don't ever hurt me like that again. You're fragging dangerous."

"I know, I'm sorry. It happened before I could stop it."

The crowd was still roaring and battering The Wall. The sky to the north was full of pods. A mass exodus had begun. But somehow, in that moment, they did feel calmer. Ellie had freaked out on behalf of them all, and they were better for it. Soon all their parents would be part of that mob and they had no choice but to deal with it.

Then the pace cranked up again. Lilian yelled in Mika's pocket. "Mika!! Mika!! Kobi Nenko's calling! He's begging you to help him! His father is planning to build a bomb and blow a hole through The Wall!"

The seven children looked at each other.

"Well," Leo said. "They're not going to get through it with their fists."

"Let me talk to him," Mika replied.

Kobi sat on his father's bed. Although he'd told Oliver not to worry, he was panicking so much he could hardly hold his companion. The whole Future Communication Building was full of adults packing bags and preparing for the journey to The Wall. He could hear them all around him. Hear roars of rage from The Shadows as the fire spread. And here he was stuck right in the middle of it, having promised Oliver he would get help. That the army was out there somewhere and would come to help them. When he heard Mika's voice, he almost cried with relief.

"Mika," he said. "I'm in The Shadows. It's a fragging nightmare here."

"I know," Mika replied quickly. "Just tell me everything. We know The Secret's out; now we need to know about this bomb so we can figure out what to do about it. Don't worry, we're all here and we're going to help you."

"Good," Kobi said. "I'm going nuts here on my own."

He explained everything, about the boy and the bolt borgs and his father. And as he quietly uploaded all this to Mika, he felt his head lighten and his muscles relax. His thoughts had been there before, coursing through The Whisper with the rest, but channeled through his friend, they became loud enough for everyone to hear.

When he'd told Mika everything, Mika said, "Don't worry. We'll figure out how to make this work for us. The best thing you can do for now is tell the adults you're going to help them. Tell your father you're sorry and stay close to him. That way you'll know exactly what's happening. How long do you think it will take before he has all the parts to build a bomb?"

"A day," Kobi said. "It usually takes him a day to source all the bits when he's building something. As soon as he's got them all, we'll follow everyone else to The Wall."

"Then I'll come to you tomorrow morning," Mika said, "while you're still in The Shadows, and we'll talk about what we're going to do. I'm so glad we've found you."

"So am I," Kobi said. "You have no idea."

The call ended.

Kobi lay back and closed his eyes, feeling relief although his world was burning around him.

At last he was part of the army.

26   The Eyes in the Trees

Helen sat by the fire in her hut, with the blanket over her knees. She'd been dozing on and off most of the night, but she couldn't sleep properly and hadn't gone to bed. She was worried about the children, she had a Northern Government minister imprisoned in her boar house, and their world teetered on the brink of war. There was far too much going on to sleep.

As she dozed she dreamed of light, of the beauty she'd seen enshrouding her house. And humbug piglets, snarling wolves, patterns in leaves, burning trees . . . Between these dozes, she stoked the fire and wondered how long it would be before the children returned.

She did not expect them so soon.

She heard a noise in the clearing outside the hut. She sat up and gripped the arms of her chair. She wondered if it was Ralph, but he could speak to her via the mansion com. It didn't make sense that he would walk through the forest in the middle of the night to talk to her. When she heard a knock on the door, she rose and opened it cautiously.

But it was the children. Seven wet, filthy children and Puck, who was fast asleep in Ellie's arms as if he'd spent the past six hours on a bouncy castle.

"Why are you back so soon?" she said.

"Everything's got difficult," Mika replied exhaustedly. "We've come here to get away from the noise and talk. Is that OK?"

"Of course," she said. "I'll put the kettle on."

She did this expecting them to gather around the fire. They looked cold. But they sat at the table and leaned on it, with their heads in their hands. She opened the kitchen cupboard and ordered a large fruit cake. They looked as if they needed cheering up. No one spoke for ten minutes.

The fire crackled.

In its dancing light they looked like two things: children who needed to go to bed and mythical beasts.

Helen placed cups on the table and warmed the teapot.

"So," she said. "Have you taken the fortress?"

"Yes," Mika replied.

"Was anyone hurt?"

"No," he said.

"Good. So then what happened? Did you manage to take the *Queen of the North*?"

"Yes," Audrey said. "We emptied it and parked it over the sea."

"Gosh," Helen said. "Well done. Then what happened?"

"We took The Wall," Mika said quietly. "That was hard; the Ghengis borgs were difficult."

"I'm sure they were," she replied, raising her eyebrows.

"Then we told our government what was happening. Leo sent them a message telling them we'd taken over."

"I bet that spoiled their suppers," Helen said.

"I hope so," Ellie replied.

"Then Leo called Raphael Mose to negotiate," Mika continued.

Helen placed the teapot in the middle of the table. "OK," she said. "That sounds promising."

"We haven't finished yet," Mika said.

"Oh dear. So what did Raphael Mose say?"

"Leo talked to him twice," Mika said. "The first time he just got furious and hung up. The second time he seemed to listen for a while, but when he realized our parents didn't know what we're doing, he laughed at us. He told us we were crazy to believe we could control them. He called them knuckle draggers."

"Sticks and stones," Helen said. "And you know that's not true. You will be able to control them when you've shown them the light. It'll take a while to fix them all, but it is possible."

"Yeah," Mika said. "We know. But we were just about to call Mose a third time and tell him that, when The Secret got out. We were standing on The Wall, Helen, and suddenly it looked as if the North was on fire! And it leaked from one of us. An implanted boy ended up in The Shadows, so sick he was ranting his head off. Now everyone's moving toward The Wall, and someone in The Shadows is building a bomb to blow a hole through it. We've got a day, Helen, just one day to get our parents under control and try to talk to Raphael Mose again."

"OK," Helen said. "What can I do to help? I've ordered a fruit cake; is there anything else you want?"

"Just sit with us," Mika said. "You're the only sane adult we know."

Awen stretched out like a hare on the hearth. The children began to talk.

It was light when they finished.

The morning was bright and the fire ash.

None of them had slept, but they felt calmer.

Mika and Audrey stood up and stretched.

"OK," Mika said. "So we'll fly the Stealth Carrier to The Shadows and talk to Kobi. Then we'll send it back for you and we'll meet you on The Wall."

Mika kissed Ellie. He was going with Audrey, and leaving Ellie behind with the others. They'd decided it was best she avoid the city where their parents lived until all this was over.

By the door, they hugged Helen and she gave Mika a piece of cake wrapped in a white napkin, for Kobi.

"Say hello from me," she said. "He sounds like a clever boy and he's going to have a difficult day."

"He is," Mika said. "But I'm so glad he's with us."

For most of the night, Kobi forced himself to sleep, if fitfully, so he wouldn't be too exhausted to cope with what was about to happen.

Just after dawn, he got up and packed their bags. Then he left Nevermore on the desk pecking them, and searched for his father.

The building was almost empty. While he was sleeping, almost everyone had left. He passed messy rooms with open doors, where families had packed and joined the exodus to The Wall. Only a few adults remained to wait for his father and the bomb parts. Kobi realized Oliver was gone and felt sad. He hadn't had the chance to tell the child that the army was on its way. He hoped to see him when they arrived at The Wall.

He found his father in a room on the eleventh floor, surrounded by boxes of bomb parts. Abe had spent the past few hours gathering them from locations around the city with the help of The Shadows network. Now he was checking each part, making sure it was right. Once they got to The Wall, it would be a major problem if any bits were missing.

When Kobi appeared in the doorway, Abe was counting a bag of micro screws. He looked up and his face hardened, ready for another fight.

"It's OK," Kobi said. "I've come to help."

Abe's features softened again. "Good," he said. "There's a list of parts on that tablet over there and I'm just checking the bits that have arrived. Those in red haven't been delivered yet. We're still waiting for them."

"OK," Kobi said.

They worked in silence, checking the parts and packing them into a box. When they'd finished, his father told him to go to one of the kitchens and eat breakfast. Kobi returned to their room and waited for Mika.

Half an hour later, he heard a quiet tap on the door.

He jumped up and opened it, but there was no one there.

Then he heard Audrey giggle.

"Audrey?" he whispered. "Where are you?"

He heard a whoosh and a flash and she appeared with Mika, right in front of him.

"Nice trick," Kobi said. He waved them into the room, looking up and down the passage.

"Kobi!" Audrey cried as he shut the door. "We've missed you so much!" She hugged him and bounced with excitement.

"I've missed you too," he said. "I shouldn't have run. I knew within hours it was a mistake."

"No," Mika insisted. "Don't think that. You're in exactly the right place. You're going to be a massive help. Here" —he held out the cake— "This is from our friend Helen. I'll explain who she is. I'll explain everything."

They sat on the beds and Mika told him the details of what had happened in the past few days. Kobi listened carefully and watched Audrey play with her kittens.

When Mika had finished, Kobi said, "So what do you want me to do?"

"Help make the North and the South listen to us," Mika said. "At the moment, Raphael Mose thinks we're a joke, and our parents are so blinded by anger, they don't even see us. So we've decided to let them shock themselves. I learned something last night while I was fighting with Ellie. Sometimes you need to shock yourself to understand what you're doing wrong. So we're going to let our parents start the war and then we're going to stop it."

"What?" Kobi said.

"It's the only way to make them listen," Mika said. "When the war starts and both sides have had a chance to realize how terrible it will be, we'll stop it, we'll save them from themselves. Then they'll see us. Then they'll listen to us."

"But are you sure you can stop the war once it starts?" Kobi asked. "That sounds dangerous, Mika. What if you can't?"

"We can," Mika said. "As long as we know exactly where the bomb is being built and what time it will detonate. The berserker borgs will attack as soon as a hole appears in The Wall, but we'll be there, all of us, in Pod Fighters. We'll let our parents see the berserker borgs attack and then we'll stop them before they do too much harm."

"OK," Kobi said. "What's my role in this?"

"Stay close to your father. Help him build the bomb, and stay in touch with us. You start the war, we'll stop it."

"Right," Kobi said. "It's a deal."

Ellie and the others waited in Helen's hut for the Stealth Carrier to return. Helen ordered breakfast and watched them eat. They were quiet now that they'd decided what to do.

She ordered pancakes and fruit and tried not to look astonished as the syrup and butter and raspberries floated across the table. She was part of them now, so they used their powers around her without even thinking about it.

Helen thought of butter and it landed in her hand. She looked up to see Colette smiling at her.

"Thank you," she said.

The girl's silver hands glinted in the morning light.

A monkey sat in the middle of the table, eating raspberries.

It was a doom-laden, magical breakfast.

As the children were helping Helen clear the table, Ralph called from the mansion. Stones slid back and his face appeared on the screen above the fire. He looked tired. He'd taken his tie off, had bits of straw in his hair, and his face was shadowed with stubble.

"Morning, Ralph," Helen said. "How are you?"

"A bit worried, madam," the butler replied.

"Oh dear," Helen said with her hands on her hips. "What's Gorman been up to?"

"Freaking out, madam," he replied. "I had to stay with him in the sty; he wouldn't let me leave."

"All night?" Helen asked. "Remember, Ralph, you're not his slave. He's lucky to have you there. And there was a nice warm bed in the mansion for you."

"He was scared, madam," Ralph replied.

"Of what?" Helen asked.

"Well," Ralph said. "First he was scared of a spider, so I had to catch it and take it away. Then he said he could see a weird face looking at him through the trees at the end of the enclosure. He's delirious. I can't reason with him. I was hoping you'd come down and talk to him. I don't think he likes the trees."

"Silly man," Helen huffed. "I thought he wanted a mansion surrounded by a forest. He's not going to get that without trees and a few spiders."

"I think he's changed his mind, madam," Ralph said. "He's not enjoying himself much."

"I'll talk to him," Ellie said. "Don't worry, Ralph, I'm coming now."

"I'll come with you," Helen said. "I want to see this."

The path through the forest looked pretty. But it was quiet and the silence felt heavy, making the forest flowers look as if they'd stuck up their heads in the wrong place.

"The birds are quiet," Helen said.

"Yeah," Ellie replied. "And Puck's behaving himself."

They walked on uneasily.

When they reached the overgrown mansion, they could hear Mal Gorman yelling. Ralph opened the door to the boar house, looking very relieved to see them.

"Oh dear," Helen said, tilting her sun hat to look at him.

In the feeding room, Gorman's face appeared at the glass of his door. He'd aged overnight. He was now about thirty and looked even more ridiculous in the Pod Fighter T-shirt.

"We'd better let him have some more Everlife-9 soon," Ellie said.

"I'll find out the correct dose," Helen replied. "He can't just swig it out of the bottle or he might vanish altogether."

"Let me out!" he yelled. "You can't leave me in here! This is abuse! This is TORTURE!"

Ellie looked past him into the sty. The sun was slanting through the door on the other side. The sty looked warm, dry, and light, a million times more comfortable than the little room she used to live in on the *Queen of the North*.

"What's wrong?" she asked. "Ralph's had no sleep because of you."

"It's staring at me!" he cried. "And it won't go away!"

"What's staring at you?"

"The eyes in the trees!"

"Stand back," Ellie said. "I'll come in and you can show me."

Gorman took a few paces away from the door and she entered. Then he crouched down and crawled through the little door leading out into the enclosure. Ellie followed him over ragged grass, past the muddy hollow, toward a clump of trees at the end. Then he stopped and pointed with a shaky finger. Ellie peered through the fence into the forest beyond. For a while she saw nothing but shifting light through leaves, then she spotted a pair of eyes staring through the foliage.

"OK, I see it," she said, backing away. "I'm going to walk around the outside of the enclosure and find out what it is."

She returned to the sty with Gorman on her heels, scared to be left alone. When she'd locked the door, he sat on his camp cot, pale and trembling.

Ellie told Helen and Ralph what she'd seen.

"How curious," Helen said. "Come on, let's go and have a look."

They left Ralph watching Gorman and walked down the path, along the line of the enclosure. When they reached the end, Helen said, "I think I know what it is. Come on, I'll show you. There's an old chapel down here."

She left the path and began to walk through the trees. At the end of the enclosure was a dense, dark area, choked by bracken and ivy.

"There used to be a little graveyard here," Helen said.

"Really?" Ellie replied, looking at her feet.

"You're not scared of a few old bones?" Helen asked.

"No," Ellie said. "I've just never been in a graveyard before."

She wasn't scared of the bones, but she didn't like it there. It felt too quiet and cold and she looked forward to returning to the path where the sunlight cut through the trees.

The chapel was hidden. It was shrouded in climbers like the mansion. There was a mossy path leading up to the porch, and inside this, a black door with a pile of old gravestones leaned against it.

"No one's used it for years," Helen said.

It felt cold, as if the chapel stone radiated it. Ellie followed

Helen around the back of the building, shivering as the bracken brushed her legs.

"There," Helen said. She stopped and looked up at the rear wall of the chapel. Poking through the ivy, under the eaves, was a large stone face. The eyes were wide and staring. The mouth gaped, vomiting a rush of foliage.

"It's the Green Man!" Ellie said. "I've seen this before on the cover of a book of poems."

"Oh yes, it's the Green Man," Helen said. "He's interesting, isn't he? There are Green Man carvings in many churches. Academics don't know where he came from, but I have an idea. I think he comes from the time when people still remembered they were part of nature. To me he looks like the cycle of life. The atoms of his body becoming something new. He looks scary or wise, depending how you feel about death."

"Gorman's terrified of death," Ellie said. "Perhaps we should cover it up so Ralph can get some sleep."

"Good idea," Helen said.

The problem seemed solved.

Ralph found a ladder and hung an old velvet curtain over the Green Man's face. Then they set off back to the hut, hurrying along the path because they could feel time pressing. But halfway, Ellie paused and looked up at the trees. Puck clung to her neck. He was still suspiciously well behaved and she could feel something, as if a ghost were watching her.

"What is it?" Helen asked.

"I don't know," Ellie replied. "Are you OK about us leaving you here with all this going on?"

"Yes," Helen said. But the question made her worry. She'd

never felt afraid of the forest before.

"We could take you with us," Ellie suggested.

"No," Helen replied. "I can't leave Ralph on his own with Gorman. Poor man, he's exhausted. I'll be OK. Don't worry about me."

27 Building the Bomb

"Careful, Kobi," his father said. "We have a serious amount of explosives here."

"I know," Kobi replied.

They were carrying the bomb parts up to the roof where the pod was waiting. It was an orange construction pod, the sort that maintenance crews used to fix traffic trunks. It was the only craft left in London. Soho John had managed to find it through his dedicated network of friends.

They piled the boxes in carefully and strapped them down so they wouldn't move during the flight. While they did this, they hoped John was a good pilot. Any hard jolts could make the pod explode, with them inside it.

It was weird up there on the roof. The Shadows was silent. The only movement around them was a single, lonely boat, chugging down the river toward the estuary and France.

Everyone was going to France, where they could get closer to The Wall.

When the bomb parts were safely strapped down, they climbed in and sat on the curved seat. There were three adults in the back, including the man and the woman who'd taken them to look at the bolt borg.

Kobi took a deep breath and closed his eyes as the pod rose and began to weave through the pillars, carrying its deadly cargo toward the river. Then they flew along its path and out of The Shadows.

It was a hazy spring morning and the waves on the Channel glittered. It would have been an enchanting view if they didn't have a heap of volatile explosives a few inches from their legs.

"Where are we going to build the bomb?" Kobi asked.

"In a city called Amiens in France," his father replied. "We've got friends waiting there for us. We've secured a tower on the front row with a good view of The Wall. Everyone's waiting."

Kobi remembered the name of the town so he could send it to Mika.

Amiens.

Amiens.

They reached the coast of France and began to fly over land toward The Wall. Now they all gazed out the windows, astonished by the view. Even twenty miles away from The Wall, the streets between the towers were crammed with people trying to get closer to it.

They reached Amiens. Here the streets were even more tightly packed. People stood shoulder to shoulder, with heavy bags piled between them. Everyone faced The Wall. It loomed in the distance like a giant gray screen, waiting for the action to begin.

They flew over no-man's-land. Here was the front of the crowd. Hundreds of thousands of people were gathered there, with the sun shining down on them. A heat haze hovered over The Wall. It looked more like the start of a music festival than a war.

"How are we going to get them out of the way when we detonate the bomb?" Kobi asked.

"We've got people on the ground," his father told him. "We've cleared a large area to the north of the city so everyone can move back for the explosion."

"Good," Kobi said. He was starting to feel hot. The pod felt like a pressure cooker with the sun beating down on it. He shook off his coat and sweater.

The pod landed gently on a tower on the front row facing The Wall.

They climbed out. The sky was blue and a warm wind whipped their clothes.

"We've got a perfect view of The Wall," Abe said, looking toward it. "And perfect weather. We'll detonate the bomb up here. It's going to be a sight you'll never forget, Kobi. You'll never forget seeing this."

"I need a drink," Kobi said. "I'm really hot."

"I'll get drinks," Soho John replied. "You unpack the boxes and we'll go down to the tower and tell everyone we've arrived."

The rest of the adults left. Abe climbed into the pod and began to undo the straps on the boxes.

Kobi sent a message to Mika telling him where they were.

* * *

"OK," Mika said. "The bomb is in Amiens, in France. Kobi's just arrived there with his dad."

"So they'll start building the bomb now," Audrey said.

"Yeah," Mika replied. "Which means we've only got a few hours to figure out what type of weapon these berserker borgs are."

They'd returned to Mainz in Germany, where they'd first landed after taking The Wall. The rest of the children were still waiting there, having slept the night in their Pod Fighters. The weather was good; a clear blue sky stretched north and south, so they could see for miles in all directions. News of the bomb had spread, so the crowd on no-man's-land was moving slowly west, toward France and Amiens.

They saw a blink in the sky and the Stealth Carrier appeared, delivering Ellie and the others. They talked for a few minutes, then gathered on the south side of The Wall and stared at the line of giant cubes. They were mirror bright in the sunshine. It was difficult to look at them for long. The forest stirred behind them in the warm wind, making its own rush of whispers.

Beneath the surfaces of the cubes were many complex elements. Each cube was made up of 729 smaller cubes, ten feet square, that could engage or disengage using electromagnetism. These smaller cubes had a variety of components. Some were solid metal with only a dense core of power cells and magnets, others contained audio speakers. These perplexed them.

What kind of weapon was this?

"Interesting," Santos said, perched on the barrier. "I don't understand the audio element, but the solid cubes are very heavy and with those sharp corners, they'll be deadly when they start moving. But I want a better look at the cubes in the center. It's difficult to see through all those layers."

"We need to make one move," Mika said.

"We could try throwing something at it," Audrey suggested. She began to search around a Ghengis borg plinth for a lump of broken concrete.

"Not yet," Mika said. "If we're going to bait one, we need to clear all the children off this section of The Wall. Just in case it does something bonkers."

They waited twenty minutes while the others returned to their Pod Fighters and flew away, to land on it again, farther west. Then they looked down on the cubes, feeling as if they were about to prod a wasp nest.

"OK," Mika said. "Throw the concrete, Audrey."

Audrey hurled the lump of concrete at the nearest cube, giving it a bit of extra propulsion with her eyes. It hit the top with a metallic thud and skidded off.

Nothing happened.

"That was boring," Audrey said.

"Try again," Santos said.

She found a bigger lump and shot it at the cube with more force. It shattered to dust as it hit the hard surface, but still nothing happened.

They paced for a while, thinking. They knew another way to make the cube move, but it was dangerous.

"We don't have a choice," Mika said. "We're going to have to put someone over The Wall to make it move. And it can't be one of us, because we're mutants."

"OK, then it will have to be one of the implanted children. Let's ask for a volunteer."

* * *

Kobi helped his father carry the bomb parts down the tower on another hover trolley. The tower was full of adults, many with guns slung over their shoulders. They talked urgently into companions as if they knew what they were doing. This tower was now the hub of the North.

"Where are all the children from the Future Communication Building?" Kobi asked.

"In the tower next to us," someone told him. "Out of the way."

Kobi imagined Oliver holding his screaming baby sister, and felt angry. Oliver would be scared, all the children would be scared, and they were right on the front row, with a spectacular view of The Wall and the start of a war.

"Is the boy with them?" Kobi asked.

"Yes."

Kobi began to panic. While he was talking to Mika and Audrey, this desperate plan had seemed like a good idea. Mika's dark determination and Audrey's bright enthusiasm had been enough to convince him to help start the war. He hadn't allowed himself to think about what would happen if it all went wrong. He had to believe in this to make it happen. But now, knowing Oliver and the other children were so close, he was scared.

Put it out of your head.

Don't think about it.

You won't be able to build a bomb if you think about that.

They were met in the lobby by a large group of men who would help them carve a path through the crowd toward The Wall. They pushed the people back, telling them what was about to come through. Then Kobi and his father followed with the hover trolley. It was a hot and dangerous journey across no-man's-land, but it was treated like a carnival procession. The people clapped and cheered as they passed, punching the air and yelling for freedom.

You won't be doing that in a few hours, Kobi thought.

Mika sat on the south side barrier, waiting for the implanted volunteer to arrive. Audrey sat next to him, trying an army ration pack. The rest of the children on The Wall had been surviving on these since they left the fortress.

"Yuck," Audrey said. Each pack contained two brown squares that looked like compressed dung. She was hoping it would taste better than it looked, but it didn't. Puck reached out from Ellie's shoulder, prepared to pass monkey judgment. Audrey handed it to him. Puck looked at the brown square, nibbled one corner, then dropped it.

"I told you," Audrey said. "Yuck."

Mika watched them and smiled. He was with a fairy girl joking with a monkey. Then he watched Ellie gaze north toward the refugee towers. Ellie, his sister, whom he'd only just found. Leo smiled at Iman, Colette watched Santos, who was still perched on the barrier like a hawk. Awen lay at his feet and beyond him were thousands of children who now felt part of him. And on the other side of The Wall were their parents. He was surrounded by beings he loved.

The sun was shining, the sky was blue, the forest shimmered. He closed his eyes and in his mind it all turned black.

"Don't do that," Leo said.

"Sorry," Mika replied.

A Pod Fighter arrived. They all jumped up, keen to see which implanted child had volunteered to act as bait for the cubes. The windshield slid back and Tom climbed out, still desperate to make amends for not listening to Mika. They could see this eagerness in his light as he ran toward them. Mika felt compassion. Tom had not yet accepted that the most important thing they had to do was forget the mistakes of the past, let them all go and start again. They would all have to do it.

The children greeted Tom warmly and they prepared to lower him over The Wall. They adapted a Pod Fighter harness and attached a rope to it so they could drop him over the south side barrier and pull him back when the cubes reacted. When this was done, he climbed up. He looked very nervous. Below him were rolls of razor wire, and the cubes looked as if they were wailing.

"Are you sure you want to do this?" Mika asked him.

"Yes," Tom replied.

They had no idea what would happen. They might all get hurt, not just Tom. Mika and Leo gripped the rope and prepared to lower him, but it was a while before they did it. It took a lot of courage, even for them. Awen whined. Audrey watched through her fingers. Ellie's pupils dilated until her eyes were almost black.

"OK," Mika said. "Let's just do it."

They let the rope out a bit and Tom lowered his legs over The Wall. No sooner had his toes passed the line dividing North from South than the cube in front of them split with an electronic *WHOMP*.

Tom froze.

In a split second it formed an orb that was suspended in the air before them. Each ten-foot-square silver cube hung in perfect geometric form, completely still. Tom pulled his legs back. Immediately, the borg reversed and settled again as one large cube.

"They're sensitive," he said shakily.

"Yeah," Mika replied. "That was good. Do it again."

For an hour Tom dropped his legs over The Wall, then pulled them back so the children could watch the cube expand and collapse. He had to be careful; if he dropped down too far, more cubes began to react and the orb in front of them flattened and made high-pitched electronic sounds as if it was charging up to attack.

When Tom was shaking so hard he couldn't do it anymore, they pulled him back and let him rest.

"They're very clever," Santos said. "Most of the cubes are solid; others contain elements of the audio system. And there's one control cube in the middle that tells the others what to do. This controls the electromagnetic field, and it also contains a randomizer that synchronizes shape and sound. 'Berserker borg' is a good name for them: They're giant, morphing, sonic demolition machines. When they're fully expanded and moving in the air, they'll be able to smash down towers like toys."

"But we can deactivate them," Ellie said. "All we have to do is look into the control cube and melt it, then the electromagnetic field will be broken and the whole thing will collapse."

"Yes," Santos said. "The only tricky part will be fixing our eyes on the control cubes when they're moving. That's not going to be easy."

"But it is possible," Ellie said.

"Yes."

"Raphael Mose will be shocked," Audrey said. "They're

coated in flex metal. If we weren't able to see inside them, they'd be indestructible."

"Perhaps when they've fallen out of the sky like sugar cubes," Mika said, "he'll reconsider talking to us."

"OK," Leo said. "Iman, Colette, you're the best strategists. Let's get the rest of the children here and you can make a battle plan."

In Amiens, Kobi and his father reached The Wall with the hover trolley. But the crowd was even denser there and they realized it would be impossible to build a bomb with all those people crushed around them.

"You must move them back," his father told the men. "Right off no-man's-land. We can't work like this; it's too cramped and dangerous. You have to clear at least a half mile in all directions or people might get hurt. This bomb is going to be huge. If something goes wrong while we're building it . . ."

"And move the people in the towers too," Kobi added, thinking of Oliver. "Move them back a whole block."

"Yes," his father agreed. "Debris from the bomb may hit that front row. Clear at least ten rows of towers, just to be safe."

Calls were made and the mammoth task of moving the crowd and clearing the first block of towers began. It wasn't easy. People didn't want to lose their spot on no-man's-land, right at the front of the queue, so they became angry again, this time with each other. Everyone was hot, tired, paranoid, and impatient.

Kobi sat on the ground and shared Helen's cake with his father. Then he tied his hair back and they began to build a set of driller borgs, following the instructions on a tablet. The driller borgs would make holes in The Wall in which to pack the explosives. The Wall was thirty feet thick, so they needed to bury them deep. It was very fiddly work to be doing on a patch of dusty earth, but Kobi worked hard and his father was impressed by him. Every time they looked up, the crowd was farther away. After an hour, it was a line in the distance, and very quiet.

The shadow of The Wall grew as the sun moved over it.

The borgs began to drill the holes.

Late afternoon, they saw a lone figure walking across no-man's-land.

"It's John," his father said. "Come to see how we're getting on."

John brought water and food: a Middle Eastern rice dish one of the locals had cooked for them. It looked lovingly prepared.

"Everyone's keen to know how you're getting on," he told them, placing it on the ground.

"We're nearly finished," Abe said. "If you wait ten minutes, you can eat with us and then we'll walk back together."

"Excellent," John replied.

John sat on the ground and watched while they attached the detonator to the base of The Wall. When this was finished, Abe showed him the remote control he would use to detonate the bomb.

Kobi couldn't watch. He started to pack up their tools, with shaky hands. The bomb was built. His father held the remote control in his hand. This was really happening.

After they'd eaten, they began the dusty walk across no-man's-land toward the towers. Kobi dropped back, and while his father talked to John, he exchanged a quick sequence of messages with Mika. Then he put his companion away and walked on. The bomb was built and the world was waiting for war. The children in the fortress, the children on The Wall, the younger children, like Oliver, in a tower ten rows back; the deposed Northern Government, the World Conservation Club; the immense crowd of people gathered in the streets; and Mal Gorman, who sat in a heap of straw with his head in his hands. Everyone was waiting. A great silence fell over the world and Helen felt it, alone in her hut. Birds sat silently in trees. Wolf borgs listened in the forest. She put the kettle on, determined to carry on until the silence broke and their fate was decided. There were worse things to be doing than drinking a cup of tea when the world was about to end. But as she turned from the fire, she saw a boy through the window. A sharp-faced boy in black uniform. She felt instantly afraid. He was looking at her as if he hated her, and she knew enough about mutant children to realize what he was.

Then he was gone. Their eyes met for a few moments, then he turned and walked in the direction of the mansion path.

Helen was left shaking. The kettle began to whistle, but she ignored it and stood in the middle of the hut, wondering what to do.

Should she tell Mika she'd seen this boy?

No.

She couldn't tell him, not now.

The kettle was still whistling alone in the silence. She grabbed it and plonked it on the hearth. Then she snatched up her sun hat, rammed on her rain boots, and followed Ruben Snaith down the path toward the mansion.

28 The Meeting of Murderers

The sun beat down on The Wall.

As the children talked, they passed bottles of water. It was difficult to stay hydrated in this heat and there was no shade up there, only lines of black Pod Fighters soaking up the sun. But they drank to stay calm, not because they were thirsty. It was something to do with their hands and mouths while they prepared for the start of this war. Iman and Colette talked strategy while the rest listened. Both girls had been chosen by Mal Gorman for their brilliance in this field and it showed now. Iman spoke assertively, Colette softly, but they knew what they were talking about, and soon a flight plan was agreed upon.

It rushed through the army like adrenaline.

Before the bomb was detonated, the implanted children would stage a fly-past along The Wall so the people of the North, including their parents, would see them. Already squadrons were leaving the fortress and taking formation over the

Atlantic. It made sense to show themselves before the war started, so in the chaos that followed, their parents would know who'd stopped it.

Then, as the bomb was detonated, six squadrons of mutants would arrive at the scene to bring down the berserker borgs coming through The Wall. The mutants would wait until their parents had seen them and realized what was about to happen, then they would fly through their midst, find the control cubes, and make them fall dead from the air.

Mutant pilots would fly through a field of spinning cubes. Mutant gunners would use their eyes instead of laser fire. This was the last level of the game, beyond Creeper Nets and snipers and rumbling freighters. Way beyond the imaginary Red Star Fleet they'd sent reeling through space like dying suns. But with all those broken humans down there, shuffling slowly toward Amiens, they faced this deadly level with a sense of inevitability.

They were born to do this. They'd been trained to do this. They'd developed the game and made it their own. They'd invented this last, deadly level.

"Are we ready?" Mika asked.

Yes.

"OK. I'll ask Kobi what time his father will detonate the bomb. Then let's fly to Amiens and have a look at the bomb site."

Kobi followed Abe and John past the first row of towers. The crowd had also moved back a block, so he could see the front line, far down the street, at an intersection. A hard shadow fell over them, cast by the towers and the mid-afternoon sun. Thousands and thousands of people were crammed wall to wall as far as he could see. As they approached the front line, they began to cheer and wave guns in the air. Kobi looked at them and realized how very fragile these humans were, driven mad by anger and suffering, but so small and vulnerable. They believed they could run through the hole in The Wall and that a few guns and their number would protect them; that they would take the South with a wave of righteousness. Kobi doubted that many would even reach the hole in The Wall. If this war was left to proceed, half of them would be dead before they'd crossed no-man's-land.

He received another message from Mika.

> **We're ready. Tell us what time the bomb will detonate.**

John was leading them toward a tower eleven rows back from no-man's-land, by the front line of the crowd. Kobi caught up with his father.

"Dad?" he said.

"What do you want, Kobi?" His father looked a bit scared now, with the crowd roaring and the remote control in his hand. His voice was kind.

"When are you going to do it?" Kobi asked. "Have you set a time to detonate the bomb?"

"Yes," his father replied. "John suggested four o'clock, so the crowd will be prepared. We've got nearly an hour. Are you OK? How do you feel?"

"Fine," Kobi said.

"I'm proud of you. You've worked so hard and I know you're sorry. I just wanted say that before—"

"Thanks, Dad," Kobi said. He felt his heart convulse with pain and wished there was some way to warn his father about the consequences of what he was about to do. For the rest of his life, he would be the man who detonated the bomb. Kobi could see this future in his eyes and it was a remorseful, sad future. It was hard to follow him into the tower, knowing this.

But he knew what time the bomb would go off. He sent another message to Mika, then followed his father up the stairs. He now felt as if he wanted to vomit; his whole body was poisoned by fear. In less than an hour, he would watch his father detonate a bomb and their world go mad.

When they were halfway up, they heard the roar of Pod Fighters for the first time. Mika, Ellie, and the other Chosen Ones wore flying low over no-man's-land, inspecting the bomb site. Kobi rushed to a window and tried to get a glimpse of them; towers blocked his view.

But they were here, in Pod Fighters.

This was real.

Mal Gorman sat in a heap of straw. His camp cot was uncomfortable; the metal edges pressed into his legs, so he'd been on the floor for several hours, staring at a patch of wall. A patch of wall pigs had scratched their rumps on. It still had bits of mud and hair attached to it. Gorman wished he felt brave enough to go outside and enjoy the afternoon sun, but he still hadn't recovered from seeing *those eyes*. And there were bugs outside. The grass was full of them. After forty-three years in the North, he'd forgotten that beauty came with bugs attached.

Ralph's face appeared at the door. Gorman stood up, desperate for news.

"I'm preparing tea, sir," the butler said. "What would you like?"

"Tell me what's happening," Gorman said.

"I don't know, sorry."

"Then bring me more Everlife-9," Gorman said. "I'm getting old."

"I'm sorry," Ralph replied. "But I don't have any. You'll have to wait for Helen. She's going to find out how much you ought to take, so you don't accidentally vanish."

"Then go away if you can't be useful," Gorman sneered.

"I'll bring you some cake," Ralph said. "Helen brought some up. It's rather good."

The butler left and Gorman kicked the wall, then slid down it and sat in the straw again. He looked at his feet and realized what a ridiculous spectacle he made wearing kid's sneakers and a Pod Fighter T-shirt. He was now about forty years old. His skin was beginning to wrinkle. He wanted to be perfect forever . . . never face death . . . get out of there. He began to fume with frustration.

But what would happen to him when he got out?

Would he ever get out?

If the war started and he was stuck in that pigsty with the forest burning around him . . .

He tried not to think about it.

A few minutes later, he heard wolf borgs snarling. Then he heard the feeding room door open and close. He got up and looked through the glass.

"Ralph?" he said.

But the room was empty. He wondered if he'd been mistaken, but he was sure he'd heard the door open and close.

He felt cold suddenly and moved away from the glass and leaned against the wall, where he couldn't be seen.

It was horribly quiet. Now he could hear the bass note of the forest. No birdsong, no animals, not even the wolves, just this low hum that seemed to come from the ground.

Then he heard movement in the feeding room. There was someone in there, now he was sure. He didn't want to look but felt compelled to, and saw a pale, sharp face framed by the glass in the door.

"Ruben," Gorman whispered.

Ruben's face was milk white. The sort of milk white made by months of confinement.

"I brought your tea," he said.

Ruben unlocked the door and entered. Gorman stood still while the boy walked around him, frozen like a puppy meeting a big, nasty dog. Ruben was wearing his black uniform and he had Ralph's tray in his hands.

"Where's Ralph?" Gorman asked.

"I think I killed him," Ruben replied nonchalantly. "He's lying on the path outside. But that's OK, isn't it? He betrayed you. He deserved to die."

Gorman began to tremble.

"Are you scared?" Ruben asked. He furrowed his brow as if he was confused, but Gorman knew he didn't need to ask that question. The boy could see exactly how he was feeling and knew the reason why.

Ruben hadn't been chosen.

He was rejected in the last round of the game.

But Gorman had tried to keep him happy. He'd given Ruben those luxurious rooms in the fortress because he understood that such a deadly boy might be useful one day, if he could figure out how to control him without getting killed. But while Ruben had been hidden like this, Gorman had never watched him in the way he watched the others. He didn't want to watch him; he felt sick just looking at him, and Ruben probably knew this. Keeping him at all had been a mistake. Now he'd turned up here and killed Ralph. What else was he going to do?

"Don't be scared," Ruben said. "I've come to rescue you. You just don't get me, I understand that now, but we're very similar, you and I, and we need to stick together. Here, sit down and enjoy your tea and cake while I tell you my plan. It's really good. You're going to love it."

Gorman sat down on the camp cot, but only because he was too scared not to. Ruben placed the tray on his knee, and the teacup trembled on its saucer.

"Mika and Ellie are doing well," Ruben said, pacing around the sty. "Really well. You'd be so proud of them. They've taken over your fortress, the *Queen of the North*, and The Wall, and they've been chatting to Raphael Mose."

"Really?" Gorman said.

"Yes," Ruben replied. "They've been talking to the leader of the World Conservation Club. You chose well. They're very bright. Shame they're so wet."

"How do you know all this if you're not with them?" Gorman asked.

"Oh, I have been with them," Ruben said.

He held out his hand and showed Gorman a silver orb, the last invisibility shield. "And my light seems to have gone out. I'm not sure why, but they can't see me. It's like I don't exist. But then, I suppose, I stopped existing at the end of the game."

Gorman ignored this last comment. It was dangerous territory.

"What are they doing now?" he asked.

"Well, they've hit a bit of a snag," Ruben said. "The Secret got out."

"What?" Gorman snarled.

"Yes," Ruben said. "The Secret got out and everyone's gone mental. At this very moment, there are billions of people pressed against The Wall, with their bags packed, ready for the smash and grab. But Mika and Ellie are still trying to help them. They believe they can fix their parents, negotiate a deal with Raphael Mose, and that everyone will come skipping over here through meadows of butterflies, for a lovely new life. Your Chosen Ones are so wet I'm surprised they can stand up. And they control your army. What a waste of all your effort."

"Yes," Gorman replied, agreeing heartily with this. Now Ruben was speaking his language.

"You've spent nearly two years working with those children and they've ruined it all for you and ruined it for themselves. Luckily, I have a plan that will really sort this mess out. Do you want to hear it?"

"Yes," Gorman replied, pouring himself a cup of tea.

"Well, first I kill Mika and Ellie," Ruben told him enthusiastically.

Gorman's hand slipped and he poured milk all over the tray.

"Mika and Ellie are the clasp holding the army together," Ruben continued. "And they haven't realized it yet. The children communicate through them like a hub. If I kill Mika and Ellie, the rest will fall apart. Then that's the do-gooders out of the way.

That's your army punished. What do you think? Mika and Ellie deserve to die, don't they?"

Ruben turned on Gorman and fixed him with pale eyes. Gorman nodded, but had difficulty tipping sugar into his cup. This boy was hard-core. He was talking about killing Mika and Ellie as if it would be easy.

"Then," Ruben said, "after I kill the twins, I end the war. But not in the same way. Not with nice chats and happy trees. I go to Raphael Mose's mansion, and I press the third button in his study and poison all the people in the North."

"Poison them all?" Gorman repeated.

"Yes," Ruben said. "Poison them. Shut them up. Leave them behind The Wall. Forget about them. Raphael Mose has had that poison button for years, but he's never used it."

Gorman felt a chill. Ruben was talking about *genocide* as if he had an ant problem in his kitchen. A list of names began to trail through his mind, Ghengis Khan, Vlad the Impaler, William the Conquerer . . . Hitler.

They were both murderers. This was a meeting of murderers, but Ruben was way up there, way out of Gorman's league. Ruben was a full-blown psychopath with mutant power.

But, with all those people in the North gone, the planet would be owned by a few thousand rich people. All that space, all that fresh air . . . and he wouldn't press the button, Ruben would. Suddenly, greed smothered the single atoms of kindness and morality in Gorman's brain and he was considering Ruben's genocide as a viable option.

"And then," Ruben continued enthusiastically, "when the people in the North are dead, I'll kill all the people in the South.

I'll go into their homes and kill them while they're sleeping in their beds."

"Really?" Gorman said.

Now he began to feel a little bit sick. This was a lot of killing talk and it was also sounding crazy. Surely, Ruben didn't need to kill everyone.

"And then," Ruben said, "you and I will own Earth. The whole fragging planet."

He stopped pacing and faced Gorman and smiled. "It's a good plan, isn't it?" he said. "No one can touch me. I'm the best."

Gorman looked up at him, stunned, with his hands clutching the tray, and tried to imagine living on Earth with only a mutant psychopath for company. It didn't sound like much fun.

"We're the same, you and I," Ruben said. "Exactly the same. Now let's start. I've got some bait to bring Mika and Ellie back. I want them to come here, because they're just about to stop the war and I know it will really annoy them to have to leave The Wall now. Really annoy them."

Dumbstruck, Gorman watched him open the stable door. He didn't want to get stuck on Earth with Ruben. And Ruben knew this. He would have seen this in his light as loud as if Gorman had yelled it. Gorman wondered if the boy was making a point and that he didn't intend to help him at all. That this mutant psychopath would force him to watch while he killed everyone, just to prove how powerful he was . . . then kill him too. He couldn't imagine why Ruben would want to keep *him* alive when he was the one who'd cast him out from the Chosen Ones. Gorman would die with everyone else.

He put the tea tray down and stood up. Ruben was

crouched over a large bundle laid out by the feeding room door. Gorman walked closer so he could see what it was, and recognized the old woman, Helen, bound up like a fly in ropes. Her mouth was covered so she couldn't speak, but her eyes were wide and bright with fury.

"Smile for the camera," Ruben said, and took a picture of her. "But I won't send it to Mika just yet."

29 I'll Be Back in a Minute

our Pod Fighters landed on The Wall in Mainz. Children in blue uniforms ran toward them. Windshields slid back. Seven pairs of hands removed headsets. A monkey slid down a wing and scampered across The Wall. He found Tom and climbed up his leg and perched on his shoulder.

The Chosen Ones had returned from their trip to the bomb site.

It was twenty-five past three on the day the world would change, and they were ready. This coursed through The Whisper.

We're ready.

Thousands of Pod Fighters turned south to fly along The Wall to perform their fly-past.

Abe stood on the roof of the tower with the remote control in his hand. He looked dignified from a distance, but Kobi could see the fear in his eyes. They were surrounded by the large crowd who'd helped organize this event. The atmosphere was intense. There was still a lot of talking going on as people communicated with their contacts on the ground, trying to control the crowd. It was pushing forward now, nudging past the intersection and into the first block. It now looked like the starting line of a race. Everyone wanted to be the first person to run through the hole in The Wall.

"Make them keep back!" adults shouted around Kobi. "Tell them not to move until the bomb has gone off!"

Kobi hid behind his hair, worrying desperately. The younger children had moved back a block, but they were still on the front line of this war, just across the street. Kobi could see their faces pressed at the windows, trying to see what was going on. He wished he'd been able to visit Oliver and tell him to stay away from the windows. Tell him not to look until this was over. To hide under something heavy and strong just in case something dreadful happened. But he didn't feel able to leave his father now that he held that remote control in his hand. The crowd was impatient and he was worried that someone would decide to detonate the bomb early. He needed to stay at his father's side so he could warn Mika if this happened.

He looked up and saw a silver swallow hovering above them. For a moment he admired its beauty. This was the kind of creature he aspired to build. Then he realized where the borg had come from and that Raphael Mose was looking down through those silver eyes. After thirty seconds, it dipped and dived down the side of the tower to fly over the crowd.

Kobi tried to forget about it.

Of course Raphael Mose was watching.

They should expect it.

And anyway, this lesson was as much for him as everyone else.

At half past three, they heard a roar in the distance. Everyone looked west and shielded their eyes from the sun. It hung low over The Wall like a great gold orb.

The heat haze shimmered over no-man's-land, and its concrete rubble began to tremble. Then the crowd felt Pod Fighters through their feet. Kobi felt them vibrating through the tower. Then they saw them coming, like a great black swarm, a half-mile-wide strip in the sky. The sound seemed to well up through all the people, making them feel a great surge of awe. Then this great bank of pods was right overhead, flying in square formation. They came down so low over the towers, the adults around Kobi ducked and put their hands over their heads. But he stood erect, watching them fly, his hair whipping in their wind, feeling proud and wishing he was up there with them.

The bank of Pod Fighters passed, and a second wave approached. These were acrobats who weaved and looped over no-man's-land, giving a death-defying display of flying skill. It lasted over a minute, while the crowd gasped below, then with a blast, they were gone. Every head turned east as the roar faded. Then someone asked, "Who were they? Was that *our children* in those Pod Fighters?"

"Surely not," someone replied. "Twelve-year-old children couldn't fly like that."

"But there were thousands of them. The old army didn't have thousands of pilots, and our children have spent weeks in Pod Fighter simulators. It must be them. Our own children have just flown past us."

They were quiet for a few moments, all heads turned east as they struggled to absorb this fact.

"It was our children," someone said. "I know it."

The fly-past left them shaken, but they soon remembered why they were standing up there.

"What time is it?" someone asked.

"Twenty-five to four."

Everyone took a deep breath and all eyes turned to fix on The Wall.

Kobi paced.

The remote control trembled in his father's hand.

The children on The Wall in Mainz gathered to watch the fly-past. Audrey whooped and gripped Mika's arm, jumping like a bean beside him. The roar of Pod Fighters was so intense, he didn't hear Lilian yelling her head off, but she was wise to him now and began to vibrate violently in his pocket, trying to attract his attention.

The acrobats had just arrived. They wove and looped not far in front of them. But Lilian's tactic had worked. Mika turned and walked to the south side of The Wall and removed her from his pocket.

He felt an instant douse of dread. There on the screen was a picture of Helen, bound up like a fly in ropes. He could see fury in her eyes.

There was a single sentence with the picture:

Come back immediately or I'll kill Helen, then I'll kill your parents, then I'll kill everyone else. Lots of love, Ruben xxx

Mika looked at the time.

It was twenty minutes to four.

"Frag!" he yelled. "Frag it!"

He sprinted across The Wall and pulled Ellie away from the others.

She had a backdrop of weaving Pod Fighters, and her eyes were as black as their skins.

We have to go, he said. *You know you said we'd deal with Ruben when he popped up again?*

Yes . . .

Well, we have to do it now.

Now?

Yes, now.

How long will it take?

I don't know. But we've only got twenty minutes, so let's say that.

OK. Let's go.

They began to run toward a Pod Fighter. The others turned and realized they were leaving.

"Mika!" Audrey cried. "Where are you going?"

"We'll be back in a minute!" Mika yelled. "Don't worry, I promise, we'll be back soon!"

He jumped into the gunner seat of the Pod Fighter, trying not to look at her, but as Ellie took off, he saw an alien fairy standing on The Wall with a borg kitten in her hand, looking as if she was about to burst into tears.

I'll be back in a minute, he thought. *I promise.*

30 War

Ruben lifted the Helen bundle with his eyes and opened the feeding room door. Through it Gorman saw wolves on the other side of the path, standing among the trees. They snarled and lowered their heads, their eyes bright with bloodlust. Ruben looked at them for a moment and, to Gorman's astonishment, the light in their eyes faded and they collapsed in the bracken.

"Mika and Ellie could have done that," Ruben said. "But they didn't want to. They thought the wolves had consciousness, so they treated them as if they were alive. They made things very difficult for themselves. Pathetic."

Ruben set off down the path, along the side of the enclosure, with Helen floating before him, her eyes twinkling with rage. She may have been trussed up like a fly, but she was determined Ruben would understand exactly what she thought of him.

"I don't care," Ruben sneered.

Gorman followed with his legs shaking, looking at the dead wolf borgs. Then he remembered Ralph and turned to look toward the mansion. He could see the butler lying facedown on the path, his hair and his suit dusted with dirt. He felt very troubled then. Ralph had betrayed him, but he'd also served him for years. Gorman didn't feel compassion for the butler's suffering, but he did feel the loss. He'd just lost something that had been part of his life for a long time. Like a leg or an arm. A part of him lay in the dirt, dead. This was a very troubling feeling.

"Where are we going?" he called after Ruben.

"To the chapel," Ruben replied. "Hurry up, Gorman, quick, quick."

Now Gorman felt fear. *Those eyes were attached* to the back of the chapel. "Why the chapel?" he asked.

"Because Ellie doesn't like it," Ruben replied.

They walked through the dense, dark trees at the end of the enclosure. Gorman followed like a puppy on a bit of string, too awestruck by Ruben's psychopathic mind to even consider running away.

They saw the chapel through the trees, silent, foliate, and cold. Ruben dumped Helen on the ground by the porch and moved the gravestones piled against the door. They floated away like slices of toast and crashed down heavily among the trees, crushing the bracken and landing flat, on the wrong bodies.

The door opened with a witchy creak. Nobody had opened it for twenty years. It was bitterly cold inside, the kind of cold that thick, damp stone, loss of faith, and darkness make. Ruben left Gorman shivering in the aisle while he searched for candles.

Gorman watched them light, one by one, on a votive stand against the north wall. Old wax candles, pitted with dust and dirt. Now he could see he was standing on a tomb, surrounded by rotting pews. Behind him was a stone altar flanked by a curved, peeling wall and three ivy-choked stained-glass windows.

He watched Ruben float Helen up the aisle and dump her heavily on the altar. It occurred to him then that he had made this happen. That he'd hunted for these children, shown them what they could do, and completely lost control of them. He was standing in a chapel, wearing a Pod Fighter T-shirt, with a boy determined to murder the world. He had less control of his future than he'd had before he started.

These were sobering thoughts. He sat on the steps leading up to the altar. They were covered in rotten, red carpet and as wet as winter grass. Ruben rubbed his hands on his smart, black uniform and said, "Mika and Ellie are here."

The candles flickered.

Gorman's heart fell. Now he was stuck in the middle of a mutant battle, and Mika and Ellie would believe he was on Ruben's side.

"Don't look so glum," Ruben said. "It will only take a moment to kill them. It will be like a gunfight. You know, the sort of gunfights they used to have in old Western movies when the cowboys walk away and turn to face each other. Only I already know I'll win, because I want to kill and they don't. Even if they manage to summon the courage to try, that split second of overriding their instinct will be enough. They'll fall like the wolves. They'll crumble like that smelly old butler of yours. I can't wait."

He looked up. Ellie was perched on the roof of the chapel like a golden bird.

He watched her through the tiles. "How sweet," he said.

Then he saw Mika walk around the back of the chapel. A bright gold light shone through The Wall.

He was expecting them to come at him quickly. They would be in a hurry, with that bomb out there. He walked down the aisle, feeling impatient. Helen wriggled on the altar like a flowery maggot.

Then Ruben noticed the silence. The chapel was silent, Gorman was silent, the birds in the forest were silent, but there was another silence cloaking theirs, a dense, focused silence that was The Roar turned inside out. The sound of pain, suffering, and anger forged into a new weapon that was polished, considered, and deadly accurate.

Now Ruben felt just a little bit afraid. He didn't know this feeling. He'd expected the twins to arrive furious. When he reached the end of the aisle, he tried to turn, to walk back to the altar and stand closer to his bait, but suddenly he found himself frozen, forced to look at the back wall and unable to move his head and legs. Now he saw their light through the stone. They were standing side by side at the back of the chapel. He felt their silent, focused power and realized he'd made a terrible mistake.

In that silence, the chapel came apart. Tiles split and floated into the air, then the rafters, eaves, beams, stone, floated up into the sky as if they were tied to helium balloons. And Ruben found himself facing Mika and Ellie with the forest around them.

A dog ran between their legs and loped quickly toward

him. A gold ghost dog, an elegant greyhound with a wake of golden light. It gained momentum as it approached him, then leaped like a gazelle over his head. Then he saw a great slab of stone coming at him, carved, round stone, the face of the Green Man from the chapel wall. It spun once, and he saw its eyes bulging, its mouth vomiting vines. Then he felt himself laid down gently on the aisle and it dropped over his head like a lid. While he was still gasping with shock, he heard Mika tap on the Green Man's nose and say, "Just because we don't use it doesn't mean we don't have it, Ruben."

"Let me out!" Ruben yelled. "I can hardly breathe in here!"

"In a minute," Mika said. "We've got something else to do first."

Ruben was left to lay on the chapel floor with the feeling of a fly that had buzzed in their faces.

The razor wire on the top of The Wall glinted in the golden afternoon sun.

"Do you want to do it?" Kobi's father asked, holding out the remote control. "You helped, I don't mind."

"No, thanks," Kobi replied. "You do it."

"OK," Abe said. "Thirty seconds."

The crowd in the streets below fell silent.

You will remember this time of day, Kobi thought. *Every time you pass it, you will feel the shock scar. Every time the sun shines, every time you smell hot concrete dust, you will remember this moment.*

The crowd in the streets began to yell:

TEN!

NINE!

EIGHT!

SEVEN!

SIX!

FIVE!

FOUR!

THREE!

TWO!

ONE!

Then Abe aimed the remote control at The Wall and pressed the button.

The crowd began to roar.

Kobi watched The Wall with his heart pumping like a bellow.

First came little flashes of light and puffs of smoke as the detonation occurred. Then the explosion began and the sound hit them:

BOOM!

It was huge.

All the towers in Amiens shook.

Then hundreds of tons of concrete erupted from The Wall and flew across no-man's-land. The heaviest boulders fell first, creating an instant lunar landscape. The smaller boulders flew farther, smashing into the first row of towers and lodging in fold-down apartments, crushing gray sofas, smashing tellies. The smallest fragments flew right up in the air and came down like a shower of hailstones on the crowd.

The people on the roof threw themselves down, with their hands over their heads.

Then the explosion was over, the hole was made, and all Kobi could hear was his father panting next to him.

They slowly rose to their feet and looked across no-man's-land toward The Wall. A mysterious cloud of dust lingered over it, tinted orange by the afternoon sun. Then a great cry rose from the crowd; a battle cry from ancient blood. Then hundreds of thousands of people began to run toward the hole in The Wall.

Kobi's father turned to look at him, his eyes victorious, the remote control still clutched in his hand. But Kobi missed this touching moment between father and son. His eyes were glued to that cloud of dust hanging over the hole.

The crowd sprinted toward it.

Everyone watched. The fastest runners broke away and poured like specks toward a heavenly hole. When they were swallowed by the orange-tinted cloud of dust, the adults around Kobi cheered again, but he held his breath, waiting.

The cloud sagged suddenly, as if something large hit the back of it.

"Dad," Kobi said.

"Come on, Kobi," Abe cried. "It's time to leave! Let's get down there and go home!"

"Dad," Kobi repeated. "Look at that cloud of dust."

His father glanced at it for a second, but his head was full of freedom. He wanted to get through that hole in The Wall and claim a good piece of land before all the best bits were gone. All the adults on the roof had begun moving toward the stairs.

"Come on, Kobi," his father insisted. "We're going to get left behind."

"No, Dad," Kobi cried. "Look at the dust!"

Abe looked again and this time his eyes stuck to it. Something huge was moving through that orange cloud. Something silver with sharp edges, as tall as The Wall. And people were running back out of it now, as if they'd seen the monster.

"Hey!" Abe shouted after John and his friends. "Stop! Come back! Look at this!"

They had only just turned when they heard a low, warping WHOMP followed by screams from the crowd.

"Frag!" Abe said. "What is it?"

A giant silver orb was floating out of the dust cloud. A silver orb made of 729 ten-foot-square flex metal cubes that spun and flashed in the sunlight.

The noise increased as the cubes gained speed, until it was deafening.

WHOMP.
WHOMP.
WHOMP.
WHOMP.

Then, as if they had finished warming up, the cubes began to make new shapes; to morph through a sequence of symmetrical forms that became increasingly complex and . . . frightening. They were like crystal formations, some organic, some geometric, and each new transmogrification was punctuated by electronic sounds: warps, thumps, punches, drills, booms, and earsplitting spikes. It was a chest-thumping display of brutal geometry.

Then two more appeared behind the first and they lined up

on no-man's-land facing the towers, synchronized, morphing, and warping with increasing speed and volume.

"OK," Abe said. "I'm impressed, that's enough. Let's get everyone back."

They began to make calls, trying to talk to their contacts on the ground, but it was already chaos down there. The people at the front of the crowd were trying to run away from the morphing cubes, but there were thousands of people behind them. They began to scream. To push on each other, forcing the crowd to compress.

Abe yelled, "They must move slowly! They must not panic or people will get hurt! There's room for them all, but they must move back slowly!"

The morphing cubes began to float toward the front line of the towers, throbbing and pulsing, as they prepared to attack.

The crowd convulsed and screamed and scrambled.

Kobi looked at the sky and thought this:

Who survives in a world of chaos is decided by so many complex variables, it's impossible to predict, no matter how hard you try.

Especially when the sky is full of spinning cubes.

And the Pod Fighters haven't arrived.

The berserker borgs contracted to form dense, spiked clumps and punched holes in the front row of towers.

CRUNCH.

CRUNCH.

Like monster fists.

The towers crumbled like sand.

This was war.

The sky was a soup of dust. The ground was a mass of screaming humans who'd forgotten about their lust for land and were trying to find the people they loved among the madness.

Somewhere above them was a milky orange sun, and adults on the roof seemed to dance against it, flailing, panicking, throwing themselves down, all preparing to die. The berserker borgs would punch their way through those ten rows of empty towers, then punch their way through them.

That a mistake had been made was a given, and at that moment even Kobi thought it. Mika hadn't come and the berserker borgs had reached the fifth row. They were choking on dust. Their faces and clothes were ghost white with it. He looked for his father, realizing that he must stay close to the man he loved, and be ready to face death in his arms.

Then he heard Pod Fighters.

He stood looking east, listening, but did not dare hope they'd come, until he saw them slip through the dusty sky like dolphin birds.

Then it was brutal, beautiful chaos. The milky orb of the sun, the giant spinning cubes, the Pod Fighters weaving with their engines roaring.

"Get down!" his father yelled. He pulled on Kobi's leg, trying to force him to lie down with the others. But Kobi stayed where he was because he was beginning to feel something he'd never felt before. As the mutants wove around him through the spinning, glinting cubes, he felt as if he was standing in an oasis of their silence; an oasis of The Roar turned inside out. And suddenly, for the first time in his life, he could *see*!

Suddenly, everything around him was a giant tapestry of

gold and blue light. A beautiful tapestry of infinite detail, a living and inanimate weave of chaos.

Then he felt heavy thuds.

The mutants were finding the control cubes and the rest of the borgs were falling from the sky.

But the battle was right on top of them.

A Pod Fighter arced mere feet from his face. Kobi saw the pilot's shoulders. He looked up. There were cubes right above them, spinning, glinting. Then they all stopped spinning and began to fall.

CRUNCH!

One came down to his left, biting the corner off the tower. Everyone screamed in shock and horror. Then another fell to his right, missing the tower but bouncing against it and falling to the street below. Then a third came down directly above them.

Through the tapestry of light, Kobi felt his mind lock on it. The Roar was in his head and it formed black rods in his eyes. He felt his pupils expand as he let them out. He felt the weight of falling metal dragging in his brain, as if it would rip his head from his shoulders. But the cube swerved, missed the adults, and clipped the edge of the tower.

Then it was quiet. All the cubes had fallen and the Pod Fighters were flying away.

The adults rose to their feet and stared at Kobi. They knew what he'd done. They didn't know how he'd done it, but they'd just watched him stand in their midst and swerve the path of a falling cube. Kobi was equally astonished: He'd left the game early; he was never shown his mutant power. He'd been born with black wings that were cut away, but inside he remained a mutant, with a latent mutant power.

He faced the shocked adults and felt a tingling in his shoulder blades. A sense of growth and fulfillment, a warmth and new light, as if his body was preparing to regenerate his mutation, his natural-born wings, and the days of hiding in a coat were over. But there was no time to dwell on that now. They could hear people crying all around them, and the dust was beginning to settle. Gradually, they began to see the devastation. All ten rows of towers before them were gone. The streets were piled with cubes and rubble, and the top of the children's tower had been punched away.

"The children!" someone screamed.

"Oliver," Kobi whispered.

Then all the adults were weeping and running down the stairs.

31 Poison

The war lasted three minutes and fourteen seconds.

Kobi followed the adults down to the lobby.

He was distraught.

Their plan had made sense before the bomb. He'd helped build it, believing their parents needed this short, sharp shock. That it was the only way they'd understand how terrible the war would be: open their eyes and ears to the army of children. But if Oliver and the younger children had died as part of this lesson, Kobi knew he'd never forgive himself.

That little boy, so young, so scared, in a Pod Fighter T-shirt ten sizes too big for him . . .

Kobi bit back tears.

They couldn't get out of the lobby. The street was piled high with rubble, so the doors were blocked. They ran up to the first floor and climbed out of a window onto the remains of the fallen towers. Among the rubble was a litter of homely things that had fallen out of apartments: smashed plates, packets of food, clothes, bedding, children's toys all twisted and broken and covered in dust. It took them ten minutes to cross a street they could have walked in seconds an hour ago, and by the time they got to the other side, they felt even more sick and sad. The crowd beyond the intersection was in turmoil. Some people were hurt, others had lost their families. The sky was full of ambulance pods carrying the injured away. It was a dreadful scene.

They reached the children's tower and climbed in through a broken window. Then they began the grim procession up the stairs, dreading what they'd see when they reached the top.

Halfway up the building, they felt a hot, dusty wind on their faces and there was rubble on the stairs, which made their progress slow and dangerous. It became lighter as they climbed, but this was because the top of the building now lay in the street below. Eventually, they reached the new top, sculpted by the berserker borgs. Trembling with horror and fear, they began to search through the rubble for their children.

They searched cautiously. They did not want to see them. They found shoes and toys among the rubble and pulled them out carefully, reverently, relieved when they didn't recognize them.

But soon they began to wonder. . . .

They gathered around the broken edges of the building and looked down to the street below, wondering if the children had fallen down there and were buried in the rubble.

Kobi stood alone, facing The Wall. He couldn't bear to

watch any longer. His father joined him, wiping dusty tears from his face.

"Where are they?" he whispered. "If I've . . ."

He trailed off.

"Look," Kobi said.

He pointed down toward the rubble of the broken towers. There was a small group climbing over it, heading in the direction of no-man's-land.

"John!" Abe shouted immediately. "Has anyone got digital binoculars? Come and look at this!"

A pair of digital binoculars was found and Abe took them. Everyone watched intently while he found the group and studied it.

"It's them!" he cried. "It's the children! And the boy's with them! The implanted boy! He's leading them onto no-man's-land!"

They passed the digital binoculars so everyone could see. Luc was holding a baby and leading Oliver by the hand. His implant flashed as his head turned, reflecting the light of the sun. The rest of the children were following, climbing carefully, determinedly, over the rubble. The boy was talking to them, guiding them, encouraging them to help the little ones scramble over the concrete.

"Where are they going?" someone asked. "I don't understand. Why would they go to no-man's-land when we're here?"

When all the adults had taken a look, Kobi was given a turn with the digital binoculars.

"There are Pod Fighters down there," he told them. "Look. In a line in front of the hole. Four Pod Fighters. That's where your children are going."

"Why?"

Kobi turned to face them. "Because," he replied quietly, "they don't trust you anymore. They've gone where they feel safe. They've joined the army of children."

Kobi walked across no-man's-land for the third time that day. Now his feet made clouds in the settled dust and he walked around the giant boulders that had been made by the bomb.

He followed the adults. The adults followed their children. Their shoulders slumped with exhaustion and remorse.

It was not a happy journey.

The sun had dipped behind The Wall, ready to set on the south side. The north face was cold and gray, but through the hole, sunlight poured, warm and bright. It made the path they followed.

When they reached halfway, they could smell the forest and see the children gathered around the wings of the Pod Fighters. They could pick out eight taller children, the red-haired boy, the rest in white uniform. The little ones were gathered around them. The babies were playing in the dust.

The adults gained pace until they were almost running.

The children noticed them and turned to watch them approach.

When adults and children faced each other, Oliver stepped forward. "We're not coming back," he said with a scowl. "Don't try to make us."

Oliver's mother crouched down and took his hand.

"We haven't come to take you back, Oliver," she said quietly. "We've come to say sorry. We're so very, very sorry. We want to talk to you."

"Really?" His face softened. "You're not going to tell us off?"

"No."

"You want to talk to us?"

"Yes. Now let us meet your new friends. We want to meet the children in those Pod Fighters. And then, we'll all sit down and talk."

The Chosen Ones walked forward. Mika, Ellie, Audrey, Leo, Iman, Colette, and Santos.

The adults looked at them, speechless.

These were *children*?

The same children who'd gone to the arcades?

"Hi," Leo said. "We're pleased to meet you."

A silver swallow hovered over The Wall. Mika and Kobi watched it and imagined Raphael Mose pacing around his study, wondering what to do.

Mose had seen everything. The crowd gathering, Kobi and his father building the bomb, the fly-past, the detonation, the berserker borgs biting chunks out of the towers, and children in Pod Fighters bringing them down with *no weapons*. The war that lasted three minutes and fourteen seconds had shocked the South as much as it had shocked the North. But Raphael Mose didn't consider it over yet.

His study was full of members of the World Conservation Club. This was the first time they'd met for many years. They'd flown from all over the South to watch their berserker borgs teach the North a lesson. And instead they'd been taught a lesson.

"Those children were telling the truth," Mose said. "Even

though The Secret got out, they've taken control of the North. And I suspect this whole event was controlled by them. The bomb, the attack, everything. That boy down there, with the long black hair, helped build the bomb, and look at those adults groveling in the dust, begging for forgiveness.

"What are they?

"How did they destroy the berserker borgs? I don't get it. I don't like it. It's weird. And they're going to want to talk to me again soon."

"But we don't want them over here," someone said. "Even if they can control their parents. There are billions of them. We don't want them."

"No, we don't," Raphael Mose said. "I want to press the second button. Does everyone agree?"

Heads nodded.

Raphael Mose swung open the horse painting and pressed the second button.

"This is our land now," he said. "And what I said before, stands. If those people take one step beyond The Wall, we'll poison them all like rats."

He swung the painting back and the World Conservation Club began to rise. The meeting was over. But as they moved toward the door, Mose heard a click on the wooden floor beyond. A hoof.

"Grace?"

He opened the door and looked out. The goat child wasn't there, but he was sure he'd heard her. He hurried through the house, searching for her, and found her in her bedroom.

"What are you doing?" he asked.

"Nothing," she replied. She was sitting on her bed, hugging her bear, but she looked at him with hot mutant eyes.

"Were you downstairs a minute ago?" he asked.

"No," she lied.

"OK, darling, my meeting's finished. Do you want to eat lunch with me? We missed breakfast together, but I could make lunch. That would be nice, wouldn't it?"

"I'm not hungry," Grace said. "Chef made me a sandwich."

"OK," he replied, feeling unsettled. The child looked different; there was a new darkness in her eyes. He closed the door and walked away.

In the North the dust settled and adults and children talked. They sat around the Pod Fighters with the setting sun pouring through the hole in The Wall. Then they heard a noise to the south that the mutant children recognized. A rumbling sound from below no-man's-land.

"We need to leave for a while," Mika said. "We'll be back soon. Kobi, do you want to come with us? We've got a spare seat."

"Yes," Kobi said.

The children climbed into their Pod Fighters, and those left behind watched them take off. The Pod Fighters rose in a line, pointed their noses at the sky, then shot up and vanished. For a while, the remaining adults and children stood around, watching the hole in The Wall and wondering what was happening. Then over the line of it they saw something come: a grid of black squares that was moving slowly toward them like a great black net cast over the sky. It passed overhead and spread toward the towers. Soon it covered the whole town of Amiens and was still moving north.

They knew enough to realize what it was.

"Poison!" Oliver cried. "The South has sent the poison!"

His mother took his hand. "It's OK, Oliver," she said. "Your friends will know what to do."

32 A Birthday Present for Grace

race Mose opened her eyes. Sunlight filtered through her pretty white curtains. As they stirred in the spring breeze, she smelled apple blossom.

It was her seventh birthday. She felt happy when she remembered, then she felt sick. She did not want to have a birthday while poison hung over the North. She could feel the people watching that grid, she could hear it in The Whisper. It cast a shadow darker than the second level of London.

She grabbed her bear and jumped out of bed and peeked through the curtains at the garden. It looked glorious. The lawn was lush and green from spring rain followed by a week of sun. The fruit trees were heavy with blossom, cherry pink and apple white. The birds nesting in the surrounding forest were singing their hearts out and there were already people on the lawn, building the marquee for her party.

But . . .

. . . somewhere out there, the children with black eyes were thinking about her.

Her curtains swayed. She stood between them, listening.

They were coming.

"Grace?"

She turned to see her mother standing in the doorway. Her beautiful young mother who knew all the lies.

"What's wrong?" she asked cheerfully. "Why so serious! It's your birthday! Come and open your presents! Daddy's in the kitchen making pancakes!"

She held out Grace's dressing gown. The goat child sat her bear on the bed and slid her arms into the robe.

The children with black eyes were coming.

She followed her mother down to the kitchen.

One end of the table was piled high with gifts wrapped in pretty paper. The other was laid for her birthday breakfast, with her favorite china and a vase of flowers. Her father was making a special effort to amuse her. He wore a flowery apron and tossed the pancakes as if there were a brass band playing in the background. Grace watched him and wished he'd stop pretending. His light was ragged with anger and fear, and his eyes were stone cold.

He slid a pancake onto her plate and she drizzled it with syrup.

Everything around her looked stolen. The flowers, the gifts, even the sunlight that gilded her mother's hair.

If she hadn't known the children with black eyes were coming, she would have burst into tears at that moment.

"I bet you can't wait to open your gifts!" her mother said.

Grace nodded and looked at them. "What time is my party?" she asked.

"One o'clock," her mother replied. "And it's going to be the best party you've ever had. *Everyone's* coming."

"I know," Grace said.

After she'd opened her gifts and shown enough interest to satisfy her parents, she dressed herself and went out with her bear. The marquee was up and the people were setting out the rest of the things for her party. They inflated balloons, tied ribbons to chairs, and unpacked boxes of china and glass. A freighter arrived and delivered a dozen giant rabbits made of white flowers. These were moved around the lawn on hover trollies until someone decided they were in the right place.

Nobody looked at her. She knew why. Her goat legs frightened strangers, but she didn't care. After a while, she wandered around to the front of the house and sat on the steps between the lions. Three borgs and a mutant child gazed down the drive.

"Grace?"

Grace turned to see her mother walking toward her.

"There you are!" her mother said. "I've been looking for you everywhere!"

"I'm waiting for my friends," Grace replied.

"Out here? Alone? I don't like you so close to the lions." She took Grace's hand and pulled her up. "And anyway, people will arrive at the back of the house, not the front. Why don't you come inside and put your party dress on?"

"OK."

As her mother helped her change, she heard the first pods come down in the garden. The party dress was very beautiful. It was made of white silk with hand-stitched white rabbits around the hem. As her mother buttoned it up at the back, Grace fidgeted impatiently.

"Hold still," her mother said. "Just two more . . . There. Beautiful." She turned Grace around and smoothed the front of the dress. Then Grace ran off to see who'd arrived.

Adults. Lots of adults with angry, scared light, who didn't realize she could see how they were feeling. They wished her happy birthday, then sloped off toward her father's study. She considered following them and looking through the door, but she was dragged away by her mother up the garden.

It *was* beautiful. Her parents had made such an effort to please her. There were twenty round tables set out on the lawn and each had a three-tiered cake stand piled with rabbit-shaped cakes, sandwiches, and biscuits. Hundreds of balloons with rabbit ears bobbed on the back of the chairs, and around the legs of the tables, *real* rabbits, white baby rabbits with ribbons around their necks, nibbled the grass. Even the waiters were dressed as rabbits. One wandered past and tripped over his feet.

"You do still like rabbits?" her mother asked.

"Yes," Grace replied.

"Good," her mother said. "But you're very quiet today. Are you feeling all right?"

"Yes."

She followed her mother up the lawn to inspect the marquee. This contained adult fare: a string quartet, champagne, and a buffet. There were always more adults than children at Grace's parties.

It got busy. Her mother took her to the terrace so they could welcome the guests. Lots of people arrived at once, and soon Grace was surrounded by a heap of gifts and everyone was talking at her, telling her how pretty her dress was.

Where were they?

The games would start soon and the only guests she wanted to see had not arrived.

She looked wistfully up the lawn, unable to listen to the people talking to her. Soon her mother was telling her off for not saying "Thank you" nicely enough, and the lawn was covered with people drinking and laughing as if *nothing was happening* on the other side of The Wall.

The rush eased off and most of the men disappeared into the house. Then her mother began to talk to a group of friends. Grace was just thinking about joining the other children on the lawn when she found herself facing an old lady, the only old lady at the party and one of the few old ladies Grace had ever seen. She was most peculiarly dressed. Instead of wearing a pretty garden dress like the other ladies at the party, she was wearing a long brown skirt, yellow Wellington rain boots, and a sun hat with faded plastic fruit hanging off it. Grace had never seen anyone like this before, but the lady's light was so warm and friendly, she smiled for the first time since the party began. The lady placed a box of colored pencils in her hands and said, "I'm sorry they're not wrapped in pretty paper, but I was in a hurry and I didn't have time."

"Thank you," Grace said nicely.

Her mother and friends had stopped talking. Grace realized that everyone on the terrace was staring at the old lady as if she were a witch who'd come to the party to turn them all into frogs.

"Helen!" her mother said in a high voice. "What a lovely surprise! How nice of you to come!"

"Thank you," Helen said. "You invite me every year . . . and I've been looking forward to meeting Grace. She reminds me of some of my new friends. I brought them with me. I hope you don't mind." She looked at Grace and whispered, "Mika and Ellie chose the pencils. They said you like drawing."

"I do," Grace whispered back. "They're coming, aren't they?"

"Yes," Helen said. "I just thought I'd warn you first, so it wouldn't spoil your party."

"It won't," Grace said. "I'm waiting for them."

"I see," Helen replied, with twinkly eyes.

Her mother was now brittle with irritation. She didn't want this scruffy old woman at her daughter's party. Helen clashed with the décor and she made everyone nervous. She'd only been invited because she was a Gelt, one of the richest people in the world, but everyone knew she was mad. And who were Mika and Ellie? She didn't know anyone called Mika and Ellie. And they weren't invited. It was very rude of Helen to bring uninvited guests.

"Whom are you talking about, Grace?" she asked. "I'm not sure we have room for more people."

"Yes, we do," Grace said. "We have lots of room."

"But I don't know who they are," her mother hissed.

"I want them here," Grace said, her eyes darkening. "They're my friends. They're like me."

"What do you mean?" Her mother's eyes suddenly glittered with fear. They'd tried to make Grace "normal" before they began to ignore the bottom half. They'd spent millions on healing chamber development that only seemed to make Grace's eyes more spooky. Their daughter was a satyr. Sometimes, in the twilight, when they saw her walking at the end of the garden with the dark forest behind her, they felt afraid. They loved her, but they did not want any more like her.

There was a bright flash at the end of the garden and a silver craft appeared.

"It's them!" Grace cried. "They're here!"

"No!" her mother shouted. "Make them go away! Someone get Raphael! Waiter! You! Go and get my husband! He's in his study! I am very annoyed, Helen! You should know that you can't just bring a bunch of strangers to Grace's party!"

A man in a rabbit costume ran into the house. All the guests stared up the lawn, and when they saw the mutant children climbing out of the Stealth Carrier, the adults put their glasses down and began to walk toward the house.

But the children remained. The rich children in their hand-stitched clothes, with baby rabbits in ribbons hopping around their feet, stayed exactly where they were, eyes glued to the uninvited guests as they formed a line before them.

Seven children in white uniform . . . and a monkey.

The rich children didn't know these *other* children had learned how to tape up their sneakers when they were five years old. Had been bullied, starved, deprived of light, taught by cartoons, and force-fed Fit Mix. Had flown Pod Fighters, overthrown their government, and won the respect of their people. But they did know this, that these were the coolest kids they'd ever seen and they wished, immediately, they were like them.

Grace tried to run toward Mika and Ellie, but her mother grabbed her by the arm.

"Help!" her mother yelled. "Where are the lions? Get guns! Wolves! They're from the *other side*! Someone HELP US!"

Bodyguards ran out of the house. Grace fought against her mother's grip.

"Grace!" her mother shouted. "Stop it! I want you to come inside while Daddy gets rid of them!"

"No!" Grace yelled. "I don't want them to leave; they're my friends! They've come to stop you from poisoning everyone!"

Her mother froze as if Grace had struck her. "Poisoning everyone? What are you talking about?"

"You know what I'm talking about!" Grace yelled. "All those people on the other side of The Wall! Stop pretending you don't know about them! I saw through Daddy's door. I watched him press the second button!"

Her mother's eyes glazed over and she released Grace's arm. Immediately the child ran away from her, up the lawn, and toward Mika and Ellie. When she reached them, she stood between them and held Ellie's hand. She could feel Awen sniffing at her fingers and Puck playing with her hair.

She looked at the house and waited for her father to come out.

Raphael Mose led the World Conservation Club down the terrace and up the lawn, surrounded by bodyguards and guns. They were not afraid. They walked with deadly confidence, their light bristling with territorial fury.

When they faced the children, Leo said, "We've come to talk."

"I don't want to talk," Raphael Mose replied. "I want you out of my garden, now. The negotiation ended when your stupid parents blew that hole through The Wall. Grace, come here."

"No," she said, moving behind Ellie's legs.

"We haven't come to negotiate," Leo told him. "We know that time is over. We've come to tell you that you can't continue with this war. You're wasting your time even trying. You can't win it because we won't let you fight it. Now that we know our parents will listen to us, the only choice you have is whether or not you listen to us."

Raphael Mose stared at Leo with an incredulous smile on his face. A thirteen-year-old boy was telling him that his hands were tied behind his back. That they would not let him fight . . . the leader of the World Conservation Club, the richest and most powerful man in the world.

"I do admire you," he said. "It must have taken a lot of guts to come here and say that when there's a poison grid hanging over your parents."

"No, there isn't," Leo said.

"Er . . . yes, there is," Mose replied. "You know those black boxes in the sky? They're full of poison."

"They don't work," Leo told him.

"Yes, they do," Mose argued. "You're in the South now. Things work in the South. We don't have vacuumbots that make more mess than they clean up. If we build something, it works."

"We broke the poison grid," Leo said. "We looked at it and broke it. Tell your bodyguards to fire their guns at us."

"Do it," Mose said. "Shoot them. But be careful with Grace. Not my Grace."

Without a moment's hesitation the bodyguards pointed their guns at the children and pulled the triggers. Nothing happened.

"Where are your lion borgs?" Leo asked. "Why haven't your lions killed us?"

Mose turned and looked toward the mansion. The boy was right; the lion borgs were nowhere to be seen.

"Summon them," Leo said.

"They're only programmed to guard and kill," Mose replied. "I can't summon them."

"We can," Leo said. "Grace, you do it. Show your dad how smart you are."

Grace crept out from behind Ellie's legs. Her father watched her eyes darken, and for a moment it felt as if the whole garden was dark. He heard the bass note of the forest and felt vibrations through the lawn as the lions dropped from their plinths. Then Mose turned and watched in astonishment as they sauntered around the side of the house, their great haunches rising and falling. At the edge of the lawn, they paused and roared so loud, the marquee trembled, then they loped through the party tables, sending baby rabbits scarpering.

The adults panicked and backed away, wondering if this would end in an attack. But when the enormous silver lions reached Grace, they lay down on the grass before her. She walked forward on goat legs, in her rabbit party dress, and stroked one down the side of its face.

Raphael Mose looked at her as if she were an alien.

"You made us," Leo said. "We're your children, in the North and the South. We are the future, so you *made* this future. You can't fight it. Listen to us. Let us show you things you've never seen."

33 We Are the Future

Helen stood in the mansion's kitchen, making a pot of tea. When this was done, she opened a hermabag and removed three rabbit cakes. They were a bit squashed; the rabbits ears were bent, but she arranged them nicely on a plate, then put them on a tray with the tea things and hobbled up the stairs toward one of the bedrooms.

The door was ajar. Leaf green light filtered through the window. It was another beautiful, bright spring day. She looked around the room and thought how much nicer it was with a guest staying in it.

"How are you?" she asked, turning to the bed.

Ralph was propped up on pillows, wearing her son's pajamas. Along the side of the bed was the healing chamber that had returned him from the brink of death.

Mika and Ellie had proved themselves experts at multi-tasking on the day of the war. They'd taken down Ruben, unbound Helen, put Gorman back in his sty, then crouched beside Ralph on the dusty path and seen a glimmer of light within him, the faintest light, a mist of gold, but enough to bring him back.

"Get a healing chamber," Mika told Helen quickly. "He's still there." Then, in a flash, he and Ellie were gone back to Amiens to deal with the berserker borgs.

If Helen had any doubts that these children could change the course of a river that had run for thousands of years, or stop the boulder of war rolling down the mountain, they vanished as she sat on the path beside the dusty butler, holding his hand, waiting for a healing chamber to be delivered. Far beyond her the war was having its three minutes and fourteen seconds of horror, but she sat on that path, feeling such hope and happiness, her heart was bursting with it.

That black-eyed boy. That tortured child who'd come to her fold-down In Barford North was a truly spectacular upgrade on the human design.

And evolved out of this! she thought, looking at the forest around her. *And concrete and floodwater and mold! A child forged in darkness out of particles that had been stardust millions of years ago. Out of stardust had evolved children born to know what they were.*

Their universe, for its chaos, was very beautiful.

From her son's bed, Ralph smiled at her.

She grinned back.

"I'm very well, thank you, madam," he said.

"You don't have to call me madam," Helen replied. "Please call me Helen."

"Yes, madam," he said. "I mean, Helen." He looked at

the tray in her hands. "I hope you haven't gone to too much trouble."

"No trouble is too much for you, Ralph," she said. "Grace gave me some of her birthday cakes. And I know you like cake."

She arranged the tray on his knee and he looked at the tea things and the rabbit cakes. No one had been so kind to him before.

"Things are going to be different now," Helen said. "The rest of your life will be different."

"How is Gorman?" he asked.

"Still frightened by the spiders," Helen said. "But he's more polite since Ruben's visit. He asks me nicely to get rid of them. Mika and Ellie are about to take him out and show him something interesting. Something they hope will fix him."

"What are they going to do with Ruben?"

"Well," Helen said. "They're not sure what to do about Ruben. They're still thinking about him. At the moment, he's in the fortress with a mutant guard and he might have to stay like that. It's most unfortunate. That's the thing about nature: Every now and then, it throws a wild card and there's nothing we can do about it. You just have to accept and adapt."

"So I ought to feel sorry for Ruben," Ralph said. "Being the wild card. He could have been like Mika and Ellie, but he's not."

"Well, I suppose we ought to feel sorry for him," Helen said. "But it's not easy, is it, after what he did to you? Doing the right thing is so very complicated."

She poured a cup of tea, and Ralph ate a rabbit cake, then they gazed out of the window and watched a bird build its nest in the ivy.

* * *

The Stealth Carrier rose from the meadow with Mal Gorman, Mika, Ellie, Puck, and Awen inside it. They flew south toward the Loire Valley, which in the days before The Wall had been called the Garden of France, with many pretty towns on the banks of the river. Now the towns were gone and it was overgrown with forest. It was the perfect place to show Mal Gorman the light.

They found a spot on the top of a hill, where they could see the path of the river twisting gently south. The valley rose in soft, green peaks, and the spring sun shimmered through its leaves.

Mal Gorman was still shaken by his encounter with Ruben, and his jump from the Stealth Carrier was messy. He was now scared of everything around him: The children, the monkey, the forest and its creatures, even the river and the sun all seemed very dark to him, very threatening.

Mika and Ellie walked ahead, looking for a spot where they had a clear view of the valley through the trees. When they found one, they waited for Gorman, who tramped toward them in sneakers, looking as if he'd rather be eaten by a wolf borg than see this thing they wanted to show him. Helen had found him a shirt so he didn't have to wear a Pod Fighter splattered across his chest, but she didn't have a pair of shoes that fit.

"Show me this thing, then," Gorman said. "Let's get it over with."

"Touch a tree," Ellie said.

"Why?" Gorman asked suspiciously.

"Just do it," Ellie replied. "We're not going to hurt you. Trust us."

Gorman tramped up to a tree and placed his hand on it. Mika and Ellie stood on either side of him and touched his back. He flinched.

"Keep that monkey away from me," he snarled.

"I will," Ellie replied. "Nothing bad is going to happen. Just relax and be quiet and watch your hand."

The wind gusted warm. The canopy stirred above. A falcon flew over their heads and dove into the valley to hover over the bank of the river. The children focused and waited. It was a quarter of an hour before Gorman stopped fighting against them.

"I feel something in my fingers," he said.

"That's good," Ellie replied. "Don't be scared of it, just watch and see what happens."

Gorman watched his hand. The tingling in his fingers felt warm and he was beginning to believe that the children wouldn't hurt him.

Then he saw it.

A golden light kindled in the tips of his fingers!

And once it started, it spread until he felt it rush right through him. He could feel it in his veins, coursing into him through the earth, rushing right through his body and into the tree, then it spread beyond him, rushed beyond him, like gold blood flowing through one great being, from tree to flower to bush to bird and down the hill until the whole valley was alight with it. The fish in the river, he could see the fish, and the falcon hovering over the bank. The gold light rushed through it all, including him.

His jaw dropped.

"You can see it now?" Ellie asked. "Do you see the light?"

"Yes," he replied. "I can see it."

Mika stood on the south side of no-man's-land, facing the hole in The Wall.

He was part of a large group of children and adults who had gathered there on a warm summer day.

While they talked, he observed.

Only a few months ago, he'd lain in Ellie's bed, feeling grief-stricken, lonely, and confused. Now he was surrounded by people who understood him and he felt calm and connected to everything: the children, the adults, the dead leaves beneath his feet, the sun overhead, even the concrete wall that loomed in the distance, with its giant war-torn hole. He felt connected to it all. As if in the past few weeks, all matter on Earth had shifted and settled, connected.

He felt its gravity.

He felt its beauty.

The people gathered around him were a ceremonial party, waiting for the first people to pass from north to south through the hole in The Wall. The key players involved in the starting and stopping of that three-minute-and-fourteen-second war had gathered.

Mika stood with Ellie, Puck, Audrey, Leo, Iman, Santos, and Colette, and Kobi, Oliver, Helen, Ralph, and little Grace. A short distance away stood Mal Gorman and a few other members of the Northern Government. And next to them, Raphael Mose and the World Conservation Club. The forest shimmered behind them. In the distance, on The Wall, was the whole implanted army, lined up and facing south. Tom, Ana, and the red-haired boy, Luc, were standing up there looking down on them. On the other side of The Wall were their parents.

It was the most unlikely party Mika had ever attended and the same sun shone down on them all. He thought about that.

The event was scheduled for four o'clock, the same time the war had started.

He watched Kobi and Oliver for a moment. Kobi had just taken his T-shirt off and shown Oliver the buds where his wings had begun to regrow. The younger boy watched in awe as Kobi put his T-shirt back on. That ragged boy everyone avoided in school had now achieved a godlike status.

"I wish I was born with wings," Oliver said.

"Stop wishing for things you haven't got," Kobi replied. "You're perfect just as you are."

"Am I?"

"Yes."

Oliver grinned.

Mika smiled.

"Gosh, it's hot," Helen said, adjusting her strawberry sunglasses. "Who wants a drink?" She had a picnic basket at her feet, full of bottles of lemonade. Immediately, Ralph stooped to open it and she slapped his hand away. "Stop it," she said. "I'll do it." Mika looked at the ninth richest person in the world and grinned. "Well, someone has to think of these things," Helen said. "It's very hot today."

"You shouldn't have worn your rain boots," he told her.

"That is a point," she replied.

"Look at them all," Audrey whispered. She slipped her arm through Mika's. She was watching the implanted army on the top of The Wall. Their implants flashed in the sunlight as they milled around and talked. They twinkled like stars.

"I want to know how the universe was made," Audrey whispered.

"Noodle brain," Mika said. "Ask Helen if you can read her books. But how can you think about that now? It's nearly time. Look — it's three minutes to four."

Awen leaned against his legs. Mika fussed his ears. The dog felt soft, relaxed and content.

A short distance in front of them stood Ellie, with Puck on her shoulder. Her eyes hadn't left the hole in The Wall for twenty minutes. Her light was all impatience softened by love. She was about to see her mother and father for the first time in a year and a half.

Mika glanced at Mal Gorman. He did not look so bright. This half-fixed man would need many nudges to remind him what he'd seen at the top of the Loire Valley. He had been broken for a long, long time. But he was starting to get it, and so was Raphael Mose. They were there, at least, with their people standing beside them, looking at the hole in The Wall. This was a start, not an ending.

At four o'clock they heard a noise.

A huge roar on the other side of The Wall.

But it was not the sound of anger, it was the sound of billions of people cheering.

Then Grace cried, "I can see them!"

And through the ragged hole between two worlds, a small group of people appeared, walking sedately, observing the ceremony of this historical event. But when they were halfway across no-man's-land, two adults broke free and began to run toward them with outstretched arms. A sari whipped in the wind, a bald man wiped tears from his eyes. Then Ellie handed Puck to Grace and she began to run too, with the light of her love reaching out to them. As she touched her mother and father, a gold flash of joy hit the connection like a bolt of lightning and made the children on The Wall glow brighter than the sun; made Mika laugh and cry.

The Beginning, said The Whisper, *not The End. We are the future.*

"We did it," Audrey said.

"Yes, we did," Mika replied.

Then he took her by the hand and ran after the others, toward the first adults they'd freed from a giant concrete cage.

Ellie sat on the nose of a Pod Fighter.

Puck sat on her shoulder, chewing a nut.

It was early evening.

She was on the north side of The Wall, by the hole, waiting for the others to arrive. They were about to fly their Pod Fighters back to Cape Wrath.

She was covered in dust. Puck was covered in dust. Everything around them was covered in dust.

She watched Oliver walk toward her, across the lunar land-scape. A heat haze shimmered around his legs. He swung his arms. He was dusty too.

When he reached the Pod Fighter, he stood at her side and drew figures in the dust on its wing. Ellie waited. He had a question to ask her. Puck climbed on his shoulder and poked a finger in his ear.

Oliver glanced at Ellie furtively.

"Yes," she said.

He stopped drawing.

"Really?" he replied.

"Yes," she repeated. "Come on, jump in."

She helped him climb into the gunner seat of the Pod Fighter and did up his harness. Then she dropped into the pilot seat and did up her own.

The windshield slid over them and icons blinked on and he sat saucer eyed behind her. Puck's head pressed warm under her chin.

Ellie wanted the child to feel this, really feel it.

"Ready?"

"Yes!"

"Are you sure?"

"Yes, I am!"

She fired up the engines.

Oliver grinned with delight.

She took off with the roar of a thousand tigers and shot through the hole in The Wall. Then she looped low over the forest and rushed toward the sea and the sun.